MURDER AT THE BINGO HALL

An Ethel Dinwiddie Cozy Mystery – Book One

By Linda Perelman Pohl

Murder at the Bingo Hall is a work of fiction. Names, characters, places and incidents are either the product of the author's imagination or are used fictitiously. Any resemblance to actual people, living or dead, places, business establishments or events are entirely coincidental.

Copyright 2021 by Linda Perelman Pohl
Cover Design by Julie Hatton
ISBN- 978-0-9625453-5-1
Printed in U.S.A.

For Stuart
My husband and best friend
I love you

Table of Contents

Chapter One
Sunday Night Bingo

Priscilla Hatfield felt lucky. It was Sunday, but not just any ordinary Sunday. Tonight, the coverall jackpot was up to $1500.00 at St. Angela's Bingo Hall. In the quaint village of Kenmore, New York those were high-stakes.

She already was imagining how she'd spend the money. Her denim blue Volkswagen Beetle had needed a muffler for ages. The rest, well, chances are she'd bank it for a rainy day.

"Yoo-hoo, over here," shouted Ethel and Nellie, as Priscilla entered the hall.

Priscilla set her things down quickly, said hello to her two bingo buddies and went up to buy her cards. The line was long, but moved quickly. "I'd like an extra $5.00 worth of coverall cards, please." It was rare for her to spend anything more than she'd budgeted for the evening. But, with the jackpot number at fifty-eight balls, she felt the risk was worth the gamble.

Although Ethel Dinwiddie and Nellie Pearce had been friends since childhood, Priscilla had met them about six years ago, at bingo, and their friendship had blossomed. Not only did they always sit together, they shared any winnings and occasionally went out to lunch or to a movie together. `

Priscilla returned to the table and began her weekly ritual of arranging her assortment of multi-colored daubers, lucky trolls and rosary beads. All were positioned in a neat row behind her cards. She picked up her two favorite trolls, Jasper and Seymour, and talked to them as if they understood perfectly well what she was saying. "Fellows, if you could sprinkle a little good luck our way tonight, we'd be much obliged!" She gave each one a quick kiss on the head before putting them back in their proper places.

"Can you believe the crowd that's here tonight? Look around. It's not just the regulars. People come out of the woodwork whenever the jackpot's high," Nellie said, as she took a bite of her pepperoni pizza. "I guess I'm forgetting my manners. Would either of you like a taste?"

"No thank you," said Ethel.

"Me neither," Priscilla responded without hesitation. "Actually, I'm feeling kind of queasy. For the past few months, Fred has been watching those cooking shows on TV. I'm sure that's what inspired him to try his hand in the kitchen! I think, now that he's retired, he has too much time on his hands. The stuffed cabbage that he made earlier isn't agreeing with me. And it's not the first meal he's cooked that's left my stomach upset. But I don't have the heart to tell him."

"I bet you'll feel better as soon as the games start. And with a jackpot of 58 numbers, I think it's going to go tonight," chimed in Ethel. "I see we all bought some extras. I think that was smart of us."

Nellie quickly surveyed the room. "Oh, my gracious. Check out how many cards *Tattoo Man* is playing."

Only a few seats down from Priscilla was a man who had occupied that same seat for as long as they'd been coming to St. Angela's. His arms, hands, legs and neck were completely covered in a variety of designs, boasting a colorful array of snakes and crosses. The three

2

women had frequently joked about where else on his body his tattoos might be. Prominent on his right shoulder was a big heart with the word *Mom* indelibly engraved in red ink smack dab in the center. They'd always thought he was a good guy, despite his unkempt appearance, because he clearly professed his love for his mother. Not to mention the fact that he played at least twelve cards every game. And, tonight it appeared he had surpassed even that number. Not an easy feat! And not an inexpensive night out either.

At precisely 7:00, the song, "Happy," by Pharrell Williams, filled the room to signal the players that the game was about to begin. People bopped their heads and clapped their hands along with the lively music. When the song ended, a hush fell over the crowd. Daubers in hand, everyone was ready to start.

Paul, known to the players as *Tall Paul*, stood behind the podium. Standing at well over six feet had earned him his nickname. His voice was strong and assured. Some players said he had a voice made for radio. He always waited the same amount of time between calls to allow those who were playing multiple cards to accurately daub their numbers. Two TV monitors, hanging on the walls at opposite sides of the room, displayed the next number to be called. Whispers of anticipation filled the hall.

"Good evening ladies and gentlemen. Welcome to Sunday night bingo at St. Angela's. I see a lot of new faces here tonight. For those of you who are playing here for the first time, we recognize five spaces in a row to make a vertical line, a horizontal line or a diagonal line. We also accept the outer four corners for regular bingo. Jackpots and coveralls are sold separately. Tonight, our final coverall will pay out $1500.00! Our workers will be walking the floor, so if you want to buy any extras, just raise your hand. And please be sure to yell loudly, if you have a bingo. And now, onto our first game of the evening. We'll be playing a $50.00 regular game. Good luck to everyone."

The balls spun around in the cage, as the crowd waited excitedly for *Tall Paul* to pull out the first one. "I 17," he called out in his deep voice.

"Got it," Nellie said enthusiastically.

Ethel and Priscilla shook their heads disappointedly.

Next up was N 44. Priscilla skimmed her card. "Gee whiz," she said in an exasperated tone. "No N 44 either." Only one thing left to do, she reasoned. And with that thought she picked up Jasper and Seymour. "Hey, I thought you two were supposed to bring us some good luck. Maybe I'll move you a little closer to me," she whispered as she stroked their crazy, wild orange and green hair.

Several more numbers were called when Nellie excitedly declared, "All I need is two little ducks." All the regulars at St. Angela's knew that was I 22.

"I 22. I 22. I 22." The three women chanted quietly in unison.

But when O 74 popped out of the hopper, *Elvis* yelled out "bingo!" with his thick, southern drawl. The threesome had given him this nickname some time ago. With his long, greased back black hair and mutton-chop sideburns, there could be no doubt who his idol was. Usually, his attire for the evening was something quite bedazzling. Tonight, he was dressed in tight black pants, a pink shirt and a black belt that was embellished with an array of brightly colored crystals.

A sigh of exasperation was heard throughout the hall, as all the players that needed only one number lamented that this would not be their lucky game.

"Better luck next time," declared Nellie, as she high-fived her two friends.

"Yes. Hope springs eternal. One of us has to win tonight. And you were mighty close, Nellie."

Several more games followed, but it seemed like luck was not in their favor tonight.

"Good grief," Nellie said. "This always happens when the jackpot is so high. People come to St. Angela's who have never played here before and these crowds wreck our chances. Not fair."

"I know what you mean, Nellie. But at least when Elvis won, we could better accept that. I mean he's a regular like we are. And there are still lots of games left. If we are going to win, wouldn't it be amazing if it were the last jackpot game."

"I sure hope you're right, Ethel."

The sound of *Tall Paul's* voice interrupted their thoughts. "Our next game will be an inner square. Here, at St. Angela's, you need to mark all the numbers around the free space. For those of you who may not be familiar with this, please look at our lit screens and you will see the pattern. The prize payout for this game is $100. Good luck to all."

The threesome loved inner square games, as they lasted longer than regular bingo. As always, once the calling started, you could hear the buzzing of the lights overhead. *Tall Paul* usually had to call several numbers before anyone started to get close. Everyone needed three I's, three G's and two N's.

"I 22," he clearly announced.

"Jeepers!" exclaimed Nellie. "Why couldn't he have called that number for me in the first game?"

"The good news is I see you have it now," said Priscilla.

Many more I's, N's and G's followed. You could feel the anticipation growing in the room.

"I only need one more number," Priscilla excitedly whispered to Nellie and Ethel. She picked up

Jasper and Seymour. "Come on now, boys. All I need is I 17. Make it happen," she wished as she brought them close to her heart.

Tall Paul called G 52. Priscilla hugged her trolls even more tightly and breathed a sigh of relief when none of the other players yelled bingo. Suddenly I 17 appeared on the screen, as the next ball to be called.

Priscilla pointed up at the monitor, her voice filled with excitement. "That's it! That's my number!"

Ethel and Nellie gave her a *thumbs up*. "Good for you, Priscilla."

But when *Tall Paul* called out I 17, Priscilla grabbed her chest and with a look of sheer fright cried out, "I, I think I've...."

And then she collapsed.

Chapter Two
Deader Than a Doornail

Priscilla's body lay slumped over the white tabletop, lying as still as Jasper and Seymour. Her frail little arms covered her neatly positioned row of bingo cards.

"Oh my God, Priscilla! Oh my God!" Ethel screamed. She ran over to Priscilla's side and grabbed her shoulders. "Wake up, Priscilla. Wake up." But she did not move. "Do something. Someone, help her." Ethel cried out to summon Father O'Leary, as tears streamed down her face.

Father O'Leary, the priest at St. Angela's, rushed over to their table. He tried to rouse Priscilla, but she was unresponsive. "Let me call the paramedics right away. It looks like she may have had a heart attack or a stroke." Concern filled his voice.

Tall Paul, a retired firefighter, jumped into action and began CPR. Ethel and Nellie huddled beside Father O'Leary.

Ethel fought back her tears. "Father, I think there's something you need to know." She took a deep breath, as she attempted to maintain her composure. "Priscilla told Nellie and me, only a few weeks ago, that she suspected someone was trying to kill her."

"What? Why would anyone want to harm Priscilla?"

Ethel shrugged her shoulders, as tears streamed

down her face. "I have no idea. She clammed up and wouldn't say a word when we tried to find out more. But she was afraid of someone or something. That I know for sure." Ethel grabbed for her purse and took out some tissues, as she blotted under her eyes. "Father, we need to call the police." Her sobs grew louder.

"With what you've just told me, I agree." Father reached for his cell phone.

Even behind the thick beige matte face powder that Nellie always brushed on her cheeks before leaving home, Ethel could see that the color had drained from her face. "This can't be real, Ethel. Tell me I'm dreaming." Nellie's hands were trembling and her voice quivered as she spoke. "I don't remember Priscilla ever saying anything about having a heart problem. Actually, I remember her telling us at lunch that she'd just had her yearly physical and everything was fine." Nellie's voice cracked with emotion. "Do you think someone killed Priscilla?"

"I don't know," Ethel stammered through her tears. "All I can say is that I recall my Leonard, God rest his soul, telling me how important it was to solve a case as quickly as possible. Being married to a detective for over thirty years, I heard a lot. So, if it was something bad and not a heart attack or stroke that killed Priscilla, the Kenmore Police are great investigators. Leonard was proud to have served on the force."

Nellie began to feel faint at the very thought of her friend dying an unnatural death. She inhaled deeply. "I know what you mean. This may sound silly, Ethel, but I watch a lot of *Law and Order* on television. They say the same thing. It's really important to catch the person before his or her trail goes cold. I hope the police get here soon," she said with despair in her voice.

A crowd had begun to form to see what all the commotion was about. Raised voices were heard. "I don't think anything is going to help her. She sure looks like she's already a goner to me."

Ethel glared at the man who'd made the cruel comment. She knew he wasn't a regular. She was so upset that she could barely get her words out. "What is wrong with you? Have you no sense of decency?"

Father O'Leary grabbed the microphone from the caller's podium. His tone was firm and solemn. "Ladies and gentlemen. May I have your attention, please. I can see that many of you are very concerned. But could you please try to remain calm and return to your seats." He paused until his request had been met. "One of our players has had a medical emergency. I'm afraid she may be dead." Sadness filled his voice. "The paramedics are on their way." He was silent for a moment. "And we've called the police."

"The police? Why the police?" Voices could be heard throughout the bingo hall all asking the same question.

Tattoo Man began to make quite a ruckus. "Come on. Enough already. I paid for sixteen games tonight and it doesn't look like she's coming back to life any time soon. That coverall is worth a lot of money and I want my chance to win." He pounded his fist loudly on the table.

Nellie took off her tortoise rimmed glasses and glared at him, as she picked up her purple dauber in anger. "You should be ashamed of yourself, young man. How can you even think about playing bingo? Have you no heart?"

"Get a life, lady," he rudely replied. "Anyone here can see she looks deader than a doornail. Nothing you or I can do is going to change that. It doesn't look like *Tall Paul* is having any luck either." *Tattoo Man* pointed at his cards. "I spent over sixty dollars on these cards. Come on. Let's play," he shouted towards the

9

podium.

For a fleeting moment, Ethel thought she saw Priscilla's hand move. "Maybe she isn't dead, Nellie. Maybe it's just a terrible mistake." Ethel rushed over and stood beside Priscilla, her cries growing louder, as she clasped her hand. "Wake up, Priscilla. Wake up," she gasped as tears streamed down her face.

Father O'Leary appeared beside her and gently placed his arm around Ethel's shoulder. "I know you're upset, but we really need to leave Priscilla just as we found her."

"Just as we found her," trembled Ethel. "You mean...dead."

Ethel and Nellie looked up to see the paramedics entering the hall wheeling a stretcher and carrying medical supplies. Shortly thereafter, two burly police officers followed.

"They look just like the cops on *Law and Order*," whispered Nellie to her friend.

The policemen spoke momentarily with Father O'Leary, in hushed tones, as the paramedics took over the CPR. Ethel shared with the police everything she'd told Father O'Leary about Priscilla fearing her life was in danger.

Seconds later, a policeman with jet black hair and a protruding stomach, addressed the crowd. "Ladies and gentlemen. I know this is very upsetting, but we'll try to make things as easy for all of you as possible. My partner, Officer Malcolm, will be taking down everyone's name and phone number and asking you a few questions. Then, you're free to go. We'll contact you again, if we need you."

"What?" yelled *Tattoo Man* in a gruff voice that captured everyone's attention. "That sucks. I came here to play bingo. Anyone here can see she ain't coming back, so why should I have to suffer. I paid a lot of money for these here cards."

Father O'Leary remained calm despite *Tattoo Man's* unsavory behavior, as he addressed the players. "We will be refunding everyone's money for tonight's games. Just stop at the front of the hall, after the police have taken down your information, and one of our workers will see that you are reimbursed. We apologize, but the police are in charge now and they want the building cleared." He paused for a brief moment. "I know this is very difficult to hear, but this bingo hall may be a crime scene." He glanced around with an uneasy look. "And with 179 people here tonight, the police are considering everyone a suspect."

Chapter Three
Nellie and Matilda

It had been three days since Priscilla had died. Nellie believed the image of her dear friend, slumped lifeless over the bingo table, would haunt her forever. She had hardly eaten or slept a wink since Sunday and the nauseous feeling, in the pit of her stomach, just wouldn't go away. The least little thing caused her to burst into tears.

Sitting in her navy-blue recliner, with a cup of chamomile tea, she awaited the eleven o'clock news. She remained hopeful that the Kenmore Police would quickly get to the bottom of things and determine what had happened to poor Priscilla. Her cat, Matilda, lay lazily across her lap atop the worn patchwork quilt that Priscilla had given her for Christmas three years ago.

The familiar sound of the music, that preceded the nightly news, brought her thoughts back to the reality of the moment. She nervously shivered, as the lead story aired.

"Police are investigating the circumstances surrounding the death of sixty-eight-year-old Priscilla Hatfield, who collapsed and died earlier this week at St. Angela's Church bingo. Police now suspect foul play, but they are not releasing specific details at this time. Anyone with information about Priscilla's death is urged to contact the Kenmore Police Department. All tips are confidential. The hotline number is (716) 877-0111."

Nellie gasped. "Did you hear that, Matilda?" she said, as she wiped the tears from her face. "The police suspect foul play." Without wasting a minute, she phoned her friend. "Ethel, did you see the news? I just can't believe it. Did you hear what they said?"

"This is one time I wish I hadn't, Nellie. I've barely been able to eat or sleep since Sunday and I know you told me you haven't either. I could use some company. Do you want to meet for coffee in the morning?"

"Sounds good."

"Let's say 9:00 at The Sheridan Family Restaurant."

"I'll see you there." She affectionately stroked her cat's back, as the sound of her purring soothed Nellie for the moment. "We've got big trouble, Matilda. Someone killed Priscilla and I really hope the police can figure out who did it soon. Ethel and I won't sleep well until we know the perpetrator's been caught." Matilda meowed contentedly.

An uneasiness overcame Nellie as she cautiously checked and rechecked to be certain that all the windows were securely locked and that all the doors had been dead-bolted, before she headed up to bed. Ever since her husband Edwin had died, over two years ago, she had thought about putting in a security system. At that moment, she regretted never having gotten around to it. Matilda was good company. But certainly not a guard cat. She was perfectly content to lay in the sunlight, eat and sleep. Nellie gave her more than her fair share of treats and table food, which probably accounted for her size. Nellie referred to her as her full-figured feline!

The murderer, whoever he or she was, surely knew they were a threesome; she, Ethel and Priscilla. And, if someone had been disturbed enough to want Priscilla dead, maybe she and Ethel were next. Perhaps they were watching her, lurking in the shadows at this very moment. Nellie was frightened and the only way things would ever be better would be when this monster, whoever he or she might be, was caught.

Nellie fluffed the goose down pillow and pulled the cornflower blue comforter up over her. Matilda curled up into a ball, purring loudly at the end of the bed. Thoughts of all the people they knew at the bingo hall spun about in her mind. Any one of them might be guilty. And, she couldn't overlook the fact that so many people who normally weren't there, had come that night because of the high payout for the coverall game. So many possible suspects, she thought. Nellie rolled over on her side, as her uneasiness grew.

The thunder and lightning only added to Nellie's restlessness, as she tossed and turned. Like the prior nights, since Priscilla's death, she found it hard to sleep. She grabbed her blue terry robe and went down to the kitchen to make herself a cup of warm milk. That was something she'd done since she'd been a child and it had always seemed to soothe her.

Having finished her drink, she brushed her teeth and slathered her Eterna 27 moisture cream all over her face and neck. "Good-bye wrinkles," she said in a monotone, sad voice that matched her mood. Then she crawled back into bed, hoping sleep would come.

What happened next seemed a blur. Nellie remembered Matilda arching her back and hissing. The thunder clapped loudly, as a streak of lightning vividly flashed and, without warning, the lights went out. She lay in total darkness. Suddenly, a tapping sound at her bedroom window caused her to bolt upright in bed. Frozen with fear, Nellie frantically tried to calm herself. She took a few long, deep breaths, a technique she had learned in meditation class after her husband had died, and slowly rose from her bed. She grabbed the flashlight, that she always kept in her night stand drawer and, fearing a prowler or worse could be outside her bedroom window, stealthily walked to the guest room. Cautiously, she drew back the curtain. The moonlight cast a wide shadow into the darkness and, although she wondered if it was just her imagination, Nellie thought she saw the shadow of a person running towards the fence.

Chapter Four
The Gold Button

Nellie awakened feeling sore and achy. She gingerly got out of bed and opened the white lace curtains. "No wonder I feel so crummy," she said to Matilda. "This rainy, damp weather is for the birds. And, I haven't seen fog like this in ages," she added as she stroked her cat's shiny coat. "Am I getting old, girl? I sure feel old, especially when this body of mine hurts like it does today. But," she quickly added, "at least I'm still here. That's more than we can say for poor Priscilla." Matilda was busy licking herself, a ritual she performed several times a day, and seemed oblivious to her owner's words.

Memories of the previous night were still pretty hazy. With the light of day, a gnawing uncertainty entered her thoughts. She remembered the sudden darkness, the tapping at the window and the possible image of someone running through her garden towards the fence. "Maybe it was just my nerves," she surmised. "Lord knows I've been on edge and upset ever since Priscilla died."

After a quick shower, she hastily threw on her gray sweat pants and bingo sweatshirt, grabbed her umbrella and headed out the door to her backyard. In the light of day, she felt much more comfortable checking things out. Minutes later, she cautiously stood below her bedroom window. Not knowing exactly what she was looking for, she surveyed the area where she believed the tapping had originated. "Hmm," she uttered to no one. "I don't see anything suspicious." She looked for footprints, but saw none. "Perhaps it was just the wind."

But her eyes were suddenly drawn to a large, gold button that lay conspicuously on the lawn beside the twisted oak tree. Could this be something important? she wondered. Nellie slowly bent over and picked up the shiny object. She quickly went back into the house where she placed the button in a zip lock plastic bag. Promptly, she placed the *evidence* in her top desk drawer for safekeeping. She put out Matilda's food and water, grabbed her car keys and hopped into her midnight blue Saab.

The Sheridan Family Restaurant was crowded, as it usually was. The two women sat at their usual booth beside the assortment of homemade pies and Greek desserts. Tammy had been their waitress for years. Whenever they came in for lunch or dinner, she would always let them know when the baklava was extra fresh and worth ordering.

"Hi, ladies." Tammy's voice was solemn. "I was so sorry to hear about Priscilla on the news last night. I could hardly believe it. When they said they suspected foul play, I was shocked. Why would anyone ever want to harm Priscilla? She was such a gentle soul."

"Thanks Tammy. That's what we're struggling with, too. We just can't figure out why anyone would want her dead," Nellie said in a dejected tone. "We miss her more than you can imagine."

"I'm not surprised. You three were like sisters. But I'm sure the police will get to the bottom of things." Tammy looked around to see the remaining booths filling up quickly. "I better take your order. The usual?"

"Are we that predictable?"

"That's a good thing," replied Tammy.

"Knowing what you like makes things easier for me."

"Okay then. Please bring us two number 5's."

"Got it," exclaimed Tammy, as she scurried off to put in the order.

"So, you won't believe it, Ethel. I may have a clue."

"What? What are you talking about?"

"It's probably nothing. But since the police strongly suspect foul play, I didn't think we should take anything for granted. Maybe it will be able to help them." Nellie related the events of the previous evening leading up to this morning's discovery of the gold button.

"Good job, Nellie. Imagine! Our very first clue."

"Don't get so excited, Ethel. I mean that button could have been out there for a long time. It could belong to anyone and just have gone unnoticed."

"True," said Ethel. "But bagging it the way you did, was pretty spiffy detective work. If Leonard were alive, I think he would have found that very impressive. I'm proud to know you."

"So, now what?"

"Now comes the hard part." Ethel pursed her thin lips together, as she brushed her silver-gray hair behind her ear. "I think it's pretty obvious from last night's news that the police are not divulging all the details. There has to be a reason why and we need to find that reason out. Maybe knowing what that is can help us help them."

"And exactly how do you propose we go about doing that?"

"I'm not really sure. Let me think a moment. What would my Leonard have done?" Furrows formed between her eyes, as she contemplated their next move.

"Ah, food for thought," Nellie exclaimed, as Tammy set the plates of eggs, potatoes and toast down before them. "Maybe once we've eaten, an idea will come to us."

As the women sat pondering what to do next, a middle-aged gentleman sat down at the table across from them. Dressed in a navy business suit, they couldn't help but notice his conspicuous red hair and oversized wide-rimmed glasses. Sprawled out before him was the *Buffalo News* and, in bold print, the headlines that clearly depicted Priscilla's untimely demise. Ethel's heart began to race. "Listen, Nellie. I know this might sound crazy, but I think we should pay a visit to the police."

"Are you kidding, Ethel? They're not going to tell us anything. For some reason, they're keeping certain things about Priscilla's case hush-hush."

"True. But what if we tell them that we might be able to shed some light on the case. Maybe their knowing that my Leonard was a former detective will gain us a little leeway. You never know. Anyway, we can offer to provide them with something they don't know in exchange for filling us in on whatever they're being so secretive about."

"I don't think the police work like that. And, besides, what detail do we know that they don't?"

"Come on, Nellie. Think! Don't you remember when the three of us had lunch at Family Tree a few weeks ago. I'm still dreaming about their chicken souvlaki salad and how good it was."

"Of course, I remember. So what?"

"So what? That was the day Priscilla shared with us that she was worried she was in terrible danger. Surely you recall how we tried our darndest to get her to share what her fears were, but she was totally tight-lipped. Remember how we begged her to go to the police. But she wouldn't hear of it."

A melancholy look came over Nellie's face. "I never took her seriously that day. I even teased her about watching too many crime shows on television. And now," Nellie covered her face and burst into tears, "now I wish I'd been a better friend to her."

"Don't be ridiculous. You were a great friend to her." Ethel placed her hand atop Nellie's. "Listen, Nellie. I don't know what happened to her. But what I do know is that Priscilla didn't tell the police she thought someone might be trying to kill her. She confided that in us. And we were the ones who shared that with the police. That was a major clue we provided." Ethel sighed deeply. "I'm sure that the police have a lot of cases to solve. And although I'm sure they'll try their best to figure out who killed Priscilla, she's certainly not their only case. Not to mention, Kenmore doesn't have a lot of murders. I recall Leonard telling me about a few murder cases over the years that were usually drug related. But, burglary, embezzlement, traffic violations and domestic violence cases were far more prevalent. Anyway, this grief is eating us alive. Neither of us has slept well in nights. So, what would be wrong with us doing a little investigating and seeing what we can find out. Maybe it would even take our minds off of how miserable we're feeling. And, if we're clever enough to discover something, we'd be helping the police find justice for Priscilla. I think it's worth a try."

"Sounds good in theory, Ethel. But I think finding a killer is way beyond us."

Ethel took a sip of her coffee. "Listen, Nellie. We were her two best friends. There are probably lots of things that we know about her that could aid in the investigation. Remember how she mentioned some kind of list that she was concerned about. And what about the gold button that you found? That could be important, too. But we don't necessarily need to share those details with the police right away. We could try to see what we can find out."

"I really think we're out of our league, but I'm willing to try." Nellie sat deep in thought, as she cut her poached eggs on whole wheat toast into bite sized portions and popped a piece into her mouth. "You know, Ethel, I was thinking about what Priscilla's activities were before bingo. Do you know where she was, what she was doing? Maybe knowing that might be helpful."

"Actually, that's a very good point. And, it's funny you should mention it. I called Priscilla right after I spoke with you on Sunday. She said she'd meet us at the bingo hall. Now that I'm recalling her tone, it was a bit uneasy. She said she had to go to confession."

"Confession?" Nellie looked confused. "I wonder why? What did she have to confess that couldn't have waited until mass next Sunday?"

Ethel shrugged her shoulders. "You've got me. For as long as we've known her, Priscilla's always gone to ten o'clock mass. I don't think she's ever varied. I mean who knows better than we do how set in her ways she was."

"True. That's odd, don't you think?"

"Definitely unusual." Ethel added.

The man at the next table looked over at the two women and, with a sinister half smile, folded up the newspaper and stood. "Ladies," he said as he nodded their way. "You two have a good day."

Ethel felt the hairs on the back of her neck stand up, but she wasn't quite sure why. She guessed it was something in his tone or demeanor that gave her the willies. In her bones, she felt something just wasn't right.

Chapter Five
Carrot Cake for Officer Malcolm

As Ethel and Nellie ascended the steep steps of the stone building that led to the Village of Kenmore, New York Police Headquarters, they were focused on one thing and one thing only. Determined to discover what had happened to Priscilla in her final hours, they hoped that, through this visit, they could garner some information that would assist them in reaching their goal. Putting the puzzle pieces together would not be an easy task. And they could use all the clues and help they could get.

Having baked the decadent carrot cake with cream cheese frosting that had won her first prize at the Erie County Fair, Nellie was quite confident that Officer Malcolm would be agreeable to the exchange of information. It was, so to speak, the icing on the cake. Armed with the delicacy, the two women smiled genuinely at the young lady who held the position of gatekeeper.

Something about her demeanor reminded Ethel of her daughter, Deborah, who was teaching English in Thailand with her sister, Sarah. She missed her two girls like crazy. But it was their dream to teach abroad and they were loving the experience. Ethel could hardly wait for the day when they'd be home.

The girl at the front desk couldn't have been more than twenty-one. Dressed in a navy and hunter-green plaid jumper, her outfit reminded Nellie of one she had worn many years ago in parochial school. The girl's thick, blond hair was pulled back loosely into a pony tail. Nellie envisioned her more as a kindergarten teacher than as a receptionist for the police department.

"May I help you?" Her voice was sweet and soft.

"We'd like to see Officer Malcolm, please."

"And whom shall I say is here?"

"Please tell him Ethel Dinwiddie and Nellie Pearce would like to see him. It's regarding the Priscilla Hatfield case. I believe we have some information he may find useful." Ethel's voice sounded strong and assured. She actually surprised herself at how easily her words flowed.

"Would you like to have a seat in our waiting area?" She motioned towards a group of worn brown vinyl chairs and a couple of vending machines. "I'll let him know you're here."

"See Nellie, I told you the police would be interested in what we have to say. Now, we have to be clever about this. I mean he has as much to gain from us, as we potentially do from him. Remember, don't tell him what Priscilla confided in us, or about the gold button, or about that strange man we saw at breakfast, for that matter, unless he's willing to help us, too. Be confident, but cool."

"Confident, but cool! Where do you get these ideas, Ethel?"

"Ah, my Leonard used to say, 'once a detective, always a detective.'" A melancholy look encompassed her face. "I miss him so much. I know I'm not a detective, Nellie. But living with Leonard for over thirty years must count for something. I like to think maybe some of his investigative skills rubbed off on me."

At that moment, Police Officer Malcolm rounded the corner and extended his hand. "Ladies, how may I help you?"

"Actually, it is we who may be able to help you, Officer Malcolm."

Nellie smiled warmly, raised her one eyebrow above the other, and handed him the cake. "A little gift," she exclaimed.

"Thank you, ladies. This looks delicious. So, what's the occasion?" Officer Malcolm's look was one Ethel could not decipher. "I hope this cake isn't some sort of bribe. You know that would be totally unacceptable."

"Nonsense, Officer. Nellie likes to bake and I don't know a man alive who doesn't like a little something sweet to eat once in a while. That's simply all there is to it." Ethel turned towards her friend, winked and exclaimed, "A bribe! Can you imagine that, Nellie?"

"Alright, then. Thank you. I'll share it with the other officers later on. For now, ladies, why don't we step into my office." Officer Malcolm led the way to a tiny, nondescript room in the rear of the building. "So, what can I do for you?"

"Actually, Officer Malcolm, Nellie and I were at St. Angela's bingo hall on Sunday night. We were the two women with Priscilla Hatfield. She was our dear friend. We've been bingo buddies for several years."

"I'm so sorry about what happened. Please accept my condolences. You both must be very upset."

Tears formed in both women's eyes, as Nellie removed her white lace handkerchief from her purse. She breathed in deeply in an attempt to regain her composure. "Sadder and more upset than you can imagine, Officer. We want you to get to the bottom of what happened to our friend. That's why we're here."

"Understandable. Our receptionist said that you had some information to offer."

"That's correct. We know from listening to the news last night and reading the morning paper that there's something the police know that you're not disclosing. As I said, Priscilla was like family to us. And, if you have information that may shed some light on what happened, Nellie and I would be most grateful." Ethel adjusted the chain on her necklace to be certain the silver cross was perfectly centered on her shirt. "You're probably not aware of this, Officer Malcolm, but my husband, Leonard Dinwiddie, used to be a detective with the Kenmore Police Department.

"Really?"

"Well, it was a very long time ago. Leonard was a police officer, like you, for four years before he was promoted to detective. He used to tell me at dinner how he had to be methodical gathering the evidence. 'Slow and steady. Don't rush things. No room for error.' I can hear his voice as if it were only yesterday." Ethel smiled at the young man who sat across from her. "I'd venture to say you were probably still in diapers when my husband worked here."

Officer Malcolm gave a hearty laugh. "I'd agree that's a while ago."

Ethel paused a moment and looked deeply into Officer Malcolm's chestnut brown eyes. "So, we have something in common. Two people both wanting to solve a crime. And I'm sure you've heard that old saying; 'one hand washes the other.'"

Officer Malcolm smiled, accentuating the space between his two front teeth. "I have."

"Well, then, I'll be perfectly blunt. You share what you're hiding from the public with Nellie and me and we'll tell you what we know. I don't know if you are aware that we were the ones who let the police know on

Sunday night that Priscilla was worried someone was trying to kill her. And we're willing to help however we can. I like to think of it as kind of an exchange of information, all for the good of solving the case. Sounds fair, don't you think?"

Officer Malcolm's face took on a puzzled look. "Ladies, I understand how very upset and troubled you must both be over this. It was a terrible tragedy. There's no denying that. And I have no doubt your friend was a lovely lady. But, as wonderful as I'm sure she was and as anxious as I can imagine you both are to bring the perpetrator to justice, this is clearly a matter for the police. Even if I wanted to, I'm not at liberty to discuss any internal details about the crime." His face took on a disconcerted look. "With your husband having been a former detective, I'm sure you understand that rules are rules. I could lose my job, even my pension."

"But, officer...." Nellie interjected.

Officer Malcolm interrupted her thoughts. "No buts about it. Police protocol plain and simple." He paused a moment before continuing. "But, if you have something that you'd like to share with me about the case, I'd certainly be happy to receive any information you have. Your assistance and input during our investigation would be most appreciated and held in total confidence. And we certainly are grateful for the tip you already gave us."

"Hmm," Ethel exclaimed. "I'll be perfectly honest, Officer Malcolm. That's not the response we were hoping for. But, if that's how you want to be, I realize there's nothing we can do about it. So, for the time being, I think Nellie and I will keep our other information under our hats, as well." Ethel collected her thoughts for a moment. "Should we find out anything definitive, that has some bearing on the case, we will certainly let you know."

"As you wish," he replied, a slight smirk crossing his boyish face.

"You men in blue aren't too flexible, are you? Well," Ethel added in a rather flippant tone, "nothing ventured, nothing gained. You can't blame us for trying. I can see that Nellie and I have our work cut out for us. And I can see it won't be easy."

"Listen, you two seem like sweet ladies and very loyal friends. But I really think you should leave the police work to the people trained to deal with these things. This case could get pretty dangerous. That's the most I can say."

The ladies stood and shook Officer Malcolm's hand. "We understand your position, Officer. And I hope you understand ours. We loved Priscilla. And doing anything short of trying our best to help solve this mystery, just isn't an option for us. No hard feelings, but we're not stopping till someone is caught and brought to justice, no matter how dangerous it might get. Come on, Nellie," Ethel exclaimed. "We've got a murderer to catch."

Chapter Six
A Person of Interest

The two ladies approached 122 Hartford Avenue with heavy hearts.

"I still can't believe she's gone."

"I know."

"God, I miss her." Nellie sighed deeply. "I couldn't sleep again last night. Then I remembered how fond Fred was of my sour creme coffee cake and, although I'm sure he won't have much of an appetite, it made me feel better baking it." Nellie smiled broadly. "I admit I tasted some of the batter." She pulled at the waist of her pants and smiled. "You don't get to be my size from not snacking!"

"I wish I could bake like you, Nellie. Remember that apple cake I made?"

"You mean the one that didn't cook long enough?"

"You're always so polite. More like the one that was raw and mushy and tasted totally disgusting. I've never seen any cake quite that pathetic."

"At least you tried. So, baking's not your forte. I stink at detective work. Thanks to you having had a husband who was a detective, you're far more savvy than I am."

"I don't know about that, Nellie. But thanks for the vote of confidence. I just feel so sorry for Fred. He worked his whole life to be able to retire and enjoy life with Priscilla." She cast her eyes down sorrowfully. "He had barely stopped working when this tragedy happened. It's awful. I just can't begin to imagine how forlorn he must be."

"I wonder if their daughter, Nancy, is in yet. I believe she lives in California. I'm sure that her being home will be a huge comfort to Fred."

"I agree with you about that. Maybe she's here already."

"Maybe. We'll find out soon enough. But, for the moment, Nellie, I just want you to know that we have to keep in mind that there might be some clues at the house." A pensive look overcame Ethel, as she continued. "Something maybe even Fred isn't aware of. Remember how Priscilla said something about a list the day she confided in us?"

"Yes. But she never elaborated. I wonder what kind of list it was."

"I have no idea, but I think it's something we'll need to try to find out about."

"Priscilla died at the bingo hall. What could possibly be at her house that could give us a clue?"

Ethel shrugged her shoulders and buttoned the top button of her burnt orange cardigan, as they approached the white shingled house. "I don't know. I'm just saying we need to keep our eyes and ears open."

Little weeds poked up from under the uneven concrete that led up the front walkway towards the home. A lamp post, with a wooden cutout of a black dog on it and the number 122, adorned the uncut front lawn.

The two women took a deep breath, as Ethel's finger hesitantly rang the front bell. A disheveled Fred greeted them, his eyes, red and puffy. The man who stood before them looked nothing like the Fred they knew.

Nellie kissed him on the cheek, as she handed him the cake. "I'm so sorry, Fred."

"I know. Thanks for the cake. It looks delicious." His lower lip began to quiver. "Why would anyone want to hurt Priscilla?" Tears began to stream down his face.

"We don't know, Fred. We can't begin to imagine how you must feel. Please accept our deepest condolences." Ethel put her arms around him and gave him a hug. "You know we're here for you and whatever we can do to help, we will."

Fred nodded his head dejectedly. "Thanks. You two were her best friends. She loved you both like sisters. I told that to the police yesterday afternoon. They sure seemed interested in the two of you. I guess since you two were the last ones seen with her, they consider you both *people of interest*, is how I believe the officer termed it."

"What?"

"I'm sure they're just doing their job. I assured them that you two would never hurt Priscilla." Fred shifted uneasily from one foot to the other. "You can't imagine how they interrogated me."

"You, Fred?'

"I guess the husband is always a prime suspect in these cases. They seemed really interested in what she'd eaten on Sunday. I told them I'd made stuffed cabbage and that Priscilla loved it so much she'd even had seconds."

"She mentioned that to us too, Fred. She told us that ever since you retired, you've been cooking a lot." Ethel intentionally did not mention that Priscilla had complained of stomach pain that night. No reason to upset him any more than he already was.

"I loved my wife. I would never hurt her. The police told me they are questioning everyone who was at the bingo hall Sunday night. Thanks to what you and Father O'Leary told them, they also called in the Erie

County Medical Examiner. Apparently, the final autopsy and toxicology reports could take several weeks to complete. But they assured me that the Medical Examiner would eventually be able to provide a definitive answer as to what killed her." Fred cupped his hands over his face and began to cry uncontrollably. "Why? Who would ever want to kill my Priscilla? It makes no sense."

"We agree with you, Fred. Why anyone would want to hurt Priscilla is beyond us. Nellie and I went to see the police yesterday. We thought maybe we could offer them some information in exchange for what they know." Ethel looked over at her friend and attempted a faint smile.

"This may sound ridiculous, Fred, but Ethel and I aren't letting anyone get away with this. If the police don't find Priscilla's killer, we will. That's how we're going to deal with our grief."

"Priscilla was lucky to have you both in her life. But finding a killer's a pretty tall order. I'm sure Priscilla wouldn't want you involved in anything dangerous."

"We're just going to check a few things out, Fred. And, we can always involve the police if, and when, we have something concrete to share."

"Speaking of the police, what were you saying about going to see them? What do you know about Priscilla's murder?"

"We don't know anything about her murder, Fred. It was more an attempt to get Officer Malcolm to tell us what he knows. If he'd been agreeable, we were prepared to tell him a few things we discovered, including Priscilla's whereabouts before the crime. But, sorry to say, our offer to barter didn't work. Officer Malcolm made it pretty clear he wasn't about to tell us anything. But, that's okay. We've done a little investigating of our own."

"I'm confused. Where was Priscilla before

bingo? She left here about four-thirty or so."

"She said she was going to 5:45 confession," said Nellie.

"Confession? Are you sure?"

"That's what she told Ethel."

Fred could not hide his astonishment at hearing those words. "That's surprising. I don't recall Priscilla, in thirty-nine years of marriage, going to confession more than three or four times. And it was always at the 10:00 mass. Never at 5:45 that I can recall. I wonder what prompted her to go to see the priest at that hour. And, whatever it was, I'm surprised she didn't mention it to me." He thought for a moment. "Are you saying the police don't know that she was there?"

"Maybe they do, but they didn't hear it from us," added Nellie.

Ethel placed her hand on Fred's shoulder. "I assume Nancy is coming in."

"Yes. As a matter of fact, she got here late last night. With the time change, she's pretty tired, so she decided to take a little nap. Having her here with me is such a comfort." Fred bent his head down and began to sob. "You probably don't know this, but it was Priscilla's wish to be cremated. Nancy and I will be given her ashes when the process is complete." His sobs grew louder. "When I retired, we discussed what we wanted to happen when we died. I never thought she'd go first. And I definitely never thought she'd die in such a terrible way. My poor Priscilla."

Ethel wished there was something she could say or do to lessen his pain. Yet, no words seemed adequate. She hugged him and said, "I'm so sorry."

"I know," said Fred as he attempted to compose himself. "Priscilla's wish was to have her ashes scattered in her garden. You know how she loved being out there with her flowers. Those were some of her happiest moments. Perhaps you two would like to join Nancy and me when we do that."

"That would mean a lot to us, Fred," replied Nellie.

"Yes. That would be very special. Please let us know when that will be. But, now, if you two will excuse me, I need to visit the little girl's room," Ethel announced. As she got up from the couch, she turned towards Nellie and gave a quick wink. She took that opportunity to stop by the study, where she knew Priscilla spent much of her time.

Ethel quickly moved the magazines on the white rattan table aside, hoping to find – she didn't know what. Her eyes darted quickly about, searching hastily for anything unusual or out of place. Beside the phone, where Priscilla kept her directory, sat a small piece of paper that had been scrunched into a ball. She highly doubted that the police had seen it or it probably would have been confiscated as evidence. Ethel slowly and meticulously opened it, to find a phone number scrawled in Priscilla's handwriting. She'd know her friend's penmanship anywhere. Beside the number, was jotted down an address. 7418 Jefferson Avenue.

Why in the world would Priscilla have a piece of crumpled up paper with *that* address? Drug dealers, pimps and prostitutes frequented Jefferson Avenue, she thought. But, Priscilla? She's more into her Thursday night bible study group or playing bingo. Why would she have ever been going to *that* neighborhood?

"Hmm," declared Ethel under her breath. "I do believe Nellie and I have a bit of serious investigating to do."

Chapter Seven
Is That Really You, Ethel?

"I'll pick you up at 10:00 tonight, Nellie."

"My God, Ethel, that's late. Matilda and I are usually in bed by then."

"So, take a nap! I mean if you want to be a real investigator, you have to be ready to go where the clues take you. Besides, I think this will be a good way to deal with our grief. We'll keep busy; all for the ultimate goal of helping the police and finding justice for Priscilla."

"I agree with you that we should try. But we can't even be sure that note was written by Priscilla."

"I can be sure. I'd know her handwriting anywhere." Ethel nudged her friend's arm, as she shook her head from side to side. "Maybe that's why I'm the lead detective and you're my assistant."

"What's all that about? I thought we were both in this together. Like two peas in a pod!"

"Okay. If you want to be equal partners, then you have to start thinking like a real detective. Try to look past the crumpled piece of paper and figure out its real meaning."

Nellie looked confused. "Honestly, Ethel, you're beyond me."

"Okay, Nellie. I'm trying to imagine what Leonard would tell me to do."

"I think Leonard would tell you to leave the investigating to the police. I think he'd tell you we're in over our heads."

"I beg to differ with you, Nellie. I think as long as we're careful, Leonard would be very proud of our getting involved. Anyway, these are my thoughts. The address is clearly in a neighborhood that Priscilla would have no reason to go to. But maybe there was some thing or someone that caused her to want to go there. We have to find that out. More importantly, we have an address, but no confirmation as to whether Priscilla already went there, or was even planning on going there."

"Okay. So, what are *we* going to do in that part of town so late at night?"

"We'll play it by ear, Nellie. Maybe the clues will come to us. But, one thing I think we should definitely do is dress for the part."

"What? Have you lost your mind completely?"

"You'll just have to trust me on this one. We don't want to stand out. You know how they dress on Jefferson."

"Not from personal experience, my dear. But I guess it would be safe to say we won't be wearing our matching bingo sweatshirts."

Ethel laughed deeply, accentuating the crow's feet around her eyes. "Surprise me. And I'll surprise you. Fair enough?"

"Okay, but no matter how we dress, we're going to be noticed. Let's face it, we're old enough to be grandmothers to most of the people who hang out in that neighborhood at that time of the night."

"So, wear some extra makeup. Remember, we're doing this for Priscilla."

Later that afternoon, Ethel rummaged about in her closet searching for the perfect outfit. "Now this is what detective work is all about," she uttered to no one, as she pulled out a slinky purple satin dress with a beaded collar that she'd worn longer ago than she cared to remember. She wrinkled up her nose and gave a quick sniff. "This dress stinks!" she exclaimed. "Time for some Febreze. Hope it gets rid of this mothball smell. But," she laughed, "that's the least of my worries. I don't know if I'll even be able to zip this creation. Lord knows I'm not the size I used to be."

Despite her best efforts, it was clear that no matter how hard she attempted to suck in her abdomen, or what type of girdle she put on, what was, was. There was no way she was going to fit into this snazzy dress any time soon. Without dwelling on her weight gain, she exclaimed, "I guess I'll put this in my Goodwill pile. There must be some other things that are suitable in this closet of mine. Back to the drawing board."

By evening, Ethel had assembled an outfit that she felt was suitable for the occasion. She had found a pair of lemon-colored capris and a pale, yellow peasant top with puff sleeves, embroidered with green and purple flowers. It had been tucked away in a box among an assortment of things she had stored away in hopes of wearing in the future. She clearly remembered having worn the clothes years ago on a trip she and Leonard had taken to Cancun, just months before he had died. Her memories were bittersweet. But, one thing she was glad about was that she could still pull the pants up over her wide hips. That, in and of itself, was a hefty accomplishment.

As she glanced at herself in the full-length mirror that hung on the back of her bedroom door, she smiled broadly at the reflection. "Is that really you, Ethel?" she declared as she admired herself. The scoop neckline of the blouse dipped low enough to reveal a bit of middle-aged cleavage. She spun about slowly, taking in her full figure from all angles. "You look ravishing tonight." The oversized gold hoop earrings that she'd added, along with far more than her usual amount of makeup, completed the total look. The hot pink lipstick and silver eye shadow were so not Ethel. "If I didn't know better, I might mistake myself for a floozy!" Ethel laughed aloud.

Had she not been such an organized, down-to-earth person, she might have wondered whether she was going a bit cuckoo. Talking to herself was one thing. But, admiring herself and dressing totally out of character was not something she was accustomed to doing. But she wasn't Ethel this evening. She was playing a role. And, if she said so herself, she'd risen to the occasion like a pro.

Carrying an oversized canvas purse, into which she'd thrown all her cosmetics, some breath mints, a snapshot of Priscilla and a hairbrush, the most important thing she'd put in was Leonard's tiny tape recorder. Maybe there were more modern recording tools available in today's world, she'd thought. But, if there were, she didn't know about them. Anyway, she'd reasoned, a simple tape recorder was what Leonard had used all those years ago and it had worked just fine for him.

Ethel actually found what she was doing that night to be rather amusing, despite the gravity of her motive for doing it. Taking out her pack of Marlboro cigarettes, that she'd bought earlier, and putting one between her lips really completed her total disguise. Cigarettes were so offensive to her. Ethel detested smoking and hated that so many people went outside during half time at bingo to indulge in the disgusting habit. But, she thought, what a perfect finishing touch to the overall look she was trying so hard to achieve that evening. Satisfied with how she looked, she set out to pick up Nellie.

Nellie stood speechless, for a moment, at the

sight of her best friend. Standing beside her car door, Ethel's intent was to give Nellie an overall picture of her idea of the *Jefferson look.*

"Well, aren't you going to say something?" She turned around slowly. "How do I look?"

"Oh my God, Ethel." Nellie gawked at her best friend and almost lost her balance, as she tried to retain her composure. "Yellow pedal-pushers! Where did you dig those up?"

"Listen, Nellie. We're not back in the 70's. These are called capris in today's world, not pedal-pushers. And, for your information, they're totally back in style. Everyone wears them."

"Not everyone. I must confess that I don't own a pair. Maybe you mean everyone half our age."

"Well, isn't that the look we were hoping for tonight? Speaking of which," she said, as she eyed her friend over slowly from top to bottom, "you look great."

"Do you really think so?"

"Yes. Your hair looks different than it did earlier today. Lighter than before. I really like it."

"Thanks, Ethel. You can be blond, too, if you want. Easy as can be. Just use Light Natural Blond by Nutrisse. Voila! A whole new look."

"Very becoming, Nellie. Honestly, you look ten years younger. And where did you find that skirt? I love the ruching. Actually, I just read in one of those women's magazines that it's the latest style."

"Really? My mother always used to say that everything eventually comes back into vogue, if you live long enough. Who knew! It's older than the hills."

Wearing a black-ruched skirt with a red silk blouse that Nellie had worn to her niece's engagement party some years ago, she had found the clothing tucked away in her basement cedar closet. She felt fortunate she could still get her body into everything. But it was the black high- heeled shoes that really completed the outfit.

Nellie teetered back and forth, putting her hands firmly against the car to stop her fall. "Whoops! I guess I'm definitely not as young as I used to be. As you can see, I'm having trouble walking in these high heels and my feet are killing me already."

"But you look amazing, Nellie. Trust me, it's worth the pain."

"If you say so. But I sure hope my bunion doesn't act up."

"Don't be such a worry-wart. Anyway, where we're headed, your bunion is the least of your worries."

Ethel sat down in the driver's seat and started the car. "Buckle up, Nellie. We're heading off on an adventure," she exclaimed. "Next stop 7418 Jefferson Avenue."

Chapter Eight
Roxy's Club

"Okay.   Maybe I'm not up on all the latest technology, but Reginald will be able to find the address we're looking for without a hitch."

"Reginald?   Who's Reginald?" questioned Nellie.

"Oh, Reginald's my pet name for my GPS. The salesman said it would come in handy one day and, by golly, he was right. Leonard and I used to name all our cars and, when we got our GPS, we thought it would be fun to name it, too. Leonard actually came up with Reginald and it just stuck."

"To each his own. So, what's your car's name?"

"Celeste Civic," Ethel replied. "Doesn't she look like a Celeste?"

"If you say so, Ethel. Maybe I should think about naming my Saab," she half-heartedly added.

"Go for it. How about Saab-rina? Or, better yet, how about Saab-astian!"

"Very funny. I guess I'll just think about it for a while. After all, I've waited this long. No need to rush it."

"Do I detect a note of sarcasm, Nellie?"

Nellie smiled. "Maybe just a little."

Ethel veered left as she exited the expressway onto Jefferson Avenue, while her friend sat speechless beside her, her mouth agape. Nellie peered out the window, becoming more and more uneasy with each passing block.

"Oh my God, Ethel. You've got to be kidding me. We can't get out in this neighborhood. Look around. There are thick iron bars over most of the windows and," she added nervously, "check out that group of kids on the corner in front of that deli. They look like a gang." Nellie slithered down in her seat. "And have you ever seen so much graffiti all over the place? It's disgusting."

"Well, Miss Worrywart, the good news is that we're only in the 4000 block of Jefferson. Maybe things will improve down the road."

"I doubt it. This is the sleaziest neighborhood I've ever been in. And that it's night, makes it even more frightening, Ethel. Haven't you heard about drive by shootings? This is just the kind of area that those things happen in."

"Chill, Nellie. We'll be fine," she confidently added, as she opened her purse. "Here, check this out."

Nellie looked in her friend's hand bag to see everything Ethel had thrown in earlier. But the one thing that left her dumb-struck was Ethel's last-minute addition; put in just before leaving her house.

"Are you out of your mind, Ethel?" Nellie's voice was agitated and, at the same time, frightened. "A gun! What would ever possess you to carry that and," she added in a confused tone, "where did you get it?"

"Actually, it's a Colt 1911. Leonard had it when he was on the force. He always kept it locked in our office safe. Said you never know when you might need to protect yourself. I guess he was right. You never do know."

"But, Ethel. Don't you think it's dangerous to have that in your purse? I mean, do you even know how to use it?"

"Remember, Nellie, I was married to a police detective. Leonard felt it was important for me to know how to protect myself. So, he took me to the shooting range several times to show me how to use it safely. He even had me get a carry permit. I never needed to use it, but I think we're wise to have it with us tonight. Carrying a gun will give us a better sense of security."

"Speak for yourself, Ethel. I'd just as soon turn around and have that Reginald thing of yours direct us on how to get back home. This is too dangerous for us."

"You've got to suck it up and be braver, Nellie. We've come this far. Remember, this is for Priscilla."

Nellie sighed deeply. "Okay. But just so you know, this is against my better judgment."

"Noted," replied Ethel, as the GPS announced that they had arrived at their destination.

Ethel slowly guided her car along the curb in front of 7418 Jefferson. The fluorescent sign above the building said *Roxy's Club* in large, bold red letters.

"I don't think it looks too bad." Ethel's voice sounded very matter of fact.

"Oh, really?" Nellie's tone was flippant. "And what makes you say that?"

"Well, for starters, I don't see any gangs."

"Oh, I feel so much better," Nellie sarcastically added. "And, exactly what kind of club is this?"

"Well, there's only one way for us to find out," Ethel said, as she grabbed her pocketbook and opened the door of the Civic.

"Wait! Close the door, Ethel. Maybe you're not scared, but I am. How do you know we'll be safe in there?"

"How do you know it's safe for you anywhere, Nellie? I mean would you ever have imagined that Priscilla would have been killed in a church in the suburbs? She might have been safer in Roxy's. Who

42

knows?" Ethel flipped her hair off to the side. "I say we go in, look around, maybe have one drink and leave. The main thing is to be alert about everything we see and hear. Come on, Nellie, we've come this far. We might as well see if anything pans out that can help us. We owe it to Priscilla."

Nellie reluctantly opened the passenger door. "I don't know how I let you wrangle me into these dangerous situations, Ethel. But, come on. Let's get it over with." She teetered back and forth as she self-consciously moved one shoe in front of the other, trying to act nonchalantly as the two entered the smoke-filled club.

Their entrance did not go unnoticed. "Well, well, what have we here?" declared the husky, muscular man who towered over them. Sucking on a cigarette, wearing a Red Sox baseball cap with the rim turned towards the back, Nellie thought if he got any closer, she was going to pass out. "I ain't never seen you two ladies in the hood before. Can I buy you a drink?" he offered in a seductive voice, as he slowly eyed Ethel up and down.

"No thank you," Ethel replied without missing a beat. "I see a table over there," she said to Nellie, as she motioned towards the corner. "Come on."

Nellie's eyes darted about, as her heart fiercely pounded. Dear, Lord, she thought to herself. If we get out of here in one piece, it will be a miracle. She tried to avoid making direct eye contact with any of the patrons, as she slid nervously into the chair.

"Okay, Nellie. I think this is really good."

"What? What are you talking about? What's good?"

"Our disguises. That guy came on to us." She bent over closer to Nellie. "Obviously, he didn't suspect we were undercover detectives," she whispered into her friend's ear.

"First of all, Ethel, we're not really undercover detectives. We're more like amateur sleuths and this sleuth would like you to know that she's not liking the feeling she's getting in this establishment. And, secondly, that man didn't come on to *us,* Ethel. He came on to *you.* And, if I were you, I wouldn't be too flattered. He was creepy, if you ask me."

"Sometimes you can be such a stick in the mud, Nellie."

"Oh really, Miss Hotshot," she exclaimed as she surveyed the group of seedy looking men. "Check out the bar. I think there's a lot more going on there than we might want to know about."

"Now you're thinking!" Ethel exclaimed.

The burly, broad-shouldered man that acted as bar tender wore a sleeveless white ribbed tee-shirt that read *Life's a Bitch* in bold black letters. Covered in tattoos, he looked even more frightening than their tablemate at St. Angela's.

Now, he's classy, Ethel sarcastically thought, knowing it was probably in their best interest to keep such opinions to herself. Undoubtedly, from the expression on Nellie's face, she had already reached the same conclusion.

The group of six or seven men, gathered around the smokey bar, all stood with drinks in their hands. Nellie wondered what it was that they found attractive about wearing their shorts half way down their behinds. But it must have been something because it seemed quite popular here at Roxy's.

A smile suddenly encompassed her face at the thought that was passing through her mind. Who am I to judge how someone dresses? She laughed to herself. They could be thinking the same thing about me and Ethel and, the funny thing is, they'd be absolutely right. We do look bizarre, no matter what Ethel thinks about our *fitting in.*

Suddenly, Nellie's eye caught one man passing an envelope to another. She made a mental note. Maybe a clue, she thought.

The pool table that sat in the far corner had two tough looking men vying for the attention of what Nellie referred to, for lack of a better word, as a hussy. The trollop was dressed in tight black leather shorts that appeared painted on her buxom body and a halter top that left nothing to one's imagination. The two men alternated between taking shots with their pool cue and kissing and fondling this woman. Has she no self-respect, thought Nellie. But she couldn't help but notice that her heels were probably even higher than hers and she found it amazing that she appeared to have no trouble zipping around the pool table. That's youth for you, she mused. I'm impressed.

Ethel appeared not to notice or, if she did, she had zoned out and pretended not to. She rhythmically tapped her fingers against the scarred, round, wooden table. She nonchalantly took out the pack of Marlboro cigarettes from her purse and lit up, as if she'd been smoking all her life. This is kind of fun, she thought to herself, as she brought the disgusting tobacco to her lips, being careful not to inhale. She was surprising herself at the skill with which she was portraying a type of lifestyle she'd only read about in books. Ethel seemed oblivious to the assortment of scantily-clothed women that paraded about cavorting with the beer-guzzling men. "Don't you just love the music?"

"I don't love anything about this place, Ethel. And, just for the record, you look ridiculous with that *thing* hanging out of your mouth. Come on. Let's order our obligatory drink and be on our way. This place gives me the creeps."

Ethel seemed to pay no attention to her friend's concerns. "My dear, Nellie. I can see clearly that this establishment caters to a far different crowd than we're accustomed to socializing with. I'll give you that. But women flirting with men is universal. Hardly something to get all riled up about. I think things are going quite splendidly."

"Oh, do you now?" Nellie's tone clearly indicated that she did not share the same opinion as her friend.

A tall, dark-haired woman wearing a mini skirt that barely covered the cheeks of her backside and a top that exposed her fleshy breasts, knelt down and placed two gin and tonics before them on the table.

"Excuse me, but we didn't order these."

Chewing a stick of gum, while twirling her hair around her finger, she replied without hesitation. "I know. These are from the man sitting beside the pool table. He said to tell you both that you look quite different from the last time he saw you. Said to tell you he thinks you both look pretty darn sexy, for two old broads." She shrugged her shoulders. "Hey, I don't get paid to ask questions. Whatever turns you on. I'm just delivering the drinks. That's it." She turned and sauntered away toward the bar.

Chapter Nine
Two Hail Marys

The room was dimly lit and the stench of stale smoke permeated the air, as the two women turned towards the pool table to see the man with the red hair smiling that same evil half-smile. Dressed in jeans and a green t-shirt, his appearance was a sharp contrast to how he had appeared at the Sheridan Family Restaurant. But there could be no doubt it was the same person.

Nellie brought her hand up to her chest. "I'm not kidding you, Ethel. I'm having heart palpitations."

"Calm down, Nellie," she said as she reached for her purse. "We'll be okay."

"I don't know if I find your saying that too reassuring," she uttered nervously, as the man who had initially greeted them appeared beside their table. Without warning, he grabbed a chair and sat down beside them.

"I'm Travis, ladies," he declared in a seductive voice, as he slowly eyed Ethel up and down. He reeked of smoke and gave Nellie the willies.

She silently said two Hail Mary's that they would not meet their demise in this seedy establishment, as she attempted to maintain her composure.

"So, you two gorgeous girls never did say what brings you to Roxy's. And I sure as hell know I ain't seen you here before. I never forget a pretty face," he boasted. "You ain't the law, are you?"

"The law? Hardly," replied Ethel, as she casually took a long drag on her Marlboro. Ethel rummaged about in her purse searching for the snapshot of Priscilla, while paying careful attention not to expose the pistol. "Ah, here's what I'm looking for," she exclaimed as she placed the photo squarely atop the nicked table, while inconspicuously pressing the 'on' button of the recorder. "We found a piece of paper with Roxy's address on it at our friend's house. To be honest, we decided to check things out for ourselves and find out if she was really ever here. I mean, we're her two best friends. Would you mind looking at the photo and telling us if you've ever seen this woman."

Travis studied the picture for a fleeting moment and then, what came out of his mouth, left the two women both mystified and frightened. "Ah, Miss Priscilla!" His broad smile accentuated his tobacco-stained teeth. "Sure, I knew her. She was one fine lady, she was. Pity she was killed."

"You knew Priscilla?" She stared at him in disbelief.

"You bet your booty I knew her."

"What? That's impossible. You can't be speaking of the Priscilla that was our best friend. She would never have come here and not mentioned it to us. Never. It makes no sense."

The burly man adjusted his cap so that the brim was now in the front, as he shrugged his broad shoulders. "Think whatever you like, but I'm telling you she was here just last week. She came on Thursday night, after her bible study class. That's the last time I saw her."

Nellie and Ethel could not believe their ears. "What was she doing here?"

"A little investigating of her own, is what she told me."

"Investigating what? I don't understand. No offense, but this isn't exactly her neck of the woods."

"Listen, ladies. I really liked that broad. So, I'm going to tell you what I know. Might be some people in here," he said as he glanced towards the pool table, "that think I should keep my big mouth shut. To hell with them." It was more than obvious that Travis had consumed more than a few drinks. He motioned to the bartender. "Another draft, Owen. And what about you two? Ready for another? I see gin and tonic's your thing."

"Not really. We don't drink very often, but we do enjoy a glass of wine every now and again. Preferably something sweet like Moscato or Riesling."

"I'd say that would be an accurate statement, Ethel. Even if we were drinkers, I don't think we'd drink *this*," she said pointing to the cocktail before her. "That man over there sent these to us and we don't have the slightest idea who he is. But I will tell you that we're quite certain we've seen him before."

Ethel silently applauded her friend for being so intriguing.

Travis looked back towards the pool table. "You talking about Red, over there?"

"If that's his name, yes."

"That's what everybody here calls him. All I know about him is that he's a thug. Comes in here four or five nights a week."

"A thug?" questioned Ethel.

"You ladies know, or maybe you don't," he said very matter-of-factly, "that sometimes people need protecting or maybe they need to be taught a lesson. Get my drift?" He gave a quick wave of the hand to the man beside the pool table.

"Are you saying he roughs people up?" Nellie innocently inquired.

49

"What's with you, Nellie? Of course, that's what he's saying. Couldn't be much clearer than that."

"You remind me a lot of Priscilla." He put his hand on Ethel's arm and she removed it as quickly as he had put it there. "You seem like a feisty woman."

"Please, Travis. This is business."

"Well, honey, in this part of town it's not at all uncommon to mix business with a little pleasure, if you get my gist." His eyes danced mischievously.

"I do," she replied feeling a bit sick to her stomach at the very thought. "But it's late and we have to be going. We'd appreciate anything you can tell us. I beg of you, in Priscilla's memory, to help us."

"Look, the most I can tell you is that Priscilla was very worried about some girl in her bible study group that she came in with that night. Annie something or other."

"Annie!" Nellie gasped. "Why we know Annie. We met her the one time we went to bible study at Priscilla's last year. She's a school teacher and a wholesome young lady." Nellie seemed flabbergasted. "What in the world would she ever be doing in a place like this? And why would Priscilla be here with her?"

"You've got me. But, looks can be deceiving, as I've learned tonight. I thought you two were undercover cops when you first came in." Travis flexed his arm muscle. "I know you're much older than the other women in this joint, but I find mature women to be a real turn on." He eyed the two slowly up and down. "I think you're both really hot." Travis chugged down his beer.

"Oh, my God, Ethel. Can you believe what he just said to us?"

"That's a compliment, honey. And, if you should ever change your minds about having a little adult fun together, you can always find me here." Travis smiled broadly. "Just so you both know, I'm not at all adverse to a menage-a-trois." He bent over and kissed Ethel on the cheek. "I have a strong feeling our paths will cross again, maybe sooner than you think."

Ethel stood, trying not to show her fear and disgust. "Thanks for the information about Priscilla, Travis. At least this wasn't a wasted trip."

"Can I walk you ladies out to your car?"

"Thanks, but we'll be okay." Ethel gasped aloud, as Travis slapped her on the backside.

"You're already okay, in my book, honey."

Nellie walked as briskly as her swollen feet allowed, swaying slightly in an attempt to keep up with her friend, whose pace was faster than she'd ever seen. "Let's get out of here," she uttered in an unsteady voice. When they opened the door to the outside, a dusting of white covered the ground and snow was gently falling. "I hope Celeste has a good heater. I'm feeling chilled to the bone."

Ethel pressed her purse close to her, as the two women made a beeline for the Civic.

Chapter Ten
Annie

Ethel returned the Colt 1911 to the safe, as soon as she returned home.

Late as it was, she hopped into the shower. "I stink," she exclaimed, unable to escape the lingering stench of smoke that remained on her hair and body. That, coupled with the need to wash away the thick make-up she'd used for her disguise, which she had to admit had turned out to be pretty darn authentic, left her no choice. She hummed *Unforgettable*, the tune she and Leonard had danced to on their wedding night, as the soap and shampoo slowly washed away reminders of a life-style she was thankful had been only temporary.

Ethel glanced at the clock beside her bed and did a double take. "One forty! I think that's the latest I've been out in years."

But, their trip to Roxy's had not been in vain. They had acquired a few clues that might provide useful leads, she thought. What puzzled her was why Priscilla and Annie were at Roxy's in the first place and what connection they could possibly have to that seedy bar. Lying in bed, she replayed the evening's events. She couldn't seem to get Travis, Red or that whole Roxy experience out of her mind, as she tossed and turned.

She realized it didn't take a real whiz of a detective to figure out that the next sensible step would be to pay Annie a visit. "Yes," she enthusiastically exclaimed. "I'll give Nellie a call first thing tomorrow morning and we can figure out a good time to go. I think a little visit with Annie might just shed some light on this whole situation." My curiosity has definitely been piqued, she thought, as she rolled over on her side and drifted off into a deep sleep.

The sunlight filtered through the partially drawn floral curtains that framed the two narrow side bedroom windows, while prisms of light danced against the butterscotch-colored walls. Ethel jolted out of bed with an enthusiasm she had not had in some time. If only Leonard was here, she thought. Not only do I miss him terribly, but he had such a good head on his shoulders. He'd know what to do, she reasoned.

With a sudden burst of energy, she declared, "Leonard, I know I'm not the detective you once were, but I learned a lot from you. After thirty years of listening to you tell me about your cases and how you handled them, a lot of information and questions are percolating in my head. And by golly, Leonard, I'm going to try my darndest to make you proud."

By ten o'clock that morning, the two women sat at their usual booth at the Sheridan Family Restaurant. Dressed in their matching bingo sweatshirts, they were ready to tackle the day. Tammy took their order for oatmeal and coffee as Ethel explained, in detail, the strategy she felt they should follow.

"So, let me just see if I have this right," mused Nellie. "We stop over at Annie's, even though we haven't talked to her in nearly a year. Oh, hi Annie, we nonchalantly say. We just happened to be in your neighborhood and thought we'd stop by to say hello. We were at Roxy's last night...oh, you know, that sleazy bar in a terrible part of town. Your name just happened to come up when we were discussing Priscilla's death and, by the way, what exactly is your connection to that hell-hole of a place?" Nellie smiled broadly at Ethel across the table. "That should go well."

Ethel shook her head from side to side. "Okay, Nellie. You do have a point. We need to be discreet. Let me just think a minute." Ethel put her hand over her forehead and looked down, as she contemplated her next idea. "Clearly we need to be very tactful and prudent when we speak with her. I think my knowing a bit about how Leonard handled himself will come in handy. He questioned hundreds of witnesses and suspects back in the day and shared information about loads of cases with me. Although I might be a bit rusty remembering what he told me, I imagine it's kind of like riding a bike. Why don't we give her a call and plan on stopping by later today, when she's done teaching?"

"Sounds like a plan."

Later that afternoon, Ethel parked her Civic along the curb of the winding road that led to Annie's townhouse. The beautiful, all-brick two story, and homes that surrounded it, seemed quite expensive. Set back from the street among towering, mature trees, in a tranquil suburban neighborhood, the area was a far cry from that of Roxy's.

They walked slowly up the long, twisting pathway, as the snow crunched beneath their boots. "It's bitter out," Nellie declared, as she wrapped the plaid scarf more securely around her neck and pulled her red knit cap down to cover her ears. She could see her breath as she spoke. Happy to reach the front door, Nellie pressed her red-gloved finger firmly on the bell, as *Hail, Hail the Gang's All Here* began to melodically play.

A young woman with curly brown hair, deep chestnut eyes and full lips, covered in a pale pink gloss, appeared. Wearing blue-jeans and a delicate rose-colored cashmere sweater that accentuated her well-endowed

54

figure, her smile seemed contagious. "Please, come in," she warmly said.

She ushered the two to a spacious family room with glass windows that stretched from floor to ceiling, offering an expansive view of the landscaping beyond. The branches of the trees, dusted in powdery white snow, gave the yard a fairytale appearance.

"May I get you something? Perhaps a cup of tea."

"I don't know about Ethel, but I'd love a cup."

"I guess that would be nice. It's so cold out today," Ethel added as she rubbed her hands briskly together.

Just then an adorable brown and white beagle entered the room. "Oh, this is Maxwell," Annie endearingly added, as she knelt down and lovingly stroked the dog's back before heading into the kitchen. "Back in a minute," she exclaimed, as Maxwell stretched out comfortably beside Nellie's feet.

"Isn't she cute?" Nellie said, as she rubbed behind the beagle's droopy ears. "Animals always seem to like me." Maxwell, who apparently could care less what these two strangers were doing at his owner's home, fell into a peaceful slumber.

Furrows formed between Ethel's eyes. "Annie sure doesn't seem like she'd ever remotely have anything to do with the goings-on at Roxy's. For the moment, Nellie, I'm stumped," she whispered.

Ethel suddenly grew silent, as Annie re-entered the room carrying a tray with a large, deep green floral teapot, three cups, some cream and sugar and a plate of what appeared to be freshly baked chocolate chip cookies. A smile encompassed her face. "I see Maxwell's made a new friend. I can move him, if you'd like."

"Oh, no. He's fine here. I'm an animal lover."

"Me, too." Annie poured everyone a cup of tea. "But I have a feeling you're not here on this cold afternoon to talk about my dog. So, if I'm not being too presumptuous, why are you here?"

Ethel took the lead. "Before we get started talking, I just wanted to say that these chocolate chip cookies are wonderful. Where did you find the time to bake them?"

"I love to cook. I baked them when I got home from school today."

"I love to cook, too," interjected Nellie. "We have a lot in common, you and I. We both love animals and baking."

Ethel shot Nellie a look that clearly meant *enough already*.

Okay, I can take a hint, thought Nellie, who sat placidly sipping her cup of tea.

"Now, where was I?" Ethel questioned.

"Complimenting my delicious chocolate chip cookies," Annie replied with a giggle. "Seriously, I think you had some questions you wanted to ask me." She put one leg over the other. "Go ahead. I'm ready."

"I'm sure you know our dear friend, Priscilla, was murdered."

Annie cast her big, brown eyes downward. "I know. It was terrible. I've been so upset about it. I think about her all the time, as I'm sure you both must, too."

"That we do, dear. Coming here today wasn't easy, but there's something we have to ask you."

"Yes. What is it?"

"Nellie and I were at Roxy's last night."

Annie's facial expression suddenly changed at the mere mention of the word. "*You* were at Roxy's?"

"We were. And we were told something by a man there named Travis that, frankly, how shall I say this, has us very concerned," said Ethel.

Annie listened attentively, as Ethel relayed the details of their visit. She fidgeted nervously with the silver charm bracelet on her left wrist, as Ethel spoke.

"I guess the easiest thing for me to do is to just come right out and ask you what's on our minds. What's been on our minds since last night. What's your connection to Roxy's?"

Annie repeatedly uncrossed and crossed her legs, as she picked away at the pale pink polish that adorned her index finger. If it wasn't already chipped, Ethel felt reasonably sure it would be now. Annie's face grew flushed and she tightened her hands together, as a guttural sound emerged from the depths of her throat. But she said nothing.

"Annie, please. We believe there may very well be some link between Roxy's and Priscilla's murder. If there's anything you can tell us, even the slightest detail, please do. I beg of you, for Priscilla's sake."

Annie clammed up even tighter than Officer Malcolm had, when they'd broached the subject of murder with him. It was clear that whatever connection she might have to Roxy's, she was not about to share it with them. A long, uneasy silence filled the room. Cautiously weighing each word that left her lips, Annie finally said, "What I can tell you is that I believe God works in mysterious ways."

"And what do you mean by that?" Ethel questioned.

She shrugged her shoulders. "Oh, I don't know exactly, but I do believe some things in life are predestined and determined by a power much higher than ours."

"You're speaking of God?"

"God and those who do God's work." Annie picked a cookie crumb off her sweater and placed it on her napkin.

57

Ethel took a sip of her tea. "I know that you and Priscilla were in bible study group together on Thursday nights. Nellie and I often thought about joining the group, but, unfortunately, we just never got around to it." Ethel sighed. "As you know, we were just there the one time. May I ask you, did the same women come every week?"

"For the most part, yes. There were six of us and aside from Clara, who moved to Texas last year to be near her daughter, it's been the same group for the past five years."

"Would you be able to provide us with a list of the women who were at the bible study group that Thursday evening before her murder?"

"Absolutely."

"And, from what I understand, the meeting was always at Priscilla's house."

"It was. We all offered to rotate houses, but she preferred to have it there. Said she'd provide the meeting place, if we'd provided the refreshments." Annie shrugged her shoulders. "Worked out well. Her house is pretty centrally located among the members and everyone took turns bringing the snacks."

"I see," said Ethel. "And, if you could think back to that Thursday's meeting, do you recall if anything out of the ordinary occurred? Anything at all."

Annie stared into the distance, a pensive look on her young face, as she blotted her moist lips together. "No. Not really. The topic that night was on the development of Godly character. The discussion centered around our choosing to do what is right by following His laws."

"Interesting topic. I recall Father O'Leary giving a sermon on that several months ago."

"Yes. And our bible study group found it so interesting that Priscilla asked him to speak before the group that Thursday night."

"Really? Did Father often partake in your study group?"

"Oh, no. Only one other time that I can recall. Father is much too busy. But Priscilla felt he had been so insightful in his approach to the topic during Mass, that she'd asked him if he'd mind stopping by. How fortunate we were to have him there that night to answer any questions we had. It was so kind of him." Annie brought her hand up to her stomach.

"Are you alright, dear?" Nellie asked. "You look rather pale."

"Oh, I'm fine. I probably picked up some kind of bug from one of my students. You know how germs go around. One of the hazards of teaching. I've had a little stomach ache on and off for a few days, but I'm sure it's nothing."

"You can never be too careful about your health. Promise us you'll take it easy. And, in the meantime, let me pour you another cup of tea." Ethel picked up the decorative floral print pot without waiting for a reply. "You know a sick teacher isn't any good to her students."

"Now who sounds like the teacher!" Annie light-heartedly responded. "You sound just like my mother. Honestly, I'll be just fine."

Ethel took the colorfully crocheted afghan from the couch and placed it over Annie's lap. "Now, that's better," she matter-of-factly stated. "So, let's get back to that Thursday night, if you're sure you feel up to talking."

"Don't be silly. I'm perfectly fine."

"Alright then," Ethel continued. "One more time. Is there anything unusual you can recall?"

Again, Annie gazed into the distance, as she contemplated Ethel's question. "I'd have to say no. Father O'Leary explained how God supplies all of us with the spiritual tools we need to be successful. But he stressed that it is we, as humans, who must each choose to follow His way."

"That makes perfect sense," added Ethel.

"I agree. I guess it all boils down to being a good Christian. Showing love, patience and kindness are only a few of the qualities that we must strive for. I think every one of us had a better understanding of the topic when Father left."

"Sounds like a very fulfilling evening. And, let me ask you, during the meeting did you ever see Priscilla act differently than she normally did? Think carefully. Anything you can tell us would be very much appreciated."

"No. Nothing. Although," Annie said, quickly dismissing her thought, "it's probably nothing."

"What you might think is unimportant, may actually turn out to be something that is very relevant. What were you going to say?"

"Just that Priscilla got a phone call in the middle of the meeting and she excused herself to go into her study. When she came back into the room, I thought something about her just didn't seem right. She looked, oh, I don't know, I guess frazzled would be the word I'm looking for. I even asked her if everything was okay and she assured me it was. But there was something about her that was off. Until this moment, I never even thought about it as possibly having anything to do with what happened."

"Do you have any idea who was on the phone?" Ethel questioned.

"No, not at all. I wish I did."

"Interesting. Well, I'm just wondering if the number I found crumpled up in her study had anything to do with who called that night. I've got it in my purse. I assumed it was Roxy's number since it turned out to be their address on the paper. Let me just get it out," Ethel said, as she removed the scrunched-up piece of paper and held the number up before her. "Should we dial it and see who answers?"

"Don't ask me," declared Nellie.

"Me, neither," added Annie. "This is all way beyond me."

"Okay, then. I can see I have no choice, but to take matters into my own hands." She turned towards Annie, wrinkled paper in hand. "May I use your phone?"

Chapter Eleven
Pretending to be Pregnant

"Good afternoon. Buffalo Women's Clinic. How may I help you?"

Ethel was speechless, as her mind tried to think of what to ask. She paused uneasily for a moment. Women's Clinic, she thought. Why would Priscilla have scrawled down *that* number, she wondered. "Yes, could you please tell me where you're located?"

"Certainly. We're just down the street from Buffalo General Hospital, on High Street off Main. 527 High Street to be exact. Did you want to make an appointment?"

"Not today," Ethel replied without hesitation. "Thank you for your time."

"No problem. I'm happy to be of help, if you should need it." The tone of the woman's voice intrigued Ethel, as she hung up the phone and turned towards Nellie.

"That's odd. I'm quite certain the woman with whom I just spoke is the receptionist for an abortion clinic."

"An abortion clinic? I don't get it. Priscilla was old enough to be a grandmother. Not to mention that she had a hysterectomy years ago. Why would she have had that number?"

"That's what we've got to find out," Ethel confidently replied.

Annie looked perplexed. "That just doesn't make any sense."

"You're right. And the neighborhood the clinic is in, off High Street, is definitely another strange fork in the road. Priscilla would have had no reason to be in that area. Although," Ethel added with surprise in her voice, "it's not too far from Roxy's."

"Do you think there's a connection between the two?"

"I'm not really sure, but I don't think it's at all unreasonable to pay the clinic a visit; take a look around. Nothing to lose." Ethel sat deep in thought. "One little hitch in our plans. If it is an abortion clinic, like I'm thinking it may be, then how do two women our age get off strolling in."

"I'd have to agree with you on that one. Somehow, I don't think, even dressed in our best disguises, we could pull that feat off," Nellie chuckled.

Suddenly Annie showed more enthusiasm than she had all day. "I've got an idea," she exclaimed. "Why don't I go with you to the clinic? I could pretend I was pregnant and thinking about aborting. That will give some legitimacy to your visit and maybe you two could poke around while I'm giving them my made-up information."

"You'd do that for us?"

Annie began to fidget with her bracelet again. "I'll do whatever I can, if you think it could potentially help you find out who killed Priscilla."

"We'll think about it and let you know. No sense dragging you down to that part of town unless we have a real plan. Meanwhile, thanks for all your help."

"I don't think I've been much help, but I would like whoever killed Priscilla to be caught and put away; hopefully for life."

Maxwell stretched and opened his mouth wide, letting out the biggest yawn they'd ever heard. Nellie bent down and stroked his back. "You shouldn't be so tired, fellow. You've been asleep almost the whole time we've been here." Maxwell looked up at Nellie and placed his paw on her lap.

"You've made a friend for life," Annie exclaimed. "He really is taken with you, aren't you Maxwell?"

The dog looked over at its owner, but remained with Nellie.

"Fickle, isn't he?"

"No more so than most men," she light-heartedly replied.

"Listen, Annie, if you're serious about going with us to the clinic, we'll try to figure things out and devise a plan."

"Alright then. I'll await your call. Come here, Maxwell," she affectionately called. "Ethel and Nellie have to go now. Let's get you your dinner."

With those words, Maxwell hastily bolted into the kitchen. Ethel and Nellie said their final goodbyes and bundled up, as they prepared to venture out into the frigid December air.

A light blanket of pure white snow had fallen during their brief visit. The wind slapped against their cheeks, as they walked toward their car.

As they approached Ethel's Civic, they noticed an old, run-down black Ford pick-up truck idling at the curb. It had not been there earlier. Unable to identify the person sitting in the driver's seat, due to the tinted glass windows, the two hastily entered the Honda and immediately locked the doors.

As Ethel cautiously maneuvered the Civic along the twists and turns that led towards home, she noticed the black pick-up truck following closely behind them.

Chapter Twelve
The Ouija Board

Nellie nervously rubbed her hands together, as she paced back and forth in her kitchen. It was troubling her more and more that the police didn't appear to be making much progress. Maybe Ethel's right, she thought. Maybe we are the ones who'll have to solve this crime. But we're going to need a few solid clues, if we have any hope of ever doing that, she thought.

She put the tea kettle on to boil and sat down on her recliner to do some thinking. Instantly, Matilda stretched her long body out on Nellie's lap, resting her head on Nellie's ample thigh. Nellie massaged behind her ears, causing her full-figured feline to purr loudly. "What are we going to do, Matilda?" She brushed her fluffy white and gold coat, as she continued to speak to her cat as if she actually understood what she was saying.

Nellie sat for a long while, staring into the distance. It was the whistling of the tea kettle that caught her attention. She gently placed Matilda on the pale blue carpeting, while she returned to the kitchen. "Back in a minute, girl, and then you can sit up on my lap again." Matilda looked up with her soulful green eyes, as if she understood.

We've got to be missing something, she pondered. Suddenly, she had an idea. She ran upstairs, as quickly as her arthritic knees allowed, and grabbed the step ladder from the utility closet. "Now you're thinking,

Nellie!" She positioned it inside the closet in the guest room that held an assortment of things that probably should have been thrown away years ago. She carefully ascended the steps and began to rummage about on the top shelf, lifting and moving the contents of each box from one place to another. Suddenly her eyes spotted what she had hoped to find. "Aha," she gasped. "Sometimes it pays to be a pack rat." Nellie grabbed the cardboard container from the shelf and carefully stepped down onto the carpeting below.

Matilda awaited her downstairs. "Look what I found girl. Can you believe it? I've had this old Ouija board for probably thirty years." She quickly brushed her hand over the top of the box. "Now that's a lot of dust!" she exclaimed, as she removed its contents. "I know many people think this Ouija board is a bunch of mumbo jumbo, Matilda. But, let me tell you, Ouija boards are nothing to fool with. Years ago, my grandmother showed me how to use it and, believe me, I had some pretty scary things happen. That's why I've had it hidden away in the closet all these years," she said as she sat back down in her recliner.

Nellie's mind flashed back to that night, decades ago, when she and Granny had asked the Ouija if grandfather would get better. He'd been sick for months, something with his lungs. The planchette had gone to the word "no" and following that, she remembered the pointer moving, as if their hands weren't attached to their bodies.

As if it were yesterday, she remembered it spelling out March 20. Chills ran up and down her spine just thinking about that night. The amazing thing is that on March 19 granddad was rushed to the hospital, where he passed away the next day. From that day on, Nellie never wanted anything to do with the board. But, maybe now, it could provide some mystical clue to help lead them to Priscilla's killer.

"It's worth a try," Nellie declared with confidence in her voice, as she reached for the telephone.

"Ethel, it's me, Nellie. Listen, I've got an idea. Maybe there is something we can do to help us figure all this out."

"Like what?"

"Can you come over tonight? Say around half-past seven. I'll tell you then."

"You sound so mysterious, Nellie. But, okay. I'll be there."

Nellie, as was her habit whenever she had some time on her hands, headed to the kitchen and took out all the necessary ingredients to make her lemon drop cookies. She knew they were one of Ethel's favorites. A wave of sadness washed over her, as she remembered how Priscilla had enjoyed them, too.

Evening came quickly. She and Ethel sat across from one another in the living room, separated by a round wooden table that held the mysterious board. Nellie had dimmed the lights, drawn the draperies and placed sage scented candles throughout the room. She recalled her grandmother telling her that sage is supposed to have a cleansing property and keep away any evil spirits.

"I've got to admit, Nellie. You've got me totally stumped here. This seems a little creepy, don't you agree?"

"Look. This is an old remedy for contacting spirits. It's even older than we are! I believe the Ouija, that's what this board is called, dates back to the late 1800's."

"Did you say contacting spirits? Have you lost your mind, Nellie?"

"Get a grip, Ethel. And don't knock it till you've tried it. Believe me, I know from personal experience that it works. And, sad as it is to say, Priscilla is a part of the spirit world now." Her voice trailed off into a whisper. "Trust me, sometimes you might even find out things you wished you hadn't."

"Really? How does it work?"

"First of all, it's important that you believe in it."

"Okay. I'm open-minded. And, if you think it might help lead us to Priscilla's killer, it's definitely worth a try."

"Good. I'll explain how it works." Nellie picked up the heart-shaped plastic pointer. "This is called a planchette. It glides over the board and forms comments or answers "yes" or "no" to questions that we pose." Nellie pointed to the woodcut style alphabet, the numbers 0 through 9 and the words yes and no on the board, as she spoke. "It's said that this board acts as an instrument to open mental exchanges with the spirit world. Kind of like a portal of communication between the living and the dead."

"But, it's just a game, right?" Ethel's voice sounded a bit uneasy.

"Let's just try it and see what happens. I'm telling you that it can be pretty powerful. Ready?" Nellie straightened the board and turned off the one remaining light that set atop a hand-croqueted white doily.

"Ready as I'll ever be," Ethel replied, as she placed her fingertips lightly on the pointer.

Stillness filled the room, as the candles flickered brightly. Both ladies inhaled deeply and closed their eyes.

"Is there anyone in the room with us?" Nellie solemnly asked. "Anyone here from spirit?"

As if being guided by an invisible force, their fingers atop the planchette moved effortlessly across the board and then, suddenly, drew to a stop.

"What does it say?" questioned Ethel.

"It landed right on 'Yes.' Come on, let's ask it another question."

"Who are you, spirit?"

The women silently and patiently waited till the pointer took control, much like it had for the previous question. Only this time it moved freely from one letter to the next, stopping only briefly at each. There could be no doubt as to what it had spelled out. PRISCILLA.

"Oh my God," exclaimed Ethel. "I've got the chills. I can't believe it. If I hadn't seen it with my very own two eyes, I would have never thought it was possible." A look of fear crossed her face. "Now what?"

"Now we ask the question that we both so desperately want to know."

The two women looked nervously at each other across the table, each taking a deep breath. Ethel had an uneasy feeling just thinking about what they were doing.

"It's time to ask," declared Nellie. She closed her eyes and began. "Priscilla, we both miss you terribly. And we both want to know what happened to you. We know you didn't die a natural death." Nellie was on the verge of crying, but fought back her tears. "We know you were murdered and we want justice for you. Can you tell us who killed you?"

The two ladies prayed that the planchette would guide them, as it had already. But, for as hard as they wished, the pointer seemed frozen.

"Maybe I need to ask the question in a different way." Nellie sat and thought for a moment. Hesitantly, she repeated the question. "Can you give us a clue that might help lead us to your killer?" Her heart was beating so quickly, she imagined Ethel could hear it thumping. As before, the pointer did not move. Ethel and Nellie closed their eyes and waited. Each concentrated as hard as she could on the question that had been posed. Without warning, the pointer suddenly took off and began to move about the board stopping at one letter, then the next. Nellie opened her eyes and made a mental note of each letter, as the planchette moved from one to another, seemingly under its own power. Finally, it drew to a sharp stop. Nellie began to tremble.

"What? What is it?" Ethel felt short of breath and far more frightened than she was letting on.

"I don't know. I mean I guess I don't want to know. It's pretty eerie."

"Tell me already. What did it say?"

"THE LIST IS KEY."

"Huh? I don't get it." Ethel looked perplexed. "What does that mean? Priscilla just mentioned the list to us in passing. She never said a word about where she got the list or where the list is or what it was a list of, for that matter."

"I know. It seems pretty cryptic."

"But it seems like that's the only clue she's ready to give us."

"Maybe. But let's try one more time."

The two resumed their positions at the board. "Can you tell us any more, Priscilla?"

This time the planchette moved quickly. Without hesitation, it stopped at the word on the Ouija board that clearly read good-bye. The sage scented candles began to flicker on and off, until the room was suddenly bathed in total darkness.

Chapter Thirteen
A Dead Bunny

"Evidence. That's what we need, Nellie."

"With what the Ouija board showed us, I think maybe we should concentrate on trying to find out what that list might be all about."

"Good thinking. You know, Nellie, I remember Leonard telling me that the least little detail might actually mean far more than you realize at the time. He always stressed the importance of really listening when a suspect was being interviewed and not letting any detail, no matter how remote, slide by."

"Your Leonard was quite the detective. And heeding his words seems like the best plan we have for now. So, what do you say we question each member of Priscilla's bible study class and see if anything about a list comes up?"

Ethel was beaming from ear to ear. "You're starting to think like a real detective, Nellie, and I'm proud to be your partner." She raised her eyebrows, accentuating the lines in her forehead. "So, no time like the present. Let's get started."

The two women set out to question each member of the bible study group to see if their remembrances of that evening were all in agreement. They had learned, from Annie, that there had originally been six women that had attended each Thursday night. But Clara had moved to Texas, leaving five. Sadly, Priscilla was dead and they'd already questioned Annie. That left Donna, Phoebe and Olive. Tedious, repetitive questioning, always done with a smile, had left the two exhausted, as evening fell. Having accomplished their goal, they decided to review everything over dinner.

Although they both loved eating out, they knew the importance of watching their budget, as they mulled over several choices. Watching their money somehow seemed easier than watching their weight! Once middle-age hit, it seemed so much harder to keep off the pounds.

"*The Red Pepper* it is," excitedly declared Nellie, as she buckled up. As usual, Ethel was the driver. "My mouth is watering just thinking about the ginger chicken with green beans."

"I know what you mean. And the orange beef is to die for."

"Everyone says Chinese food is healthy, so there you go. The perfect ending to a very productive day. I think we accomplished a lot."

"I agree. And, once we go over everything, we might even find that we have a clue or two."

Martin Tu, the owner of the establishment, greeted the two by name with a warmth and enthusiasm that probably contributed to the large number of people awaiting a table. He seemed to know every customer's name who dined there and made a point of making every patron feel welcome. Excellent food and a friendly proprietor seemed a winning combination.

The waiter, who efficiently scurried from one table to the next, quickly brought the preliminary crunchy dipping noodles with plum sauce and spicy mustard, along with a pot of sweetly scented jasmine tea. Ethel and Nellie were in heaven. Once they had ordered, Ethel brought out her notes listing the name of each bible study member whom they had interviewed and what her comments had been. Although Ethel had also taped each encounter, because they were at a restaurant, it seemed more appropriate to verbally review their notes as they dined.

"Phoebe and Olive's recollections of that night were pretty consistent with Annie's, wouldn't you agree?"

"I would. They seemed very distraught and eager to do anything they could. But, unfortunately, not one of them remembered anything about a list. So, that clue is still a mystery." Ethel popped a piece of orange beef into her mouth and paused for a moment. "But there was something about Donna that just didn't set right with me."

"What do you mean?"

Ethel paused a moment. "Oh, I don't know. She seemed pretty eager to defend herself. Almost like she thought we were accusing her of something. None of the others reacted that way. There's something haughty about that woman, in my opinion. Not at all someone I'd describe as being a good Christian. And she was the only one who didn't seem genuinely upset and disturbed by what happened."

"But she said she was sorry."

"True. But words are just words. There was no feeling, no hint of sincerity behind them. She was just parroting what she knew we expected to hear her say, if you ask me."

"You're the lead detective. So, what if she wasn't as sincere as the others. What does that prove?"

"Maybe nothing. I don't know. We'll have to wait and see." Ethel popped a crispy green bean, coated in the tasty brown sauce, into her mouth. "This is wonderful," she exclaimed. "You know what really turned me off about her."

"What?"

"That story that she told us about her garden,

when we complimented her on how the other women had raved about all her flowers, was really unsettling. I guess, from all we've heard, she has one of the prettiest collections of petunias and pansies anywhere. But at what price?"

"I know. It was nice of her to invite us to come and see the garden next summer, but I found her story very disturbing. Frankly, I'd be embarrassed to admit that to anyone."

"That's just what I mean. Something about her just isn't normal. What person in her right mind would do something like that? Imagine holding a garden hose over a defenseless little bunny till it was gasping for air and continue blasting it with water, till it lay dead. And she had no remorse. She actually seemed proud of her perverted actions." Ethel felt a wave of sadness pass through her, as she thought about the poor animal meeting its death in such a cruel way, merely for trying to eat from Donna's beloved garden. "Did you see how smug and self-righteous she was when she described the killing? Animals are God's creatures, too. I really think she's mentally ill."

"I'd have to agree, but that doesn't mean she had anything to do with Priscilla's death. A rabbit is one thing; a human's another."

"I didn't say she necessarily had anything to do with Priscilla's death, although, we can't rule anyone out. I just think that we should go over the tape again and listen very carefully to everything she said about that night. She's different than the others in the group. Maybe it's just good-old woman's intuition, but I think there's more to Donna than meets the eye."

"I remember Priscilla commenting once, months ago, about how nobody's husband was as hen-pecked as Donna's. Priscilla said the poor guy just yes's her constantly, because she's impossible to live with if things

74

don't go precisely her way. I guess she's bossy and mean."

"Now we're the ones who don't sound too Christian. We're being rather judgmental, wouldn't you say?"

"Maybe so. But we're not doing or saying anything malicious. We're merely discussing what we saw or heard. Speaking of which, maybe this is just fueling the fire, but I also heard she's a hypochondriac."

"I'm not surprised. From what I know about her, she likes to be the center of attention. She's an odd one alright."

"She was surely my least favorite among the three women we talked with today. Speaking of Donna, we can check her out again next time we're at bingo. She volunteers at the snack bar every few weeks. And, if I'm not mistaken, I think I've seen her selling cards at the table up front sometimes."

"Yes. You're right. I've seen her there, too."

"Okay, then," Ethel said, as she put her notebook and pen back into her oversized bag. "Enough shop-talk. There's still a smattering of beef and a little chicken left on these platters. And being a sleuth has sure given me quite an appetite!" she exclaimed as she scraped the remaining bits of food onto her plate.

Chapter Fourteen
The Black Truck

Matilda sat comfortably perched on the cushioned window ledge, as Nellie prepared a pitcher of lemonade to serve with her double fudge brownies. Every time she baked them, she thought of Edwin. They'd been one of his absolute favorites. Thoughts of him and their life together flooded her mind. How she had hoped they'd grow old together. But his heart attack had changed everything, leaving her a widow. Her heart felt an emptiness that could not be filled. Just as Father O'Leary had promised, the pain had lessened with each passing year. But not a day had passed since he'd died, that he wasn't in her thoughts. Maybe it was because they had never been blessed with children that she doted so on Matilda.

"Company's coming, Matilda. Maybe we should put on one of your bandanas," she exclaimed, as she opened the desk drawer and removed a pink scarf with the words *kitty princess* scattered about. "You look so beautiful in this, my pretty girl," she added as she gently tied it around her cat's neck. Matilda did not appear to share her enthusiasm, as she jumped down and headed off towards the kitchen. "Sometimes you can be so aloof! Go ahead. Have your dinner. Ethel should be here any minute."

The doorbell rang shortly thereafter, as Matilda whisked off abruptly to hide. For as much as Nellie loved her companion, she definitely wasn't the friendliest of cats.

"So, we really need to get down to business," Ethel exclaimed as soon as she stepped through the door. "Put our heads together and try to make some progress; any progress."

"Well, I believe we'll think better with a bit of sustenance," Nellie exclaimed as she brought over a platter of her double fudge brownies and set them down beside her friend.

"These are decadent, Nellie. And," she added as Nellie poured a glass of her homemade lemonade, "everyone knows you make the best lemonade in the county. Your winning first prize at the fair was pretty impressive. It's so refreshing."

"Glad you like it," Nellie replied as she settled down across from her friend. "But you didn't come all the way over here to talk about my culinary talents," she said with a cheery tone.

"There's just so much to digest. I don't know." Ethel's voice trailed off as she continued. "Don't get me wrong, Nellie, I'm not saying we should give up. To the contrary, I think we have some significant leads to investigate. I just want to know we're on the right track."

"I know. But the only way that can happen is with some good old-fashioned detective work. Don't forget, Ethel. I learned from the best."

Ethel laughed. "So now whose sounding like the lead detective!" Ethel paused a moment. "You're right Nellie. We need to explore every possible clue. And," she added as she took a bite of the scrumptious brownie, "two heads are better than one."

"So, let's review."

As the two women discussed everything that had happened thus far, Matilda appeared out of nowhere.

"Well, doesn't she just look like she could win a contest for best dressed kitty. Love her bandana. Very chic, Matilda."

Matilda ignored the compliment and nonchalantly jumped back up on the cornflower blue, upholstered window ledge without so much as a tiny meow. But unlike her usual ritual, where she would find her spot, stretch out her long, lean body and fall asleep in the blink of an eye, Matilda began to bat her little paw against the window.

"Well, that's something I don't see every day," exclaimed Nellie. "Whatever has gotten into her?"

"It's snowing pretty hard out there. Maybe she's grabbing at the snowflakes."

"Maybe. Let me take a look."

Nellie stroked the back of Matilda's neck, as she gently spoke to her favorite feline. Since Edwin had passed away, Matilda had become her best friend and confidant. "What are you grabbing at, sweet girl?"

Sometimes, Ethel believed that Nellie thought Matilda would truly respond.

Suddenly, Nellie shrieked. "Oh my God!"

"What's wrong, Nellie? What's the matter?"

"Maybe it's nothing," her voice trembled. "But I'm nearly positive that black truck parked in front of my house is the same black truck that followed us home from Annie's house the other day."

Ethel popped out of her seat quickly and joined her friend at the front window. "It sure does look the same," her voice quivered. "But, why would that truck be following us?"

"That, my dear friend, is the million-dollar question. And that is what we need to find out." Nellie gave a deep sigh, as she attempted to regain her composure. "There's only one way to know for certain. Let's investigate."

"It could be anyone, Nellie. That's just it. We don't know what kind of person we're up against. This is getting much too scary for me. And I think it's far too dangerous. I know we both want nothing more than to find Priscilla's killer, but we don't want to get ourselves killed doing so. That wouldn't solve a thing. This is a job for the police, Nellie."

"Ethel, have I made a grave error in thinking you were following in Leonard's footsteps? I mean a clue, a big clue, may be sitting right outside my house. And you want to back down at a time when clues are at a premium? No, not acceptable, Ethel." Nellie paused and gazed out the window. "I know you're our lead detective and I know you usually call all the shots, but I just feel it in my bones that this is something we need to do. Usually I'm the nervous one, but this opportunity is staring us in the face. I think we should proceed with caution."

"But, Nellie, I......."

"I don't want to hear it, Ethel. You got us into this. We may only be amateur sleuths, but we vowed to bring justice for Priscilla." She placed her finger gently over Ethel's lips. "Just listen. I have a plan."

"You just listen, Nellie! Being at Roxy's was dangerous. I think we both would agree on that. But having that strange truck following us is really giving me the willies. And now it's here. Here at your house. I don't like this, Nellie. I don't like it at all. I'm frightened and no plan of yours can change how I'm feeling."

"There's nothing wrong with feeling anxious and really getting the adrenaline flowing. That's the sign of a real detective, Ethel. Isn't that what you always say to me?"

Ethel wasn't sure what to think, at that moment. It seemed to her that their roles had suddenly reversed.

"Now grab your coat and hat because we, my dear friend, are stepping out into the blustery snow to do what we were born to do. And, if we're very lucky, we may even get an important clue."

"Oh sure, Nellie. That's a great plan you have. Let's just stroll out into the snowy night and confront whoever is in that black truck." Ethel sighed loudly. "It's more likely, Nellie, that we could get our first real bullet. So, let it go on the record, that I, Ethel Dinwiddie, am strongly opposed to your brilliant plan."

"Noted," responded Nellie. "Never forget that I'm quite aware that I've been trained by the best, Ethel. And this is how I believe we should proceed. A significant clue may be just outside my doorway. It would be a shame to not at least check it out. Now follow my lead."

In a matter of minutes, the brisk December air slapped their faces as they cautiously stepped out onto Nellie's front porch.

Chapter Fifteen
The Warning

The cold air beat against their cheeks as the wind howled and the snowflakes fell. For a split second, Nellie questioned her decision. Maybe she was being fool-hardy, she thought to herself. Perhaps she should have called the police and reported a suspicious vehicle in front of her house. She kept her thoughts to herself. She couldn't let on to Ethel that she was having any doubts. What kind of detective would she be then?

"So, tell me the plan again, Nellie." The air was so frigid that Ethel could see her breath as she spoke.

"It's simple. Nothing complicated. Sometimes basic is best."

"Okay. Basic it is. Review, if you would."

"Of course. Not a problem." Nellie gathered her thoughts and began. "We need to catch him or her off-guard. So, we walk down the driveway and make a sharp left."

"Left? Away from the black truck?"

"Yes, the opposite way. That way whoever is in the truck won't suspect that we noticed them. We're just out for a brisk stroll."

"Oh sure. That seems plausible. Two old ladies out for a night-time walk in this freezing, snowy weather. Now, that's believable! And then what?"

"Stop being such a killjoy, Ethel. After we continue nonchalantly down the street, we turn and walk the opposite way which will take us right beside the truck. We can peer in and, hopefully, see who the culprit is."

"Are you nuts, Nellie? That plan sounds ridiculous to me."

"Well then, can you come up with something better?"

"I feel like I'm getting frostbite out here. What kind of idiots are we anyway? What if we do see who's in the truck? What then, Madame Detective?"

"You don't need to be so sarcastic. I'm just trying to keep our promise to Priscilla. Come on. Let's head that way."

As the two women approached the truck, the door opened and a muscular, tall man approached them.

Nellie gasped, as the imposing figure placed his hands firmly on Ethel's shoulders. The man's grip tightened. Ethel froze in fear. His voice was low and monotone, but his words were clear. "Stay out of things that don't concern you. Consider this a warning. Next time someone may get hurt. Badly hurt." And with those words he pushed Ethel with such force that she fell to the frozen ground beneath her. Nellie cried out, as the man got into his black truck, revved the engine loudly and drove away.

Without hesitation, Nellie bent over to help her best friend up. "Oh, my God, Ethel. Are you alright? I'm so sorry. This is all my fault. I should have never suggested confronting that man. He was so creepy." Nellie put her arm around Ethel as they slowly walked back into the warmth and safety of Nellie's house. "My plan backfired. That's for sure. We were supposed to catch him off guard. Instead look what happened. Can you ever forgive me? Are you sure you're alright?"

"I will be. I think my ego is more bruised than my body, although I'm feeling pretty sore right now."

"No wonder. That pig gave you quite a push. But, thank goodness that's all he did. It could have been a lot worse."

"That's for sure. I'll be fine, Nellie. Actually, now that we're back in your house, I can't believe your plan actually worked. I'm glad you were so persistent."

"What are you talking about, Ethel? My plan totally backfired and, worse yet, could have gotten us killed. You were right."

"I'd have to disagree. I was pretty scared out there, I'll admit. But it was worth it. I got a definite clue."

"I'm confused, Ethel? What kind of clue?"

"It must be from a case Leonard once told me about. The idea just flew into my head. I'll admit that I was scared silly. But, a part of me was thinking about doing my job; about getting a clue. So, when he was squeezing my shoulders so hard, I focused on his license plate. That bully didn't have any idea that's what I was doing." Ethel took a deep breath. "EJP 6979."

"So, where does that get us?"

"With a little luck, that license plate number will get us the name of the person who owns that truck. And," she added, "knowing that may lead us a step closer to finding Priscilla's killer."

"And exactly how do we find that out?" Nellie asked in a very confused tone.

"That's the easy part. Let's talk about it tomorrow. I've had about as much detective work as I can take for one night."

Chapter Sixteen
Black and Blue

The following morning, Ethel woke up feeling achy and bruised. She probably should have stayed in bed longer, but she had things to do. Important things. Her shoulders were quite sore from the event of the previous evening and a good-sized bruise was visible on her leg from when that hooligan had pushed her to the ground. The mere thought of it made her quiver. She gingerly stepped out of bed and winced, as she slowly moved towards the bathroom. She went directly to her medicine cabinet and grabbed two extra strength Tylenol. "These should help what ails me," she said aloud, as she gulped them down with a full glass of water. "Now, a cup of coffee and my bowl of oatmeal and I should be almost as good as new."

When the phone rang, Ethel had a pretty good idea who it was. Nellie had been so worried and concerned yesterday that she had begged her to spend the night. But Ethel felt the greatest comfort would be the security of her own bed. And so, she'd gone home; carefully watching to be sure no one was following her.

The voice on the other end of the phone sounded a bit frantic. "Ethel, how are you? I've been worried sick, thinking about you every minute."

"Nellie, calm down. You are such a wonderful friend to worry about me like this, but I'm going to be just fine. I promise." Ethel took a deep breath and continued.

"A little black and blue, but so worth it. Nellie, we got a clue. And a great one at that."

"I know that's what you're telling me. But I still don't understand how getting a license plate number can help us find our killer."

"Listen, Nellie. I need to take a shower and get dressed. Can you come over in an hour? I'll explain everything."

"Sure."

"See you soon and I'll fill you in on the next step. Let me just assure you that I have something in my bag of tricks that I think will be very helpful."

"You've piqued my curiosity, Ethel, I must say."

Ethel and Nellie sat facing each other on the mauve wingback chairs that always made Ethel think about her dearly departed Leonard. How many evenings they had sat visiting or reading on these very chairs. But sad as it was for Ethel to face, he was gone. And, as Father O'Leary had said, life goes on. How she wished Leonard were there. But, maybe sitting in the same spot that she used to share with her beloved husband would bring her some strength and clarity. She knew finding Priscilla's killer was no easy task. And, from what happened last night, she was surer than ever, that something sinister, something she probably could never have imagined, had happened to Priscilla.

"I was up most of the night worrying about you and thinking about what we should do."

"And, detective, your verdict?"

"Don't be flippant, Ethel. This is no joking matter. You know, as well as I do, we could have been killed last night."

"True. But we weren't, were we? And I believe that was for a reason."

"A reason? What do you mean?"

"I mean that if that thug wanted us dead, we'd be dead. But I think he thinks we'll be scared off and stop investigating."

"Maybe that's a good idea. His warning spooked me and just look at what it did to you." Nellie paused a moment. "You didn't mention the bruise on your face. That's not so easy to cover up, is it?"

Ethel brought her hand to her cheek. "I'll be fine. This mark will be gone before you know it. Let's do what we set out to do. What kind of detectives would we be if we were intimidated by that lowlife?"

"Maybe smart ones," chuckled Nellie. But, if you're sure you want to continue with this, I'm with you." Nellie placed her hand on her friend's knee. "But, you know, Ethel, anytime you want to back out or go to the police, it's fine with me."

"Fair enough, Nellie. But, for now, let's see where our clue leads us. Before we talk shop, how about if I make us both a nice, hot cup of coffee. It will calm our nerves."

"Sounds good."

Ethel set the coffee mugs on the oak coffee table that separated the two chairs and took a deep breath. "Ready?"

"Ready as I'll ever be."

Chapter Seventeen
Baby Steps

"There's a lot we don't know. But, lucky for us, I still remember some of Leonard's old contacts in the police department. I'm quite certain that once they hear our plight, they will help us get the information we need." Ethel sounded confident, as she spoke.

"Okay," Nellie replied in a perplexed tone. "And then what?"

"Sometimes you can really be a stick-in-the-mud, Nellie. What do you mean and then what?"

"Dear Lord, Ethel. I am confused. I wasn't married to a detective, like you were. I was never privy to all this inside information. So, forgive me for being a little mixed up. I mean if we do get a name that matches that license, what are we going to do?" Nellie smiled and continued with a sarcastic edge to her voice. "Do we casually stop by his house and say, oh we know you are the guy that pushed Ethel to the ground. So nice to meet you. And, as long as we're chatting, do you happen to know anything that could help us find our friend Priscilla's killer?"

Ethel folded her arms and shook her head. "Nellie, Nellie. You were making such progress, but I'm starting to wonder if you forgot how to think like a real detective."

"Okay, then. Enlighten me."

"Baby steps, Nellie. No need to get ahead of ourselves. We take it nice and slow. And where do you think the next step leads us?"

Nellie shrugged her shoulders. "Got me."

"Come on, Nellie. You can do this. Think."

"Well if you say you have contacts that may be able to find out who the black truck belongs to, maybe we should start there and see where that lead takes us. If there is a lead."

"Bingo." Ethel smiled broadly. "Now you're thinking."

"I still have Leonard's old directory from his last year on the force. Let me look up a few names that may be able to help."

"Sounds like a plan," Nellie said as she took a sip of her coffee.

Ethel skimmed the pages quickly, seeming to know just who she was looking for. "Got it," she exclaimed. "Bill Sullivan. He was one of the finest officers in the department. Thorough, honest, smart and just an all-around good guy. Leonard and he were great friends. If anyone can help us, I'd put my money on Bill."

"But that was a while ago, Ethel. Anything could have happened to him. He could have moved or, worse yet, he might have died."

"Who are you anyway? Should I nickname you Detective Nellie Negative?"

"Well, all I meant was that anything is possible."

"True. But why do you have to think the worst. Have a little faith."

"It has nothing to do with faith, Ethel. Life happens."

Ethel's countenance took on a look of sadness. "I guess you're right, Nellie. I lost Leonard and never expected that he'd die when he did. Anything's possible." She stared into the distance for a moment, as she gathered her thoughts. "No use dwelling on what might have happened to Bill. Let's find out." Ethel picked up the phone beside her and carefully dialed the number in the directory. "No time like the present, Nellie."

The phone rang and rang until, as Ethel was just about to hang up, a husky voice said, "hello."

"Is this Bill? Bill Sullivan?"

"Who wants to know?" questioned the voice on the other end.

"I don't know if you remember me, Bill. It's Ethel. Ethel Dinwiddie. Leonard's wife."

"Ethel Dinwiddie! Why of course I remember you. Leonard and I were best of friends. He was one of the finest detectives I ever had the good fortune of working with. How have you been? What can I do for you?"

Bill listened carefully, as Ethel filled him in on everything that had happened so far. She made sure not to leave out any pertinent details.

"That's quite a story, Ethel. But I think you just might be in over your head. I'd hate for anything to happen to you or your good friend."

"I thought you might say that, Bill. But I, or should I say we, made a promise to Priscilla to find her killer. It's haunting us that she died the way she did and that no one has been held accountable. It's such an injustice."

"I understand. But, from what you just told me, your lives may be in jeopardy if you pursue things further." An uneasy silence filled the line between them.

"Bill, are you there?"

"Yes, Ethel, I'm here. If you're determined to investigate this, I have contacts who can trace the license plate. They should be able to find out who owns the truck." He cleared his throat. "Why don't I do that and see who comes up. I can see if the owner has any violations. Then we can talk more."

"Sounds good, Bill. I was telling Nellie how you were one of the best officers back in the day. I'm so glad I reached you and that you're willing to help us."

"I'll check it out and get back to you." His voice became solemn. "In the meantime, Ethel, be careful. Any man who would push you to the ground and maybe even be involved somehow in Priscilla's death, is no one you should mess with."

"We'll be careful, Bill. I promise. And thanks so very much for doing this. I'll be on pins and needles till you get back to me."

"I'll try to get it done quickly."

Ethel looked at Nellie and smiled. "Baby steps. What did I tell you? One step at a time."

"Okay, Ethel. But, until we hear from Bill, let's agree to lay low. Depending on what he finds, that may be one giant baby step."

"Fair enough." Ethel walked over to the liquor cabinet and took out a bottle of vodka that she and Leonard used to bring out for special occasions. She removed two cut crystal Waterford glasses from the breakfront and poured them each a drink.

'Let's make a toast," declared Ethel, as she handed a glass to her friend. "To Priscilla. And to catching her killer."

Chapter Eighteen
The Mysterious Phone Call

Nellie just couldn't sleep. She tossed and turned and finally decided to get up and do something. Fred had been on her mind a lot lately. She pictured the last time she had seen him and how forlorn and gaunt he had appeared.

Since they'd decided to take a little break from their detective work until Bill got back to them, why not bake something decadent and fattening for Fred. Without wasting a minute, she grabbed her bathrobe and slippers and headed to the kitchen. She recalled how he had loved her rich chocolate fudge pie that she had brought over to their house on several occasions when the foursome had played canasta. It seemed so long ago.

"The pie it is," she declared with joy in her voice. With Matilda by her side, she assembled her ingredients and in a little over an hour, the dessert was ready and the aroma that filled the house was delicious. Seeing as it was not yet three o'clock in the morning, she went back upstairs and drifted off to sleep. It was close to 10:00 when she awakened. She phoned Ethel and suggested they stop by to visit Fred and drop off the pie.

"What a good idea, Nellie. And we know how he loves your baked goods. So, when do you want to go?"

"Do you want to grab a quick bite for lunch and then stop over?"

Ethel couldn't resist. "I am never one to pass up eating out. You know that. How about if we go to Teds. I've been dreaming about their hotdogs and onion rings."

"That does sound good. And I love their loganberry drink."

"Great. I'll pick you up around 1:00."

The two women sat across from one another at the cozy establishment that they believed had some of the most delicious fast food in Kenmore. Their hotdogs, dressed in mustard, relish, pickles and onion, were a real treat. Unlike other places, Ted's char-broiled them. They shared an order of their homemade onion rings that were greasy and decadent, but worth every calorie.

"Do you want to be really bad?" asked Nellie.

"That depends. What do you have in mind?"

"Well, we've already abandoned Weight Watchers for the day. What do you say we drive across the street and get sundaes at Andersons?"

"Oh, that sounds so good. Being bad sometimes is just what we need. I know how much you love their chocolate ice cream with hot butterscotch. And I adore their cinnamon ice cream with double hot fudge sauce. Let's do it."

As they delighted in every spoonful of their luscious desserts, their thoughts turned to Fred.

"Do you think Fred has lost more weight? He looked so thin."

"I know. I'm sure he's not eating right with Priscilla gone."

"Maybe I should have made a dinner rather than a pie."

"I'm sure he'll appreciate whatever you bring. But we could always bring him a dinner next week, if you want to."

"Let's do it."

"Okay. I'm actually a little nervous to see him. He was so distraught and now he's all alone."

"I know. It's so different without Priscilla here." She paused and continued in an unsteady voice. "But it's the way she died and the not knowing who killed her that must weigh on him something awful. Poor Fred."

As they headed over to his house, the two women wondered how he would appear. When the man whom they'd been friends with for years opened the door, Nellie and Ethel barely recognized him. He forced a smile. "Nellie. Ethel. How good it is to see you." He hesitated a moment. "Please, come in."

Nellie handed him the fudge pie and Fred seemed genuinely touched by the kind gesture. "What a treat this will be. Thank you so much."

"Enjoy it, Fred." Nellie quickly looked around and couldn't help but notice that the inside of the house, that Priscilla had always taken such pride in keeping just so, looked as unkempt as the man who lived there. Newspapers were strewn about and empty plates and glasses were left on the table. Although this was certainly not a laughing matter, Nellie couldn't help but think that Priscilla would roll over in her grave if she ever saw her house looking the way it looked this afternoon.

"Sit down, ladies," Fred said. His voice sounded monotone and both women observed a Fred they had never seen before.

Ethel placed her hand on Fred's shoulder. "You look tired, Fred. And so thin." Her voice was empathetic and sincere. "Nellie and I are worried about you."

"No need to be," Fred replied. "I'm grieving, that's all. I miss Priscilla so much." His voice quivered and his eyes welled up with tears. "I....I just can't help thinking that somehow what happened to Priscilla was my fault."

"Don't be ridiculous, Fred. Priscilla's death had nothing to do with you. You were one of the kindest husbands around. You can't possibly blame yourself."

Fred bowed his head. "But I do. If only I had gone with her to confession that night. If only...."

Ethel cut him off mid-sentence. "That's nonsense, Fred. You and Priscilla were married a long time."

"Thirty-nine wonderful years." He began to sob. "We would have celebrated our fortieth anniversary next October, if she hadn't died. We were planning on taking a cruise to celebrate. Priscilla had always dreamed of taking a cruise."

"I know how much losing your loved one hurts. My life has never been the same since I lost Leonard. I know right now this may not give you much comfort, but you do have many years of wonderful memories. And no one can take those from you."

"For all the years that you and Priscilla were married, I never remember you going to confession with her. So, please, don't blame yourself for that one night." Nellie's voice took on a somber tone. "Unsettling as this is to think about, maybe Priscilla wouldn't be the only one who was ...." Nellie found it too painful to complete the sentence.

"Murdered. Is that the word, Nellie?" Fred cupped his hands over his face and wept uncontrollably.

The persistent ringing of the phone brought them all to the reality of the moment. "I'll get that. It's probably Nancy. She calls me several times a day and plans to come back for a visit next month." Fred stood and picked up the phone from the adjoining table. "Hello."

The silence that followed was disturbing. Then Fred's hands began to quiver, as his face lost all its color.

94

"Stop it. Stop calling me." Fred's voice was frantic. "I told you I don't......."

Within seconds, Fred gasped, grabbed his chest and fell to the floor.

"Fred, Fred," Ethel called out in a panicky voice. But he did not reply. "Quick, Nellie. Dial 911."

The ambulance arrived in record time and rushed Fred to the hospital. He'd had a major coronary event and was whisked into the operating room. Unfortunately, he needed bypass surgery and, from what the doctor said, he was fortunate to have arrived at the hospital when he did. Blockage in four arteries could have had a very tragic outcome. And he was not out of the woods yet.

Chapter Nineteen
An Unwelcome Visitor

"Dad." Nancy's voice was loving and concerned. She held her father's hand, as she spoke. "You gave me quite a scare. Ethel phoned to tell me what had happened and I was on the next plane. We should count our blessings that she and Nellie were at the house and that they acted so quickly."

Fred was still quite weak and hooked up to an assortment of IV's and monitors. But he was alive and that was a blessing.

"I guess so, Nancy. I think I almost joined your mother."

"Dad, don't talk like that. I don't know what I'd do if anything happened to you." She squeezed her father's hand. "You're all I have."

"And you're all I have, Nancy."

"I've been doing a lot of thinking." She gazed lovingly into her father's eyes. "Maybe you could move to California or I could move back home. I don't like you being alone."

"I appreciate that, Nancy. You're a wonderful daughter. But strange as this may sound to you, that house, our house, brings me a certain comfort. It's where your mother and I raised you and I have lots of wonderful memories there."

"I get it, dad. But, times like this make me think we should be together. Maybe I could move back here.

I'm not married and I'm sure I could get a teaching job in the area. It would help you and be a new beginning for me."

"That is very kind of you, Nancy. But you have your own life and I would never want to become a burden."

"Please, dad. If I didn't think it was doable, I never would have suggested it."

Fred looked up at his only child and was overcome by such love and gratitude that tears filled his eyes. "I guess your mom and I did something right. You are an amazing young woman and I'm so happy and proud that you are my daughter."

"I love you dad. Just promise me you'll think about it. We don't have to decide anything today."

"Fair enough," Fred replied, as he closed his eyes and drifted off to sleep.

Nancy decided to drive back to her childhood home and clean up the house a bit, while her dad rested. When her mom had been alive things had always been just so. But, with her dad living there alone now, the house was definitely in disarray.

She started by gathering up his clothing that was strewn in little piles in the bedroom. He had probably remembered that his wife had always sorted the wash into two piles. And he had tried to follow what she had done. Whites and colors were separated, but there must have been four or five piles of each haphazardly thrown around the room. She organized the clothing and, without hesitation, headed to the laundry room to start a load of whites.

Then, she set out to throw away the piles of miscellaneous newspapers that had accumulated and had been left everywhere. "What a mess," she said aloud. Crusty dishes and used coffee cups were on the tables. Some of the plates had remnants of food on them. "Dad, this is disgusting," she said aloud to no one. She gathered them up and took them to the kitchen where she promptly rinsed them off and put them in the dishwasher.

The two plants that sat on the kitchen ledge were droopy and looked as if they hadn't been watered in weeks. It made her sad to think of how her mother had loved caring for her garden and plants and how everything now was on the verge of dying. She gave them a good drink of water and made a mental note to check on all the plants and flowers when she had more time. But, for now, she had at least made a dent in cleaning things up. Her mother would be happy.

She decided to get ready to head back to the hospital when the doorbell rang. A muscular man with slicked back black hair and a large tattoo of a cross on his neck stood before her. Nancy immediately checked to be sure the screen door was locked.

"Yes. Can I help you?"

"Where's Fred?" His voice was gruff and he gave her the creeps. There was no way in the world her father would ever be friends with this man. That she was certain of.

"I'm sorry, but he's not here."

"Where is he? I need to talk to him."

"I'm sorry, but that won't be possible." She refused to divulge where her dad was. After all, she thought, what business could he possibly have with her father.

"Won't be possible, you say. And just who are you to tell me what is and is not possible."

Nancy was becoming extremely uneasy and frightened. She tried to remain calm, but her heart was beating quickly and her palms felt sweaty.

"I can give him a message, if you'd like."

The man gave a hearty laugh. "A message. Oh, now that's big of you."

Nancy did not like his tone or his demeanor. She was scared. "How does my father know you?"

"That is none of your business. You just tell him that he's running out of time." He smirked an evil grin. "He'll know what I mean. And, little lady," he added with a look that sent chills up and down Nancy's spine, "tell him I've had the good pleasure of meeting you." He paused. "And the next time *we* meet may not be as pleasant." With those words, he turned and walked away.

Chapter Twenty
A Visit to the Clinic

The phone call to the suspected abortion clinic had been on Ethel's mind ever since their visit to see Annie. She often lay awake at night thinking and wondering what possible connection there could be between Roxy's and the clinic. Maybe it's nothing, she thought. But, then again, a good detective leaves no stone unturned.

She had been in touch with Annie who, thankfully, was still eager to help. They had agreed that she should schedule the appointment on a day convenient to her. With winter recess just around the corner, it had been an easy enough task.

The day that they were to meet was blustery and the temperature was below freezing. A perfect day to wear their matching bingo outfits, thought Nellie. She quickly called Ethel who thought the idea was great. The wind and snow were threatening. Ethel considered postponing the appointment, but decided it was well worth the inconvenience of the frigid weather to perhaps gather a clue. Annie agreed, as did Nellie. Cancelling was not an option. Finding a killer was.

Annie preferred to meet the two women at the clinic. She had a 1:00 appointment. Ethel picked Nellie up with plenty of time to spare, as she knew the driving would be tedious and slow. As they approached High

Street, Nellie sighed. "Dear Lord, Ethel. What are we doing in this kind of neighborhood again?"

"You know darn well why we're here, Nellie. We have to go where the leads take us."

"I get it, Ethel. But, why do you think all of our so-called leads are in these dilapidated, rundown parts of the city. It's so unsettling to look around and see windows boarded up and groups of hoodlums standing on street corners."

"I'm sorry, Nellie. Would an upscale neighborhood with tree-lined streets and children building snowmen be more to your liking for investigating a crime?"

Nellie recognized the sarcasm in Ethel's voice. "Okay. Point well made." Nellie spotted the parking garage coming up and breathed a sigh of relief that they had arrived safely. She glanced at her watch. "It took us nearly an hour, but you did it, Ethel. You got us here safely. Good job."

"Thanks, Nellie. I know I drive like an old lady, but that's just how I roll. Slow and steady." She pulled her plaid scarf up tightly around her neck. "The clinic is just across the street. Let's go find Annie and see if we can discover anything of interest."

Getting from the parking ramp to the clinic left the two women shivering. "My God, Ethel, I feel like I'm in Alaska. This weather is for the birds."

"Maybe when we solve the case, we can reward ourselves with a trip somewhere warm. Doesn't that sound like a great motivator?" A melancholy tone filled Ethel's voice. "Leonard and I always talked about spending winters in Florida, but" she said with sadness, "some things just weren't meant to be."

Annie sat in the row of brown vinyl chairs, positioned neatly along the wall. She nervously paged through a magazine. The office seemed clean, but spartan.

All the women waiting seemed so young. Annie's face lit up when she spotted the women coming through the door. However, the response of the receptionist was definitely not the same. She displayed a rather startled, confused look as she asked the women if she could help direct them to the correct office. Ethel chuckled to herself, knowing full well that no amount of makeup or disguise could ever have made this woman believe that Nellie or she was carrying a child.

Ethel smiled warmly, as she approached Annie and gave her a hug. No sense keeping the receptionist wondering, she thought to herself. "Just here to support my niece," she said to the woman behind the front counter. Quick thinking, Ethel thought to herself.

The woman nodded and smiled for the first time. "We'll be with her shortly."

When Ethel and Nellie took off their winter coats, Annie couldn't contain herself. "You two look adorable," she blurted out. "I love your matching bingo sweatshirts!"

"Thanks, Annie. Kind of our logo. Glad you like how we look."

"Most original. I think Priscilla would be very impressed."

As Ethel studied the few women sitting in the compact room, she couldn't help but notice that almost all of them were teenagers.

When Annie was called back, Nellie said a silent prayer that she wouldn't be discovered. Annie had told them that she had made it clear that she was just there to discuss her options, not for a physical. That would be too revealing and would definitely arouse suspicion. It was Ethel's guess that Annie would speak with a social worker today and see the doctor next time. Only the three of them knew there would be no next time.

While Annie was gone, Ethel went to the ladies-room. She didn't really know what she was hoping to find, but nothing of interest or out of the ordinary surfaced. But, when she returned to her seat, she couldn't help but overhear the conversation between two young girls. Ethel imagined they were probably about thirteen or fourteen.

"I still can't decide what to do."

"I know. Me neither. It's a really hard decision."

"Five thousand dollars is more money than I've ever had. I could sure buy a lot of stuff."

"That's true. But then you'd have to keep the kid in you for another seven months."

"Yeah. And that would suck."

"Big time. But he told me I don't have to decide yet. I've got a little more time before I no longer can get rid of it. But I'm having a hard time deciding because of the money."

"Me too."

The receptionist called out the name Jasmine and the young girl, whom Ethel had been eavesdropping on, stood and walked away.

Shortly thereafter, Annie appeared. She looked flushed.

Once they were well away from the office, she asked if they could talk. A quiet coffee shop was adjacent to the parking lot and the hot coffee tasted unusually welcome. They spoke in quiet tones.

"Something's not right in there. I feel it in my bones."

"What do you mean, Annie?"

"The woman I met with was pleasant enough. We talked and she answered all my prepared questions. I was quite the actress," she exclaimed. "For a minute, I actually had myself believing I was carrying a baby and that I wasn't sure if I wanted to keep it." Annie paused a moment. "She asked me a lot of questions about myself and my background. She wanted to know how much schooling I'd had, my hobbies and a little bit about the father."

"The father?" questioned Nellie.

"Well, clearly there would need to have been a man involved if I were truly in the position that I'm claiming to be in." Annie paused a moment. "I decided to make it good. I told her he was a gorgeous teacher where I worked and that, although I knew it was a sin, I'd had an affair with him. I told her I didn't know what to do. I put my hands up over my face and pretended to cry."

"Wow, Annie. That was clever of you."

"I know she believed my story. I must have been pretty convincing. She even brought me tissues and said she was there to help. I just seemed a bit taken aback when she started to ask me about Brian's height, weight, eye color and other questions that just didn't seem relevant to why I was there. I named the teacher Brian because he was an old boyfriend of mine. I made him a biology teacher and married. Thought that was fitting."

"You did great, Annie. We're really proud of you."

"The strangest thing was right at the end of my visit."

"What do you mean?"

"Well, the counselor with whom I was speaking said I should come back in a few weeks for a physical. I think she actually introduced herself as a social worker. I just nodded and went along with her." Annie got a confused look on her face. "It's what she said next, that I wasn't expecting."

"What was it she said?"

"She told me that an abortion wasn't my only option. She said that many couples are looking to adopt healthy babies and that mine would be in big demand because of my education, race and other factors."

"Really? That's interesting."

"I know. She even said that I'd be well paid for my troubles. She told me I'd be doing a godly act by not ending a life, but by giving a newborn baby a chance at a wonderful life. She concluded by saying the choice was mine and to think about it. She rescheduled my next appointment in three weeks, but of course I'm never going back there again."

"Blow me away. I think this visit has given us a lot to think about." A look of great concern clouded Ethel's face. "I can't begin to imagine what connection Priscilla could have had to all of this. But, if it's the last thing I do, I'm going to try to find out."

"Count me in, too," said Annie. She placed her hands over her coat, atop her belly. "Maybe some-day, when the time is right, I won't have to pretend. But, for now, I'm happy to be your assistant detective."

Chapter Twenty-One
The Man with the Tattoo

"I think we should pay a visit to Fred and see how he's doing. That phone call really spooked him. Thank God he's still alive."

"I know. And it's wonderful that Nancy is here now. That has to bring him great comfort."

"I just can't get the expression he had on his face, just before he fainted, out of my mind. It was truly a look of pure horror."

"I know. Maybe Nancy will be able to tell us something about that."

"Maybe. So, do you want to head over to the hospital now?"

"Sure. No time like the present."

The hospital, with its stark hallways and antiseptic smell, brought back unpleasant memories for both the women. It was at this very hospital that each of their husbands had died. Ethel prayed that Fred would not have the same outcome.

"Do you think we should stop at the gift shop and pick up a little something?"

"That's a great idea, Ethel. I hate to go into his room empty-handed."

The gift shop was filled with a variety of things, but it didn't take the two women long to decide on several magazines and a big bag of hard candy. "I know how Fred likes reading and I think he'll enjoy these."

"He's in room 679. I think the whole sixth floor is the cardiac wing. We can take the elevator right over there," Nellie said pointing ahead.

When they entered his room, Nellie could hardly believe her eyes. Fred looked like an old man, lying in bed hooked up to tubes and monitors. Somehow, she had imagined he would look better than he did.

A genuine smile encompassed his face when he saw the two women. "Why Ethel and Nellie," Fred exclaimed. "How wonderful it is to see you both. Thank you so much for coming."

"We've been worried about you, Fred, ever since that afternoon at your house. That was so frightening."

"I'd have to agree. I think I almost died. In a way though, it was a blessing in disguise. If I hadn't been brought in when I was, I might never have known about the blocked arteries until it was too late."

"I guess it's true that God was looking over you."

"Yes." Fred managed a wistful smile. "I'm living proof of that."

"Is Nancy still here?"

"Oh yes. She's been a godsend. She just went down to the cafeteria to grab a little lunch. I don't know what I'd do without her."

"You're lucky to have her, Fred. She's a wonderful daughter."

As they spoke, a grateful Nancy entered the room and hugged the two women with such sincerity that it brought tears to Fred's eyes. "It's so good to see you both. I can't help thinking how lucky my dad was that you both were there." She walked over and sat down in the chair beside her father's bed. "Dad and I both agree that you two were life savers. And we are very thankful."

"As are we. We were just in the right place at the right time. Thank God everything worked out for the best."

"Amen to that."

"Fred, we almost forgot. These are for you," Nellie added, as she handed him the gifts.

"Thank you." His voice had a tone of true excitement. *"Sports Illustrated*! My favorite. I know I'll enjoy these."

"Fred, would you mind if I stole Nancy away for a minute. We'll be right back. In the meantime, Nellie will visit with you."

"Sure." Fred motioned to the chair that his daughter had occupied. "Come. Sit here, Nellie."

Ethel and Nancy found a quiet room down the hall where family would often congregate to wait for a loved one to come out of surgery. At the moment, they were the only two there.

"I can't begin to tell you how truly grateful I am that you were with my dad and that you called me so quickly. You have no idea what that means to me."

"Nancy, we're just happy we were there when we were and that your dad got help right away," Ethel said without hesitation. "Your mom and I were best friends. You know that."

"Of course. Mom loved you and Nellie like sisters."

"And I want to be perfectly honest when I share with you what I'm about to say."

A worried look came over Nancy. "You sound so serious, Ethel. What is it?"

"I really don't know. But I can tell that right before your dad collapsed, he received a phone call that was obviously very troubling to him."

"From whom?"

"I have absolutely no idea. Wish I did. But, when your father heard whoever was on the line, his hands began to shake and every bit of color drained from his face. He went white as a ghost and then he passed out." Ethel breathed in deeply. "I thought maybe you'd have some insight as to what the call might have been about."

Nancy shrugged her shoulders. "I have no idea, Ethel. But I will tell you that something very troubling happened when I was cleaning up the house. And, by the way," she added with a bit of levity, "the house was a total disaster. My dad really is clueless how to take care of things. Mom did everything."

"Believe me, I understand. I think most men are pretty helpless when it comes to housekeeping." Ethel thought about what Nancy had just said. "Can you tell me what upset you?"

"As I told you, I was cleaning up and there was a knock at the door. No big deal, right?"

"I guess not."

"Well, there was this scruffy guy standing there. He was a big man, very muscular with greasy black hair and a tattoo of a cross on his neck. Lord knows there were probably others, but that was the only one I could see. I was sure he had the wrong house, but then he specifically said he wanted to talk to my dad. He called him by name. He really gave me the creeps and, of course, I had no intention of divulging my dad's whereabouts to him."

"What else did he say, Nancy?"

"That's the weird thing. He said dad was running out of time." Nancy shrugged her shoulders. "What does that mean? Running out of time for what? I can't imagine dad would ever have had anything to do with someone like that."

"I can't imagine it either. Have you brought this up to your father?"

"No. He is so frail now. I don't want to say or do anything that could jeopardize his recovery. But I will tell you that guy really scared me." Nancy wrung her hands together and bit down on her lower lip. Ethel could clearly see how upset and frightened she was.

"I guess I should tell you what else he said that I just can't get out of my mind."

"What? What did he say?"

Nancy fidgeted with her hair. "He said that the next time we meet might not be as pleasant."

Ethel gasped. "What an evil bully he is. I wonder if he's the thug who frightened your dad?"

"That I don't know," exclaimed Nancy. "But he definitely threatened me and I don't think, judging from his looks and his demeanor, that he'd give a second thought to doing something that could hurt me. Or worse."

"This is nothing to take lightly, as I'm sure you know. How about if you come and stay with me till your dad is released from the hospital. I don't like the thought of your being alone in the house. Besides, I have plenty of room and I'd love to have the company." Ethel thought a moment. "You know, Nancy, it might just be a good idea to report this to the police. There are so many crazies in the world today."

"I was thinking about reporting it, Ethel. It really unnerved me." Nancy inhaled deeply. "I actually thought about going to the police yesterday, but wanted to get back to the hospital to be with dad. But, when I leave here today, I think I'll stop and let them know what happened."

"I think that's a good idea."

"And, about your offer, Ethel. I just might take you up on it."

"I'd like that."

"I'm so glad we talked. I feel much better having shared what happened." A look of worry overcame her face. "Do you think there's a connection between the phone call and the man at the door?"

"I definitely think it could be a possibility."

"I am stumped, Ethel. I can't make any sense of how my dad would ever know or have anything to do with a man like that."

"I don't either. But you can rest assured, Nancy, that your mom's murderer will be found and made to pay for what he or she did. I have no idea what connection, if any, the man you're talking about has to any of this, but I'm going to find out, if it's the last thing I do. And that's a promise."

Chapter Twenty-Two
T-Bone

"Aren't you two a sight for sore eyes." As she refilled the coffee brewer, Shirley, the owner of Shirley's Diner, smiled warmly at the two women who had been customers at her neighborhood restaurant for years. "It's so good to see you both. I heard about Priscilla. I'm so sorry. Do the police have any leads?"

"Not that they're sharing with us. But Nellie and I are meeting someone here today who may be able to shed some light on things. Can we take that empty booth in the back?"

"Sure. Sit wherever you like. Do you want me to bring over a carafe of coffee?"

"That would be great, Shirley."

"My pleasure. And I'll bring over a few menus, in case you want something to eat."

The phone call from Bill Sullivan had come more quickly than they had anticipated. He had been able to trace the license plate and wanted to meet face to face to discuss his findings.

A balding man, dressed in a dark brown parka and jeans entered the restaurant. Ethel immediately recognized him. She stood and they exchanged a long hug. Old friends are often the best friends, thought Ethel. When he sat in the booth across from them and she introduced him to Nellie, she wondered how she could have ever forgotten his eyes. Oh, his eyes! They were almost an indigo shade of blue and reminded her of a perfect spring sky.

"It's a pleasure to meet you Nellie," he declared, as he extended his hand to hers.

Nellie smiled sincerely. "The pleasure is mine. Ethel and I are so grateful that you agreed to help us. We really appreciate it."

"I'm glad to help." Bill took a sip of the black coffee. "I have to say that what I found is a guy with quite a rap sheet. Certainly not anyone I would expect you two ladies to have ever had the opportunity to cross paths with." Bill paused. "Some pretty gruesome charges."

"Like what?" Ethel questioned.

"Like drug trafficking, extortion and sexual battery, to name a few. But even more frightening is that, in two neighboring states, he's been arrested for being involved in baby selling."

Ethel and Nellie gasped. "Baby selling. That's unbelievable. Whatever would he want with two little old ladies? I mean we're harmless, Bill. You know that."

"I know that and you know that, but maybe Jimmy doesn't. You've riled him, or someone he's working for, big time and you don't want to get on the wrong side of this guy. Trust me, he's dangerous."

"You called him Jimmy. Are you sure that's his name?"

"As sure as I can be. His full name is James Jesus Monzaro. He is from Mexico, but came to the United States about eleven years ago. His friends call him Jimmy. His nickname on the street is T-Bone. He's spent quite a bit of his time here in prison. A real low life." Bill took a long, slow sip of his coffee. "I recommend that you try not to be anywhere near him. He's bad news and very dangerous." He looked solemnly at the two women who sat aghast across from him. "Am I making myself perfectly clear?"

"You are, Bill, but that is easier said than done. It was not Nellie and I who sought him out. Rather, it was Jimmy, or should I say T-Bone, who found us. And, I'm beginning to wonder if he is the same man who threatened Fred's daughter, Nancy, yesterday." Ethel took a moment to explain to Bill the conversation she had shared earlier at the hospital.

"It certainly sounds quite possible. This creep wears a lot of different hats."

"What do you mean?"

"Just that he's used for whatever his employer needs him for at the moment. Could be as an enforcer, a bodyguard, a thief, whatever."

"Sounds like a dreadful person. I seriously wonder what ever led him to lead a life of crime like he does."

"Well, don't wonder. He is what he is and you're not going to change him. Just do yourselves a favor and try to steer clear of him. Capeesh?"

Ethel and Nellie chuckled. "Capeesh!" It was a word they were both familiar with.

"Oh, I almost forgot. The only identifying body marks noted on his rap sheet were his many tattoos. Apparently, one that is clearly visible is a fairly large cross on his neck."

Ethel could hardly catch her breath. "That is the precise tattoo that Nancy told me was on the man who threatened her yesterday. This is getting too weird."

"Listen, ladies. You are clearly involved in something that someone, for whatever reasons, does not want you involved in. I really think you should go to the police. This is beyond your expertise and far too dangerous." Bill sighed deeply. "I would be willing to help you, if you want, but only if you share everything about this man with the police." His face took on a worried, solemn look. "I really like the two of you and I would hate to see something bad, I mean really bad, happen to either of you."

"Okay, Bill. I think you've spooked us enough. We agree it's probably the wisest thing to let the police know what's happened and that we've been threatened."

"I think Leonard would be proud of what you're trying to do. But I know he'd want you to put your safety first. Let's face it, many heads are better than two and I think it's a good idea to have backup, if you need it."

"Understood. And Nellie and I welcome your kind offer. Your assistance could be invaluable. We are so grateful that you found out the information you did about Jimmy. It gives us a lot to think about."

"My pleasure. Glad I could be of help. I'll be in touch in a few days and we'll see where this takes us. In the meantime, please be careful." Bill stood to leave.

"That's a promise. And tomorrow Nellie and I will pay a visit to the police department."

"Shall I bake Officer Malcolm another cake?" Nellie joked.

"Couldn't hurt! Not that it did us any good last time. But you never know."

"Alright then. Let's get going, Ethel. I've got some serious baking to do."

Chapter Twenty-Three
Granny Smith Apple Cake

The same young receptionist that had greeted them a few months ago was stationed at the front desk of the police department. Although she was not wearing what Nellie and Ethel had perceived as a Catholic school girl's uniform, like she had been on their initial visit, she was dressed quite prim and proper in a navy skirt and pale blue sweater. Her hair was swept into a ponytail that she'd tied back with a floral scarf. She smiled at the two women. "Back again?" she questioned.

"You remember us?"

"I would never forget two ladies as lovely as you. Especially since you always seem to be bearing wonderful smelling baked goods!"

"Ah, my homemade apple cake," exclaimed Nellie. "I do hope Officer Malcolm enjoys it. It was one of my husband's favorites."

"I'm sure he'll love it. Have a seat," she said, as she motioned towards the chairs that lined the periphery of the room. "I'll let him know you're here."

Within moments, the young officer whom they had met on their prior visit appeared. A genuine smile came over his rather round baby face, as his eyes eagerly took in the cake. "So, ladies. It is good to see you both again. How's the investigating coming along?" Ethel detected a note of sarcasm, but decided to ignore it.

"Can we speak privately, Officer Malcolm? Nellie and I have some concerning events we feel compelled to share with you." Ethel cleared her throat. "It's pretty heavy stuff."

"Pretty heavy stuff," repeated the police officer. "Well, let's go back to my office and we can discuss what this is all about." He smiled at Nellie, as he eyed the cake again. "Is that for me?"

"Baked it special! The secret is in the apples." Nellie smiled broadly. "Granny Smith are my go-to apples whenever I make an apple cake."

"Can't say I know one apple from another," Officer Malcolm replied. "But, if it's half as good as that carrot cake you brought in, it's a winner for sure." He gestured for the two women to be seated.

"Flattery will get you everywhere officer."

He looked Ethel squarely in the eyes. "So, tell me about this *heavy evidence* you have."

"Unfortunately, we've come up against some dead ends. Things aren't going as swimmingly well as we'd hoped. Being a detective is not an easy job, that's for sure."

"Don't beat yourselves up, ladies. Even the police department is finding this case difficult to crack. That's about all I'm at liberty to say."

"We're making some progress, but ...." Ethel's voice drifted off as she attempted to pull herself together. "To be honest, officer, we're scared. Really scared. And we think the wise thing for us to do is to make you aware of what's happening. Of how we've been threatened." Ethel's voice choked on her next words. "We don't want to join our dearly departed friend, Priscilla."

"What? Someone threatened you?"

Ethel took a deep breath and proceeded to tell Officer Malcolm how she and Nellie had ventured out to see who was in the black truck and how she had been pushed to the ground. She cleared her throat and added, "The scary thing is that this hoodlum told us to stop our meddling or something bad might happen to us. And I don't think he was kidding around. He said this wasn't anything that two little old ladies should be sticking their noses in."

"He called you two little old ladies. Imagine that!"

"Do I detect a note of sarcasm, Officer Malcolm?" Ethel smiled as she collected her thoughts. "Listen, Officer, we just learned who this guy is and he's not someone we want to mess with."

"How did you learn his identity? I must say that finding that out displays some pretty impressive detective work."

"Thanks, but we had some help. Actually, Bill Sullivan used to work for the Kenmore police, too. He and Leonard were good friends. I was fortunate to reach him and lucky that he was agreeable to helping us." Ethel paused a moment. "Actually, it was Bill who strongly suggested we confide in you. It's a long story, but the man who tried to intimidate us is a convicted felon. My informant says he's served time and has committed assault and battery, among other unsavory crimes. He's not our cup of tea, that I can tell you."

"He's a big bully," Nellie added. "He isn't one to take lightly which is why we wanted you to know where we stand."

"You did the right thing coming in, ladies. I believe, when we initially spoke, I cautioned you that things could get dangerous and turn ugly quickly."

"You did."

"Well, what you're telling me is the very reason that I so strongly advised against your trying to solve this crime on your own." His voice became even more solemn. "This is a police matter, ladies. Plain and simple.

If he comes near you again, I want you to promise me you'll call for backup. Understood?"

"Yes, we understand, officer. And we promise that if the going gets tough, we will call you."

"Call anytime you feel in danger. We are here for our citizens. And I can't stress clearly enough that I believe you two are in way over your heads." A look of true concern washed over his face. "Would you be willing to share the name of the person who intimidated you. I'll see if we have anything on him."

"Glad to, Officer Malcolm. His name his James Jesus Manzaro. But he goes by the street name T-Bone." Ethel went on to inform Officer Malcolm about the threats to Priscilla's husband and daughter. "I'm quite sure that it was T-Bone. He's pretty creepy."

A smile washed over Officer Malcolm's face. "Pretty creepy. I do like how you describe things, Ethel. You've got a real way with words."

"I'll take that as a compliment."

"So, why don't you let me do a little poking around and I'll see what I can find out about this character. Maybe we can somehow tie him to Priscilla in some way."

"My, my Officer Malcolm. Have you had a change of heart about helping us? I mean we don't want to get you in any trouble for doing anything you shouldn't. You made that pretty clear the last time we were here. And, I might add, I still can't begin to fathom what our lovely friend Priscilla could have ever had in common with that low life. It is just inconceivable to us."

"I'm not divulging anything about our investigation. But you have clearly come here with a very valid complaint and it is our job, as public servants, to do what we can to keep you safe and well protected. I'd say looking into this matter is definitely in the line of duty."

"Well then, duty calls! Thank you, Officer."

Nellie placed the cake, that she had been holding on her lap the entire visit, on Officer Malcolm's desk. "Enjoy, officer, and don't eat it all in one sitting."

"I must say that you two ladies are refreshing. Stay safe and please stay clear of T-Bone."

"That is a promise we can easily make. But the problem is, we need to pray that T-Bone stays clear of us."

Chapter Twenty-Four
Skylar

The phone call from Annie came from out of the blue. "Can I meet with you two later today?" Her voice had a ring of urgency to it.

"Absolutely," Ethel replied without skipping a beat. "What's this about, Annie?"

"I'd rather tell you face-to-face. Listen, I'm at school now, but I should be home by about 4:00. Can you meet me then?"

"Yes, we'll be there."

Ethel immediately phoned Nellie. The two women were perplexed as to why Annie wanted to see them so quickly. But they wouldn't have to wait long to find out what was on her mind.

The weather was a bit more forgiving than the last time they had paid her a visit. Maxwell eagerly greeted them and, as he had on their prior visit, snuggled up beside Nellie.

"Maxwell has really taken to you."

Nellie rubbed behind the beagle's floppy ears. "That's a good fellow. You just stretch out and relax. It's a dog's life."

"That it is," added Annie. "But I really thought it was important to talk to you two ladies face to face." Her tone became quite serious. "I heard something at school today. Something that gave me pause and made me think about Priscilla."

"Priscilla?" questioned Ethel. "I'm confused."

"I am as well. And I really have no idea how, or even if, this ties into what happened to her. Just a feeling I have. That's all."

"Maybe you know more than you think you do."

"I don't know about that. But you both know that I teach English and that I love my students. Sadly, most of them have not had many advantages in life. But, for the most part, they are truly hard-working young ladies who are trying their best to turn their lives around." Annie breathed in deeply. "I have a really good rapport with them and they know that they can trust me."

"Okay. So, what happened?"

"Well, I have a particular student. Her name is Skylar. She comes from a very dysfunctional family. Her dad is in prison for armed robbery and her mom is an alcoholic. Skylar has had a really tough time of things her whole life. She has two younger sisters that she pretty much takes care of. But she is trying her best to turn her life around and to not follow in her parents' path. But, it's hard for her. There is a lot of temptation out there."

"That we know. Must be very difficult for a young girl with so many obstacles to overcome."

"I have worked really hard to earn her trust and to try to do what I can to help her to make good, positive choices. But I'm afraid I've failed her." A melancholy look encompassed Annie's face.

"Sounds to me like you're just the kind of teacher that she needs. You seem to be in her corner and I'm sure she knows that."

"I thought so, but now I'm not so sure. She confided in me today and I just can't get what she shared out of my mind. I don't know how to help her."

"It can't be that bad, Annie. What is it?"

"Skylar is a beautiful girl. Gorgeous deep green eyes, long thick red hair. She is stunning, but I don't think she realizes just how attractive she is."

"What do you mean?"

"Well, she confided in me that when she got home yesterday, there was a man waiting for her beside her back door. She said she had no idea who he was and was confused as to what he wanted with her."

"Go on."

"He grabbed her shoulders and pushed her against the back door. She was frightened, but he told her not to make any noise and that he wouldn't hurt her. He just wanted to talk. Said he had a message for her."

"A message?"

"Yes. He told her he knew what a hard life she had and that he could help make things better for her, if she'd cooperate."

"I don't understand. What are you saying?"

"I didn't get it either. He told her she was beautiful, but that she'd never get out of the slums without some help. And," he added, "he knew how to help her." She was really scared.

"Who wouldn't be."

"But it's what he said next that is more worrisome. He told her that lots of rich families want to adopt healthy babies and that they are willing to pay generously. He said she seemed like the perfect person. She was young, healthy, beautiful and smart. And, God knows she could use the cash. He told her all the ways a big sum of money could change her life. He said she'd be surprised how many girls like her are happy to take his offer."

"Is Skylar pregnant?"

"No, that's just it. She said this man told her he'd take care of finding the perfect donor and pay for all her medical care. She'd just need to take her prenatal vitamins and deliver a healthy baby in nine months. He made it sound like nothing but a reasonable business deal. But he is clearly exploiting her and preying on her vulnerability."

"Do you have any idea who this man was who tried to coerce her?"

"All she remembered was that he was really strong and that he had red hair."

"Red hair?" A chill passed through Ethel and Nellie. They immediately wondered if it could have been the same man whom they saw sitting beside them at the Sheridan Family restaurant and then at Roxy's Bar.

"This is getting even more creepy with everything we're hearing. So, what happened next?"

"Skylar said she pushed him away and said she wasn't having a baby for anyone. He was pretty angry when he stormed away. Told her he had ways to entice young girls like her."

"And what do you think he meant by that?"

"I sure don't know, but I am worried for her. I fear that this guy with the red hair is doing this to other girls whom he thinks he can control."

"And I remember that day at the clinic when that young girl stated she could get a lot of money for her baby. I wonder if that abortion clinic and the man with the red hair are all tied together somehow."

Nellie shrugged her shoulders. "Even if they are, whatever would that have to do with Priscilla's murder?" Maxwell rolled over on his back and stretched out, as Nellie petted his furry underside.

"You did the right thing sharing this, Annie. And Skylar's secret is safe with us. We'll do some snooping around and see what we can find out."

Chapter Twenty-Five
The Threat

"We have a lot of food for thought, Nellie. Finally, some clues are coming our way. But it's going to take a lot of spiffy detective work to put them all together."

"Couldn't agree more. That's where two heads will be better than one. And now that we have some extra help from your friend, Bill, and Officer Malcolm, maybe we can move forward a bit."

"I hope so, Nellie. Finally, we're bombarded with some solid evidence, but I'm still stumped."

"Okay. Let's assess."

The two women reviewed all the clues that they had collected. "We need to write everything down, Nellie. Keep a log of what we've gathered and what events have happened that might provide a lead. It's vital that everything is recorded in an orderly way, not willy-nilly. Maybe then we'll have a better idea of what our next step should be."

"Good thinking, Ethel. That's why you're our lead detective and I'm your backup! Let's get on it."

The women felt a sense of accomplishment at having logged everything of significance in a sturdy yellow ledger.

"Now what, Ethel?"

"Now we decide our next step. I've been thinking about it all day."

"And?"

"And, although I know that this is not what either of us wants to do, I think a trip back to Roxy's would be prudent. Sniff things out a bit. See where our clues take us."

"But, every time I allow myself to think about our last time there and that creepy bouncer named Travis, I get a knot in the pit of my stomach and an uneasy feeling like nothing I've ever had before. And what if that red-headed scumbag is there? He scared the bejesus out of me. Do you really think that's what we need to do?"

"I do, Nellie. I don't know what we'll find, if anything, but something in my gut tells me that someone at Roxy's is somehow involved."

"Well then, Roxy's it is. But please tell me we don't need to dress up again in those ridiculous looking outfits. I felt like such a fool, Ethel."

"Nonsense, Nellie. You looked adorable." Ethel could hardly contain her huge smile, as she spoke. "And, as you may recall, we were quite well received. I think that alone warrants another dress up night!"

Nellie shook her head. "What am I going to do with you? You are losing your mind, Ethel. But, although this may sound crazy and I know how dangerous what we're doing might be, I must say that this is more adventure and excitement than I've had in a lifetime. And, the thought that we may actually catch Priscilla's murderer, or at least try our best to, is reason enough to pursue things."

"Now you're talking, Nellie. That's the spirit. Let's plan on going tonight. No time like the present."

"Okay, Madame Detective. But I'll need some time to gussy up. It takes more than a few minutes to transform myself into the woman you want me to be."

"Hey, don't I know it. Plus, I need time to assemble my purse with all the *necessary* tools, if you get my drift."

"I don't think I'll ever forget that night when you carried your gun, Ethel. That was a real shocker to me. And the cigarettes were pretty out of character, too."

"Nellie, Nellie. Authenticity counts for so much in our line of work. And you've got to admit that last time we pulled off the part like two pros. I was quite proud of us. Hopefully, tonight, we'll be just as convincing."

"I guess time will tell."

"That it will, So, I'll pick you up at nine and we'll see what we can find out."

"I'll be ready. Heaven help me."

It didn't take nearly as long as they had thought to spruce themselves up for their repeat visit to Roxy's. And, by 9:45, they approached the decrepit establishment with a sense of determination and fear. Travis was clearly delighted to see the twosome and let them know that he was still up for his proposed menage-a-trois.

"Come on, ladies. Let's have a little fun. I promise I'll make it worth your while. I'm quite the ladies' man."

"I'm sure you are, Travis. But Nellie and I are just here for a quick drink and a little conversation. But," she added not quite knowing whatever prompted her to say such a thing, "if we ever have the desire for such an arrangement, you're the man we'll call."

"Now you're talking, honey. I knew you were a feisty dame with a great sense of adventure. One of these days, I think you'll come around. Good things are worth waiting for. And I'm not going anywhere. So, whenever you're ready, I'm ready."

Ethel thought she could hear her heart beating outside her embroidered blouse. She felt like screaming, but maintained a calm, cool exterior. She gestured towards the table they had sat at the previous time they'd been there. "I see our table is free, Travis. May we sit there?"

"You can sit anywhere you damn well like. And I insist on buying you two sexy broads a drink. What'll it be?"

"What do you think, Nellie?"

"Oh, I don't know. Maybe a glass of wine. Moscato, if you have it."

"Two glasses of Moscato coming up." Travis smiled cunningly. "And with those two glasses, I think I'll pull up a chair beside you. We really need to get to know each other better."

Oh no, thought Nellie. He'll cramp our style. Why can't he just go back to where he was?

Travis placed his hand over Ethel's. "How about the truth, gorgeous. What really brought you two broads back here tonight? I'm not so stupid as to think you were in this neck of the woods and just decided to stop by."

Ethel gave a stifled laugh. "You're pretty sharp, Travis. I can see that."

"So, level with me."

"Fair enough. We are still trying to figure out how Priscilla died and why. The mere fact that she was here so close to her death makes us think that there may very well be some connection." Ethel took a drag on the cigarette that Travis had lit for her just moments earlier. "I mean if your best friend died, wouldn't you try to get to the bottom of things."

"You are good women. You do remind me a lot of Priscilla. And, because of that, I'm going to share something with you. But you didn't hear it from me, understand?"

"Understood." Ethel gave a deadpan look and shrugged her shoulders. "Don't have a clue where I heard what I heard. Not the foggiest notion."

"Good. You're a quick learner. And now that we understand each other, I'm really going out on a limb for you two. I am kind of the eyes and ears of this place. Not a lot gets by me, if you get my drift."

"And?"

"And the night Miss Priscilla came in, there was a lot going on. Not your typical night here at Roxy's."

"How so?" questioned Ethel.

"Well, there were a lot of people here that night that weren't *regulars*, so to speak. They kind of stood out to me."

Ethel sucked in on her Marlboro and blew the smoke towards Travis. "Like who? Anyone we'd know?"

Nellie took a long, slow sip of her wine. She was definitely feeling uncomfortable and all she could think about was leaving. Her uneasiness only grew with what happened next. She was startled to feel two strong hands on her shoulders. She turned around and gasped aloud to see Red standing behind her. Seeing his chest hairs popping through the top of his unbuttoned shirt made Nellie want to puke. He was so disgusting. She tried her best to remain nonchalant.

"I see you two ladies seem to get around. Don't you think maybe you're getting involved in something that you should stay out of. Things happen. Bad things can happen to little old ladies that snoop around where they're not welcome." His grip tightened. "Am I making myself perfectly clear?"

"Is that a threat? Because, if it is, Nellie and I may just have to report it to the police."

Red gave a deep belly laugh that spread throughout the tiny bar. "Oh, I'm really scared of you two doing that." His voice was filled with an irritating sarcasm. "I'm shaking in my boots, ladies. Look, I'm just trying to give you a little friendly advice. Go home and bake a pie. Do something you were cut out to do. Being here is dangerous. I can't be any clearer." He turned and walked away.

Nellie could feel her hands trembling and she was beginning to hyperventilate. "Can we leave, Ethel?"

"Soon, Nellie. Soon. But Travis here was going to share something with us when that despicable Red interrupted our conversation. So, Travis, what stood out that night?"

"You are one tough broad, Ethel. I think most women would be scared shitless by Red's threat. But, not you. You're all business and I can't begin to tell you what a turn on I find that."

Ethel smiled at the man who clearly was frightening in his own right. "You said there were people here that night that weren't regulars. What did you mean by that?"

Travis tapped his fingers against the nicked tabletop. Then he put his hand atop Ethel's and looked her deeply in the eyes. "Men were here that stood out like sore thumbs." Travis gave a deep belly laugh and took a gulp of his beer. "Imagine coming to this joint in a three-piece suit. Those guys might as well have painted signs on themselves saying look at me. Anyone with half a brain knew it wasn't your normal night here at Roxy's."

"Men in suits?" Ethel looked perplexed. "And add to that Priscilla and Annie being here. What in God's name was going on that Thursday night?"

Travis shrugged his broad shoulders. "Damned if I know. But you've got to admit that I've given you a lot to think about." He leaned over so close to Ethel that she could smell the beer on his breath. "You owe me, baby."

Ethel tried to remain calm, in spite of everything.

130

"Okay. I'll keep that in mind." Ethel zipped up her purse and stood. "Come on, Nellie. I think we got more than we came for. Let's head home."

Travis, as he'd done the prior time, slapped Ethel on the behind. "Safe travels and I hope to see you ladies again real soon. And don't forget my offer still stands. I think we'd have quite the time."

Ethel could think of nothing but getting safely out of this place.

But as they attempted to exit, Red stood in front of the door and blocked their way. "Drive safely, ladies, and remember our little chat. You wouldn't want to have an accident in this part of town." He paused for what seemed a long, drawn out few minutes. And with a tone that sent shivers through the two women casually said, "just saying."

Chapter Twenty-Six
A Visit with Father O'Leary

Father O'Leary sat at his desk in the rectory of the church and seemed surprised to see the two women. He raised his head from the paperwork he was engrossed in and smiled a genuinely warm smile. "Ethel, Nellie. How nice it is to see you."

Ethel cleared her throat nervously. She had gone over this meeting repeatedly in her mind, but now that she was face-to-face with Father O'Leary, she seemed hesitant to confront him.

"What brings you here this afternoon?" It was clear from the worried looks on their faces that this was not a social call. "Is it about Priscilla?"

Ethel took a long, deep breath. "It is, Father. Nellie and I are so deeply troubled by her death. We just can't wrap our heads around what happened to her. And I guess the hardest thing for us is knowing that..."

"That what, Ethel?"

"Well," she hesitated, "that it wasn't a natural death." Suddenly, tears streamed uncontrollably down her face. It seemed that everything was just becoming too much to cope with. "That someone wanted her dead is so frightening and we are trying to figure things out, but we seem to be getting nowhere."

"I know what dear friends you both were to Priscilla, but I firmly believe this is a matter for the police."

"We can't say we don't agree, Father. We know they are trying to solve the case. But we just can't sit idly by and not try to help. You do know that my husband, Leonard, was a former police detective and I learned a lot from him over the years."

Father O'Leary smiled broadly. "I'm sure you did, Ethel. But that doesn't make you a detective."

"I'm not claiming to be a real detective like my Leonard was." Ethel fidgeted nervously with her silver cross. "But I think Nellie and I are doing a pretty good job as amateur sleuths." Ethel paused and collected her thoughts. "As a matter of fact, Father, that's why we're here. We need to ask you something."

"Ethel," interjected Nellie with a slight tone of annoyance in her voice. "Father has a million things to do. I feel really uncomfortable; like we're bothering him. Why don't we come back another time?"

"Nonsense," replied Father O'Leary. "You are two of my most cherished parishioners. I'd certainly be glad to help you in any way I can. But I really don't think I know anything that could shed light on what happened to Priscilla. It was a tragedy."

"Yes, a terrible tragedy. But Nellie and I have done a little investigating of our own and we haven't made a lot of progress. But we have discovered some things that may prove helpful. We believe we did find a connection to Roxy's."

It didn't take a savvy detective to clearly notice the look of surprise on Father O'Leary's face and the uneasiness that seemed to come over him at the mere mention of the seedy bar.

"Roxy's, you said?"

"Yes. And I guess the best thing for me to do is to just come right out and ask you if you know why Priscilla and Annie were there the Thursday night before

Priscilla was murdered. I know you spoke at Bible study class at Priscilla's house that night."

Father O'Leary stared at the two women without speaking. "Who told you they were at Roxy's?"

"That's something we'd rather not share, Father. But, suffice it to say that our curiosity has most certainly been piqued. All I can say is that we heard it from a very reputable source."

Father O'Leary contemplated his next words for, what seemed to Ethel and Nellie, a very long time. When he eventually spoke, his voice was solemn. "I probably shouldn't be sharing this with you both, but I know how much you loved Priscilla and that your motives for finding her killer are sincere and honorable." He inhaled deeply. "I believe breaching my vow of confidentiality is something God would forgive. I think it is the right thing for me to do in this case."

Ethel and Nellie sat quietly, eagerly awaiting his next words.

"Priscilla confided in me that she was very worried about something that involved Annie. She told me that she'd gone with her to Roxy's that night to offer her support."

"Really? Support for what, I wonder."

"I'm not sure." Father looked confused. "The only thing I know for certain is that Roxy's is in a most undesirable part of our city." Father sighed, as a look of sheer exasperation filled his face. "I will share with you both that I've been there once or twice in the past because I believe, if I can save the souls of any misguided, troubled individuals, I will be doing God's work. I like to think of my work there as community service."

"I don't doubt that there are many there who could use some spiritual guidance. And, we agree with you that it is most definitely in a frightening area. That Priscilla and Annie were there so close to Priscilla's murder may be more of a coincidence than we'd like to believe." Ethel adjusted the cross on her necklace so that it was centered on her blouse. "I suppose we should tell you that we've been to speak to Annie a few times. And I don't think it would be breaching our confidentiality to say that she is very concerned and worried that some of her students are being intimidated and threatened."

"Really?" Father's voice was filled with concern.

"Yes. She even shared with us that the perpetrator is a real thug who scared one of her student's half to death. He wanted the girl to agree to have a baby and give it up for adoption. He tried to motivate this girl with the promise of money. More money than she has ever seen."

Father O'Leary appeared perplexed, as he stared silently into the distance. "This is very troubling to hear."

"Basically, these young women are being coerced into doing something they may or may not wish to do."

Father O'Leary's face became even more solemn. "So, it's not just an isolated one or two girls. Is that what you're telling me?"

"Unfortunately, that's how we see it, Father. And, from what we surmised from speaking with Annie, her school is being targeted by these lowlifes who are preying on the economic misfortune of these students. It's wrong. Plain and simple. Something must be done."

"But what?" questioned Father O'Leary. "What can we do to help these young women and prevent them from being exploited? I think this is most assuredly a matter for the police."

"The police are a definite resource. But I don't believe we, as Priscilla's closest friends, can turn a blind eye knowing what we know. Wasn't it at one of your last church sermons that you spoke about helping others?"

Father O'Leary smiled broadly. "I'm glad my sermon made such an impact on you. But, I'm not really sure which sermon you are speaking of."

"I think it was two or three weeks ago and it really hit home with me."

Father thought a brief moment. "Ah, yes. Ethel. As I recall, I quoted Proverb 19:17. It says, 'Whoever is kind to the poor lends to the Lord, and he will reward them for what they have done.'"

"Yes," Ethel excitedly declared. "That was it! And I think that proverb perfectly captures the problem before us. We must help these young women, Father. I believe it is a sign from God that you chose to speak about a topic which has such relevance now. But I remember you also quoted a proverb that I think was from The Book of James. Do you recall that one?"

"I do," said Father. "And I am quite impressed that you remembered it. It basically states, 'what good is it, if someone claims to have faith, but has no deeds? Can such faith save them?'"

"I clearly recall those words, Father."

"It goes on to say that if one of you says to them, 'Go in peace, keep warm and well fed, but does nothing about their physical needs, what good is it? In the same way faith, by itself, if it is not accompanied by action, is dead.'"

"That speaks to my heart, Father," said Nellie.

"Yes, and it really sends a message loud and clear, don't you agree?" asked Ethel. "We cannot stand idly by and do nothing."

"True, added Father. "But words are merely words. What actions can we take to help? That is the question."

"You're right, Father," Ethel firmly said. "And now, comes the hard part. We need to put our heads together and decide on our next step. It may not be easy, but I think we can all agree that it's the only way we'll have a chance of solving things."

Father O'Leary crossed himself. "There is one other thing that Priscilla said to me at confession that I have kept to myself. But, in light of our discussion, I feel she would want me to share her final thoughts with you both."

Ethel and Nellie sat silently, with great anticipation, awaiting Father's words.

Chapter Twenty-Seven
The Troubling Confession

"Are you alright, Ethel?" Father O'Leary's voice was gentle and kind. "You look pale."

Ethel managed a faint smile. "I'm okay, Father. Maybe what you're about to tell us will provide an important piece of evidence that we've overlooked."

With a solemn look, Father spoke in a hushed voice. "The night Priscilla came to confession I was truly taken aback. For all the years I have led my parishioners and for all the times I have interacted with Priscilla, I never once recall her coming to confession on a Sunday at 5:45. It seemed so unusual to me. So out of character for her. I knew there must be something deeply troubling her that had brought her there at that time." Father O'Leary cleared his throat. It was clear to Ethel and Nellie that this was not easy for him. "What she said clearly was nothing I was prepared for or ever expected to hear."

Ethel and Nellie could not imagine what Father would say next. They both sat speechless, as they waited for him to continue.

"I am well aware that by my breaking the seal of confession I am committing a grave sin. I can even be excommunicated. I have never, in all my years of service to God and to my parishioners, been so torn. I have always taken the Sacrament of Penance very seriously. And I still do."

"We understand, Father, how troublesome this must be for you." Nellie's words flowed easily.

"I'll never forget my conversation with Priscilla as long as I live." He inhaled deeply and looked upwards. "God forgive me, but I believe this is the righteous thing to do."

Ethel wrung her hands together and sat awkwardly awaiting his words.

"Priscilla was clearly a very troubled soul. She was overwhelmed with so much uncertainty in her life. To be honest, there were two reasons she came to see me that night."

"Really? We had no idea she was so distraught."

Father hesitated and then crossed himself before beginning. "I don't know how long you've known Priscilla or what she's shared with you about her marriage."

"I don't understand, Father. We've been bingo friends for the last six years and have occasionally gone out to lunch or to a movie. We know she was happily married to Fred and that they have one daughter, Nancy, who lives in California."

"And I'm sure that's all she wanted you to know." Father's look became pensive. "Several years ago, Fred had a real gambling problem. From what Priscilla shared with me, they almost lost their house. It was a very dark period in their marriage. But through extensive counseling and his going to Gambler's Anonymous things eventually got resolved."

"So why was that a problem now?" Ethel questioned.

Father inhaled deeply. "Priscilla felt reasonably certain that he'd fallen back into his old ways. He was going out a few nights a week and she found him talking on the phone at all hours. Whenever she'd ask him who it was, he'd always reply, "wrong number." She had come to confession that night to discuss what I thought she should do. She also hoped I might be able to offer Fred some spiritual guidance. She was clearly extremely upset."

"Poor Priscilla. We had no idea," said Ethel.

"I'm sure it was something she chose to keep very private." Father stared into the distance for several long minutes before speaking. "But perhaps, even more troubling than that, is the next thing she shared with me." Father struggled with his words. "Priscilla feared that she might be killed."

"What?" Shivers ran through Ethel and Nellie's bodies, as the hairs on their arms stood on end. "I know we shared with you at bingo that Priscilla had confided the same thing in us. But that she came to you on the very day she was murdered is really frightening."

"Priscilla believed the threat was real and could be imminent." Father bowed his head. "She sought guidance as to what I thought she should do. I suggested she go to the police, but she didn't seem too eager to do that. I even told her I'd go with her, if that would make it easier. But she was emphatic that was not an option. I really didn't know what other guidance I could offer, so I suggested that she try to relax after confession. I know how the three of you always play bingo together every Sunday night. I encouraged her to do so and felt it might take her mind off her worries. And," he added with sadness in his voice, "I imagined the church bingo hall would be a safe haven for her. It seemed like the best choice at the time."

"You'd think so, Father." A pensive look appeared on Nellie's face.

Father's tone seemed ominous, as he continued to speak. "Priscilla added that she had stumbled, quite innocently, onto something that some very bad people were involved in." He paused. "People," she said, "that would go to any length to get what they wanted. Even murder."

"Murder? My God. Did she tell you anything more? Did she mention any names? Anyone specific?" Nellie suddenly felt as if a light bulb had gone off, as her next thought popped into her mind. "Now I'm wondering if these threats had anything to do with Fred's gambling problem. I know from all the crime shows I watch on television that those loan-sharks can be pretty vindictive if they don't get their money back on time."

"Never really thought of that, but it certainly is a possibility," said Father. "And she did start to say something about Roxy's Bar, too, but then she stopped as quickly as she had started."

"Roxy's Bar? Are you sure?"

"Yes." Father's voice was choked up and tears were in his eyes. "Sadly, we now know that Priscilla's instincts were correct. It was almost as if she knew her demise was coming. A premonition of sorts. But figuring everything out is not going to be easy."

"That's for sure. Poor Priscilla. So, what do you think we should do now, Father?"

"I guess the police are doing everything they can to catch the culprit, or culprits. But I shared this with you both because I know how committed you two are to solving this crime. I know how much you both loved Priscilla. Between her worrying about Fred's possible gambling problem and the threat on her life, no wonder she was so frightened."

"Absolutely." Ethel's voice was filled with sadness. "I had no idea about Fred's addiction, Father. I can't imagine the Fred we know being a compulsive gambler. But I guess you never know." Ethel wiped a tear from her eye. "Actually, that might account for that despicable hoodlum showing up at his house and threatening Nancy when Fred was in the hospital. And the fact that Priscilla was at Roxy's Bar before she was killed makes me even more curious about what's going on there." Ethel bit on her lower lip. "You know, Father, Nellie and I have been to Roxy's a few times to do a little investigating of our own. But we haven't found any evidence yet that ties anything about that decrepit place to why someone would want Priscilla dead. I am perplexed as to why she'd ever be at a place like that, even if it was for Annie's sake."

"I share the same thought," replied Father O'Leary. "A fine, upstanding Christian woman having any connection to a place like *that* is something I just cannot come to terms with. And I don't think that the possible link to what she told me about Fred can be ruled out." Father O'Leary placed his hands over his face for several long moments before he spoke. "This was not an easy thing for me to share. I only pray that God will forgive me for divulging to you something said in confidence in the Sacrament of Reconciliation. But I truly believe in my heart that Priscilla would want you to know whatever you could that may potentially help you."

"Thank you, Father. And, as God is my witness, Nellie and I will not rest until Priscilla's murderer is brought to justice."

"Amen to that," declared Father O'Leary.

Chapter Twenty-Eight
An Unwelcome Visitor

The days passed slowly for Fred, but he was grateful to be alive and even more thankful that Nancy had taken a leave of absence from her teaching job to be with him. He was thrilled that it was finally time for him to be released from the hospital. Nancy's stay with Ethel had been pleasant for both of them. But now it was time to get on with their lives.

Nancy had cleaned her father's home and prepared a delicious welcome home dinner to which she had invited Ethel and Nellie. It seemed only fitting that she should invite the two women, who had saved her dad's life, to celebrate his safe return home. Nellie and Ethel would be arriving any moment.

Nancy helped her dad to the recliner that had always been his favorite place to rest. She placed a cup of green tea on the table beside him.

"Dr. Galler said you need to take it easy, dad, and I know that's hard for you to do. You've always been so active. But I think it's important that you follow your doctor's advice. He deals with heart problems every day and knows what's best. Promise me you'll let me pamper you for a few more days."

Fred felt such love and gratitude towards his only daughter at that moment that tears filled his eyes.

Nancy couldn't help but notice and bent over to give her dad a big hug. "I love you, dad. You're all I have. I want you to be around for a long time."

"I love you, too, Nancy. And I can't begin to tell you what having you near me during all of this has meant to me. You are, without a doubt, the best medicine any father could hope for."

"I'm just so happy that you're home and doing so well."

Fred took a sip of his tea. "You need to get back to your life in California, Nancy. I appreciate everything you've done for me and I promise you, if another emergency comes up with my health, I'll give you a call." Fred smiled broadly. "And, let's face it, if I don't call you, we both know Ethel and Nellie will!"

"I'm sure you're right about that. Speaking of Ethel and Nellie, there's the doorbell. I'll get it."

Nancy opened the front door and couldn't believe her eyes. Her hands began to tremble. The same frightening man, who had greeted her just weeks earlier, stood smugly before her. She instinctively began to push the door closed, but he placed a firm hand against it and said, "No one closes the door on me, bitch. Do you understand?"

Nancy could not speak. She stood breathing heavily, her heart pumping rapidly and waited. Her father called out in a weak voice from his chair in the living room.

"Are they here, honey? Show them in."

"Well, well. I guess your dad has better manners than his daughter does, wouldn't you agree? You heard the man. Show me in." He pushed with more force and the door fully opened.

"Please. I beg of you. My dad is not a well man. He just got home from the hospital today. Please leave us alone. I'm begging you."

"Oh, you're begging me, are you. Am I supposed to care? I have unfinished business with your dad."

"What? What is wrong with you? Have you no feeling? I told you that he just got home from the hospital. Can't you leave him alone?"

"Not an option. Simple as that. Now, I'm through being nice."

Just at that moment Nancy saw Ethel's Civic pull into the driveway. She wanted to call out to her. In minutes, they were approaching the front door, where they noticed the imposing figure pushing his way in.

"Nancy," Ethel called out. "Are you okay?"

Before she could reply, the man with the huge cross tattooed across his neck turned towards the two women. "Well, I guess this is my lucky day. One big, happy party! Come in, ladies. You don't want to be late." Sarcasm dripped from his voice.

Ethel didn't know what to do. She thought about running, but where would that leave Nancy and her dad. She tried to whip out her cell phone to call Officer Malcolm or Bill, but the thug pulled a gun from out of nowhere and pointed it at Nancy.

"I'd think again about using that phone of yours, grandma. Probably not the best idea, if you get my drift." He nuzzled the nose of the gun into Nancy's neck. "Now everyone do as I say, and no one will get hurt. No funny business. Do I make myself perfectly clear?"

Nancy felt as if she were about to pass out, but she focused on her father and the importance of being strong for him. She didn't know what she could do or how this ordeal might turn out. But one thing she was sure about was that she would do everything in her power to keep her father safe and calm.

"After you, ladies," T-Bone said in a gruff voice. He herded them all into the living room, smiled evilly at

Fred and said in a frightening tone, "Let's let everyone know why I'm here. Shall we, Fred?"

But Fred did not hear him. He looked as if he had passed out, or worse.

Chapter Twenty-Nine
Ethel's Quick Thinking

"Well, well," uttered T-Bone. "Who would have ever thought this little party of ours would get off to such a great start. Everyone's here," he smugly added. "But, what's with this deadbeat?" he added as he glared wickedly at Fred. He gave a self-righteous laugh and continued. "Oh, well. He'll join us in time. I didn't even need to send out invitations, did I? Couldn't have worked out better." He inhaled deeply. "Is that chicken I smell? One of my favorites. I do hope you'll add an extra seat at the table."

"What do you want with us?" asked Nellie in a terrified voice.

T-Bone grunted and again looked displeasingly towards Fred. He walked over and placed his hand firmly on his shoulder. "Listen, I don't owe nobody an explanation. But it sure don't take no genius to see that this old piece of crap don't look too good."

"How dare you speak about my father like that. Leave him alone," cried Nancy. "He's recovering from surgery and seeing you has clearly upset him."

"Oh, now isn't that just too bad. Daddy's upset, is he? What a pity. It would be a real shame if the old geezer croaked."

Ethel mustered up every bit of courage and ran over to try to remove T-Bones hand from Fred's shoulder. But she was no match for the muscular bully. He snorted loudly. "You're pretty funny for an old broad. Did you honestly think you was any match for me? Please. Don't embarrass yourself, Granny."

Ethel tried to imagine what Leonard would do, but this was one situation she didn't remember him ever discussing. She had only her own wits to rely on. Sink or swim, she thought to herself. It was a split-second decision and her timing would have to be just right. "You're right. I'm no match for you. Just don't hurt Fred."

"That's entirely up to Fred. When he comes to, we'll see if he's willing to cooperate. It sure would make his life easier and all of yours, too," he said as he squeezed his shoulder with greater force.

Nancy began to cry. "You're hurting him. Stop it."

"Listen, little lady, I'm in charge here. And if you don't want your father or any of you to get hurt, I suggest you shut up. I'm getting pretty tired of listening to your whining."

Silence filled the room.

Fred's eyes slowly opened and it was clear that he was not happy to see James Jesus Manzaro standing before him. "Nancy, are you okay?" he called out weakly to his daughter.

"Dad, don't worry about me. I'm fine. Just tell this man that he's made a terrible mistake. Tell him you don't know anything that could be of use to someone *like him.*"

"Watch it, bitch. I hope you weren't insulting me, cause if you were, I....." He placed the revolver beside Fred's head. "Hi Fred. Surprised to see me again?"

Nancy gasped. "Dad, how does this awful man know you?" Nancy fought back her tears.

"Okay. You win. Just tell me what you want."

He looked at Fred with hatred in his eyes. "You know what I want, old man. And reckoning time is now. You can either tell me what I want to know or this lovely daughter of yours may just be the one I decide to kill first." His tone was cold and matter-of-fact. Ethel and Nellie had no reason to doubt him. "The choice is yours."

"Okay, okay. Put down that gun and I'll talk." Fred was so weak that you could barely make out his words. "I can't think with that thing pointed at my head."

In the meantime, Ethel's mind was whirling, trying to figure out how and when she could implement her plan. She realized if it backfired, they might all wind up dead.

T-Bone reluctantly complied, as he placed his gun on the coffee table beside Fred. "Okay. I done what you asked. Now, spill your guts. I ain't got all day."

Fred's hands began to tremble. Nancy's sobs grew louder. T-Bone glared at her and she realized that her crying might put her father in greater danger than he already clearly was in. So, with every ounce of will power she had, she bit down on her lower lip and breathed in as deeply as she could. She had never been so frightened in her entire life.

Fred began to nervously tap his fingers against the arm of the recliner, as he moved uneasily in the chair. His face lost what little color it had. "It's in the office." He spoke in a hushed, monotone.

"Yeah. Where in the office? Be specific, old man."

"Okay." Fred was clearly rattled and afraid. "Second desk drawer, behind the folder that is labeled tax information."

"Now we're cooking."

It seemed to Fred as if T-Bone's eyes pierced through him.

"Is it all there? Every name?"

"As far as I know."

"As far as you know? You better hope it's all there. I've about had it with your bunch of delays and attempts to slow me down." He grabbed his gun from the table and began to walk towards the office.

At that moment, Ethel lunged at the thug and, with every ounce of strength in her body, brought her knee up to his genitals. "Call the police, Nellie," she screamed, as T-Bone dropped to the floor and lay writhing in pain.

"You'll pay for this, bitch. And, I'll get even with you. Fred. You're a dead man."

Without a moment's hesitation, Ethel grabbed his revolver from the floor and pointed it squarely at his body. "Just stay where you are, you scumbag. The police will be here any minute and we'll just see how tough you really are. Intimidating a sick, old man really shows what a lowlife you are."

T-Bone continued to moan in pain, as the sound of sirens grew closer.

Chapter Thirty
Confronted by a Creep

Annie was sitting at her desk grading papers when Skylar knocked on the door. She looked up to see her student with a look of worry on her young face. "Is everything alright, Skylar? Please, come in and," thinking about what Skylar may have to say added, "close the door behind you."

It was easy to see that Skylar was on the verge of tears and very nervous. Annie got a chair and pulled it up beside hers. "Please, sit down, Skylar. What's troubling you?" Annie's voice was kind and filled with compassion. "You can tell me anything. I promise I won't judge you."

Skylar tried to speak, but the words would not come. She put her hands up to her face and began to sob.

Annie leaned over and gently placed her hand on Skylar's knee. She reached onto her desk and grabbed a tissue. "Here. Take this. You don't have to share anything you don't want to talk about. I just want you to know that what you tell me is just between us."

"I know," Skylar said between sobs. "But I don't know what to do. I've never been so confused."

"Just relax and take your time. I'm here to listen whenever you are ready."

The two sat beside one another for a long time without speaking. Skylar finally broke the silence with words that were alarming. "He was at my house again.

He was waiting for me and tried to intimidate me even more this time. He is very insistent and doesn't like to be told no."

"When, Skylar? When did you see him?"

"About a half hour ago. He was waiting for me when I got home. Thank God my two younger sisters weren't there. I worry about them."

"What did he say, Skylar?"

"Pretty much what he said to me the first time he cornered me. He's such a creep. He wanted to know if I'd changed my mind about having a baby. He asked me if I'd had time to think about his offer and to come to my senses. Imagine that."

"That's pretty despicable."

"I know, but he's a powerful man. I think he's used to getting whatever he wants."

"You're probably right about that, but you don't have to do anything you don't want to do, Skylar. And, what he is asking you to do is not legal. He is breaking the law."

"I'm sure he could care less. He wants what he wants." Skylar wiped her eyes with the tissue. "He told me I could cooperate and, if I did, getting pregnant would be a pretty pleasant experience or...." Skylar began to sob.

"Or what, Skylar? What did he say?"

"He said if I refused to cooperate with him that he'd make all the arrangements and it might not be a memory I'd want to remember. Either way, he told me, he'd get what he wants."

Annie sat speechless, not knowing what to say to comfort the young girl. "That is a pretty serious threat, Skylar. I think we should go to the police."

"No," Skylar said with more determination in her voice than Annie had ever witnessed from her. "No police."

"But, they could...."

Skylar cut her teacher off mid-sentence. "I know you mean well and you're the only one I trust to share this with. But we've had some really bad experiences with the police. I don't want them involved." She began to bite on her lower lip and to nervously twist her beautiful shimmering red hair around her finger.

"Okay, Skylar. The last thing I want to do is to upset you any more than you already are. The decision is yours."

"Thank you for understanding." Skylar's eyes filled with tears. "Do you think that awful man with the red hair was implying he, or someone he would send, was going to rape me? That's how it sounded to me."

Annie couldn't disagree with her student's interpretation of the words that had been spoken. Plus, Annie knew that Skylar was one of her brightest, most promising young students and, if that was her gut feeling, it most likely was correct. To make matters worse, Annie knew that Skylar's father was serving time in prison and that her mother was drunk more often than she was sober. Life can be so unfair, Annie thought to herself.

"Listen, Skylar. I have a thought. I don't really know if it will be very helpful, but I respect your decision not to go to the police." Skylar sat clinging to every word her teacher was saying. "I have two very close friends whom I think could help you. The one was married to a detective. He died several years ago, but she learned a lot from living with him. And I can assure you she is kind, well organized and discreet. Do I have your permission to fill her in on everything and see what she thinks? She may have some ideas that you and I don't." Annie paused for a moment. "I think it's worth a try.

"Okay. If you promise me that she's not connected to the police department," Skylar nervously added.

153

"I promise." Annie leaned over and grabbed a piece of paper and a pen from her desk. She quickly jotted down her own home phone number and handed it to Skylar. "Call me any time, Skylar; night or day. I want you to know that you're not alone."

Skylar had never experienced the kindness and genuine concern she was feeling at that moment. Instinctively, she bent over and hugged Annie. "How can I ever thank you for helping me and, more importantly, for not judging me."

"No thanks needed, Skylar. I'm more than happy to help you. But I must say that my curiosity has been piqued. If he's doing this to you, I wonder what other girls he's doing the same thing to."

Skylar looked downward to avert Annie's gaze. And, at that moment, Annie believed Skylar knew far more than she was saying.

Chapter Thirty-One
A Tough Nut to Crack

Annie shared what she had found out from Skylar with Ethel and Nellie.

"This is getting more complicated and dangerous then I'd imagined," said Ethel.

Nellie looked up with an appreciative gaze towards Annie. "But thanks to you, Annie, we have some new evidence to look into."

"Now, the question of the day. How to proceed?" Ethel stared into the distance. "This is a tough nut to crack. Harder than I'd ever thought," she added. "Not being able to at least consult the police makes it harder yet. But, I'm still confident, if we chip away a little at a time, we can figure it all out."

"I knew I could count on you," Annie replied with genuine sincerity in her voice.

"Thanks for the vote of confidence, Annie. I'm thinking our next step should be to try and find that piece of paper at Fred's house that T-Bone wanted to get his hands on so badly. Maybe, somehow, all of this is related in some way or another. I mean he was like a crazy man."

"Crazy and dangerous," chimed in Nellie. "But, thanks to your quick thinking, Ethel, and Officer Malcolm's fast arrival, he's out of the picture for a while. I bet that's not at all how he envisioned things going down." Her voice was solemn as she continued. "Whatever it is in that desk drawer, it must contain some pretty important information. Information worth killing for. And now that T-Bone's in police custody, we're safe to investigate without any interference."

"And I think Officer Malcolm will view us with a bit more credibility after what happened," Ethel uttered.

"Maybe," retorted Nellie. "Or he could be annoyed with us that we didn't heed his advice and not get involved. I mean we could have all been killed. And, we don't really know if T-Bone was acting alone, do we?"

"True. But Officer Malcolm can't ignore the fact that he has a big-time thug in custody, with no one having been hurt, thanks to us." Ethel grabbed her sweater. "Come on. Let's head over to Fred's house and see what evidence we can find." She turned towards Annie. "Thanks for sharing. We'll be in touch."

Ethel and Nellie walked slowly up the walkway to 122 Hartford. The landscaping looked even more overgrown and shabby than the last time they had stopped by.

"It's sad how things change so quickly. Priscilla would be so disappointed to see how her prized yard has deteriorated."

"I'm sure that's true. But circumstances changed everything. Nothing is the same and I doubt Fred will ever get over the fact that his beloved Priscilla is gone. I just hope that whatever we find inside provides a clue as to why Priscilla was murdered."

"I hope so too," added Nellie, as she rang the front door and waited. "Or, maybe, the list will confirm what Father told us about Fred's possible gambling problem."

"No matter what, it is potentially a huge lead and we need to find it."

Nancy greeted them warmly. "I'm so glad to see you. My dad has been asking for you both. He wants to......" Nancy's voice trailed off as Fred called out from his recliner.

"Is that Ethel and Nellie?"

"It is, dad."

"Please show them in."

Without delay, Nancy ushered the two women into the living-room where Fred sat with a concerned look on his face. But his color was far better than it had been the last time they'd seen him.

"I wanted to say thank you to both of you. I'm starting to think of you two as my guardian angels. I am so grateful that you seemed to be with me again at a critical moment. You saved my life and my daughter's life and I can never repay you for that."

"Fred, there's no need to......."

Fred cut Ethel off before she could complete her sentence.

"I need to say this. Please." Fred composed his thoughts. "You two ladies were Priscilla's best friends. And I know how hard you've both been working to try to right the terrible wrong that was committed against her." Fred's eyes filled with tears. "But I need to tell you something. Something that I probably should have told you earlier."

"What is it, Fred?"

Fred's voice was weak and choked up. "I really don't know how to say this. I still can't believe it myself, but I think Priscilla may have been involved in something shady."

Nellie and Ethel exchanged concerned, uneasy glances.

"Dad, what in the world are you talking about? Mom was as upright and honest as the day is long. You know that and I know that. What would ever possess you to say something like that?"

157

"I didn't want to think it or believe it, but she started being very secretive the last several days of her life." Fred began to weep and took a moment to compose himself before finishing his thought. "That wasn't the first time I'd had a visit from that thug."

"What? I don't understand." Panic filled Nancy's voice. "What business could you possibly have had with a criminal like that?"

Fred gazed downward and paused for a moment. "It wasn't me, Nancy. It was your mother."

"That's impossible, dad. I don't believe you. Mom would never associate with the likes of a man like him. Never. He's a disgusting creature with no sense of right or wrong. What could he possibly have wanted with mom?"

"That's what I'm still trying to figure out." Fred shivered, as he spoke. "I feel a little guilty telling you this, but I listened in on one of your mother's phone calls. I could hardly believe my ears. The man on the other end was gruff and crude. He said he wanted that list. I'm telling you that I've never heard anyone speak with such foul language as he did to your mother. I was appalled." Fred began to cry. "I thought to myself that whatever list he was referring to and whatever was on that list must be pretty important for her not to share it with me. I guess I just assumed she eventually would. I mean, when you've been married as long as we have, you share everything." He took on a melancholy look. "Or, should I say, I thought you did. Obviously, I was wrong. Can you ever really know someone?"

"But you said he paid you a visit. Was mom here, too?"

"No. She was out. He told me that I better encourage her to give him the list or she could wind up getting badly hurt. I'll never forget, till the day I die, that greasy hair, those awful tattoos and the way he spoke. I couldn't imagine my wife, your mother, having anything to do with the likes of him."

"I'm so sorry, dad. I can only imagine how frightened you must have been."

"I was actually trembling, Nancy. So, when your mother got home, I confronted her about everything."

"And?"

"And at first she wouldn't say a word. But, when she realized that creep had come to our home and specifically asked me for the list, she said she'd tell me where it was hidden. But she made me promise, on our Nancy's head, that I would never tell anyone. Said she was trying to piece things together and that she, eventually, was going to go to the police. She was upset that she had no idea who had sent the list to her and what its implications were. And she seemed even more baffled as to how T-Bone knew she had the list. Priscilla told me she loved me and that I'd have to trust her on this." Fred bent his head down and began to sob uncontrollably. "What did I do? I wish I could have just given him that damn list when he first asked for it. Maybe then my Priscilla would still be alive."

Ethel and Nellie exchanged glances and, with kindness in her voice, Ethel spoke. "Fred, I think, if it's alright with you, I'd like to get that envelope with the list from your office and see just what's on it." She patted his shoulder gently. "It just might provide a major clue for catching Priscilla's killer."

Chapter Thirty-Two
The List

Ethel and Nellie were eager to try to locate the missing list.

"If there's anything I can help you with, just holler."

"Thanks, Fred. But the only thing you can do to help us is to get better. We'll handle things from here."

"What would I ever do without you two? You've been a godsend to me in so many ways."

Nancy smiled broadly at the two women. "I'd have to say I agree with my dad. I share his sentiments about you both. I believe my mom is looking down from heaven and feeling blessed that you are in our lives."

"Nancy, all this talk is going to make me cry. Nellie and I loved your mom, you know that. We're trying our best to help the police and we're determined not to give up. So, here's hoping we can find the list and figure out why someone would be willing to kill for it."

The two women headed off into the office that they'd been in more times than they could remember. But, seeing the family pictures that adorned the walls and table, knowing Priscilla would never be there to admire them again, caused a surge of sadness to pass between them.

The antique mahogany desk, with its numerous nooks and crannies, was the focal point of the room. Priscilla had told them, on more occasions than one, that it had belonged to her grandmother and her mother. It held great sentimental value and she imagined one day it would belong to Nancy. Family had always been so important to Priscilla.

As she pulled out the second drawer of the desk, her heart fluttered with nervousness. Whatever list this was must be pretty important, she thought. So valuable, in fact, that T-Bone was willing to kill for it.

"Are you okay, Ethel? You look kind of flushed."

"I'd be lying if I said I wasn't worried. This may be the clue we've been waiting for." Ethel inhaled deeply. "I have to say I feel kind of uncomfortable rummaging through Priscilla's private papers. But I have to believe we're doing what she'd want us to do."

"We've got no choice, Ethel. How many times have you told me how important it is to go where the clues take you? Well, the clues have definitely taken us to the second drawer of this desk."

"You're a good detective, Nellie. I'm glad we're partners."

Nellie grinned broadly. "Partners in crime. That's us, Ethel."

The files were all neatly arranged in alphabetical order. It didn't take long to find the one labeled tax information. Ethel took a deep breath and looked behind it. She hastily pulled the file out, so she could get a better look. "Nothing," she exclaimed with disappointment in her voice. "There's nothing that in any way resembles an envelope," she uttered as she hastily pushed back the other files.

"Nothing?" questioned Nellie. "That just can't be. Fred said that Priscilla told him that's where it was hidden. And, if that's what she said, it's got to be there."

"Okay, then. I agree. Let's stay calm. Let's try to think like detectives. Maybe Priscilla was giving Fred

161

some kind of a clue that only he would know the significance of."

"Like what?"

Ethel threw up her hands in desperation. "Like, gee Nellie, I don't know. Why don't we go talk to Fred? Maybe he can shed some light on the missing envelope."

The two women did not want to upset Fred in any way. Ethel asked him as gently as she could if those were Priscilla's exact words. Was he sure she had said the second drawer behind the tax file?

"That's what she said, alright. I'll never forget the frightened look on her face and the fear in her voice. She was spooked. That I know for certain." Fred stared into the distance, not really focusing on anything. "Let me think. Are you sure you opened the second drawer and looked behind the tax file?"

"Positive, Fred. Nellie watched me do it."

"Okay then. I don't think Priscilla would have made a mistake about something this important. I suggest you take out all the files and look through them. Maybe she thought she put it behind the tax file, but she was pretty upset that day. I suppose it could be somewhere else in that drawer. I can help you, if you'd like."

"No, Fred. You've helped us already. You rest. Nellie and I will go back and check things out more carefully."

They didn't want to accept the possibility that Fred may have put Priscilla's life in danger through some gambling problem he still had. Considering that possibility, they preferred to search without him.

Ethel and Nellie crouched down beside the desk and, with great care, removed one file at a time. They checked and double checked. All of a sudden, they noticed an envelope that had been placed lying flat fairly close to where the tax information had been. They had not seen it earlier because it was more under the file than behind it.

"Bingo!" exclaimed Ethel with great delight. "We've got it Nellie."

The two women sat together eagerly reviewing the paper before them. But what they saw made no sense to them.

"I don't get it, Ethel. All this seems to be is a list of names with notations beside each one. I can't really decipher anything. It looks almost like a foreign language to me." Nellie squinted behind her tortoise shell glasses to try to make out the notations. "Looks like 25,000 beside this first name and 45,000 beside this other name. But, it's scratchy at best. What do they all have in common? And how could they have anything to do with Priscilla's death?"

"I'll be darned if I know, but one thing's for sure. We're going to find out. These names may help us catch the killer."

The two women sat on the brown and beige plaid couch, as they intently reviewed the list.

"Hmm," declared Ethel. "Do you notice anything similar about all these entries, Nellie?"

"Not really."

"Well, if you look carefully, you'll see that each line belongs to a couple. There are no single names on this paper."

"So? What does that mean?"

"I don't know. Maybe nothing. Or, maybe something. It could be people Fred borrowed money from or people Priscilla spoke to about something that led to her murder." The furrows between Ethel's eyes deepened. "Really no idea at this point. We've got our work cut out for us, Nellie."

"Let's take a minute to review. There appears to be six couples on this paper with different notations

163

beside each one. But I believe someone intentionally made whatever is beside each name very difficult to read. Maybe it's some type of shorthand or foreign code."

> Dr. and Mrs. Harry Rockland
>
> Mr. and Mrs. Stuart Joslin
>
> Mr. and Mrs. Joseph Lerner
>
> Mr. and Mrs. Gary Bloom
>
> Dr. and Mrs. Samuel Sussman
>
> Mr. and Mrs. Anthony Farmington

"Let's show the list to Fred and see if he recognizes any of these names."

Fred studied the list with great interest. "I wish I could help you. If only I knew even one of these couples. But, I'm reasonably certain that Priscilla didn't know them either. Why would that list ever be worth killing for?"

"We have no idea, Fred. But, one thing's for certain. Nellie and I are going to get on this pronto."

"Ethel, do you think we should make a copy of this list and hide the original in a safe place? I once saw them do something like that on *Chicago PD.*"

"Nellie, you are becoming one heck of a detective right before my eyes. That's a great idea. Can we use your copier, Fred?"

"Of course. Whatever you need. And," said Fred with more enthusiasm than they'd heard in a long time, "I know the perfect place to hide the original list."

"And where is that, Fred?"

Fred smirked ever so slightly. "Let's hide it under the mattress on Priscilla's side of the bed. I know you probably think that sounds ridiculous, but that way it could almost seem like she's involved in the case."

"I think that's a wonderful idea, Fred." Ethel put the duplicate list safely in her pocketbook. "We'll call you if we make any progress. For now, Detectives Nellie and Ethel over and out."

Chapter Thirty-Three
Glove Lady

Ethel and Nellie approached the church bingo hall with curiosity and sadness.

"I can't believe we're here," Nellie exclaimed, as she clutched the bag of multi-colored daubers firmly in her hand.

"I know," added Ethel. "But we've put it off long enough. It's been over three months since Priscilla was murdered. Maybe there is something we'll notice that might give us an important clue."

"We can always hope. But I honestly don't expect any great revelations." Nellie shrugged her shoulders. "I mean the police have interviewed everyone that was here that night and the crime scene tapes are down now. But, you're right, Ethel. You never know. Besides we haven't played bingo in forever."

A moment of deep sorrow overcame them, as they set their purses and bingo bags on the table. The seat that Priscilla had once occupied sat painfully empty. As they quickly glanced around, they noticed that most of the faces were the same. *Tattoo Man* was in the same place he had occupied on that dreadful night.

"I guess life goes on," said Nellie. "I wonder if anybody here ever thinks about Priscilla or about her not being here anymore."

Before Nellie could utter another word, they were approached by *Glove Lady.* For all the years they'd been coming to bingo, *Glove Lady* had sat at the table adjacent to theirs and they had rarely exchanged a word.

"How are you two doing?" she inquired. "I was so sorry about your friend."

Glove Lady always wore a long white glove that extended from her left hand clear up to her elbow. If anyone spoke or made any noise during the games, she reprimanded them. She had even been known to raise her voice and tell players to find another table, if they couldn't follow her rules. No matter what the season, *Glove Lady* never abandoned her hand wear. It was a peculiar fetish and one that the threesome had often commented on. *Glove Lady* was definitely weird. But, on that night, they appreciated her concern.

"We're struggling to come to grips with what happened and hoping the killer is caught soon," was all Nellie replied.

"I hope so too," she added, as she turned to return to her seat.

As Ethel and Nellie glanced over to where she was sitting, they noticed that she'd put a variety of colored daubers at the two seats to either side of her, as well as at the two seats across from her. She may be able to fool some people, but they were on to her and her wily ways! It wasn't the first time that *Glove Lady* had tried to make players think that those seats were taken, so she'd have the whole table to herself.

As they organized their cards, being careful to put them in the right order, they were approached by Father O'Leary. His smile was warm and genuine. "It's so good to see you here, ladies. I've missed you both. Bingo just hasn't been the same without you."

"Thanks, Father, but I don't think bingo will ever be the same for either of us."

He placed his hand gently on Ethel's shoulder. "I understand. It must be very difficult for you both to be

166

here but I, for one, am very glad you are. Maybe, in some small way, being here tonight will be a good thing for you."

"We hope you're right, Father. But the only good thing we want is to figure out what happened to Priscilla and how she died."

"That is what we can all hope for. But, in the meantime, you two deserve a little fun in your lives. I know how much you enjoy a game of bingo, so why not think of tonight as a night to put all your worries aside. I think that would please Priscilla."

Ethel managed a faint smile. "Maybe that's not a bad idea, Father. We'll try our best."

Father O'Leary turned and walked away.

"How about visiting the snack bar and seeing if Donna's volunteering tonight. Remember we were going to talk to her again, if we had the chance."

"Sure, why not. I could go for a bag of popcorn and a diet coke."

As the two women approached the snack area, they were pleased to see Donna. She was putting a piece of pepperoni pizza on a paper plate for none other than *Tattoo Man*. The two women smiled at each other. "Some things never change," said Nellie in a quiet voice.

When *Tattoo Man* noticed them standing there, all he said was, "Sorry about your friend." Then, he flexed his tattooed-shoulder and added, "Mom and I are feeling lucky tonight." With those words, he turned and walked away.

The two women rolled their eyes at each other. "Speaking of weird."

"Well, you two haven't been here in quite a while. Any progress tracking down who killed Priscilla?" Donna's words seemed matter of fact and cold. Not the sentiment they would have expected from someone who had known Priscilla as long as she had.

"We're still investigating. It's not easy, but we won't give up till her killer is brought to justice. We were hoping maybe you could help us."

Donna responded with an exasperating sigh. "Me? How?" A confused look encompassed her face. "I told you when you spoke with me after the murder that I didn't know anything. I told the police the same thing. Nothing has changed."

"Sometimes the littlest clue might be a lead, Donna. Something you think is nothing might turn out to be something."

Donna looked dumbfounded. "What could I possibly know? I was right here that night. Right here working the concession stand like I do every few weeks." Donna shook her head from side to side. "Do you two expect me to pull something out of thin air?"

"That's not at all what we're saying. We're just asking you to think really hard about that night. Did you see or hear anything, anything at all, out of the ordinary?"

Donna suddenly got a befuddled look on her face. "Actually, there was something a little odd, but I'm sure it was nothing."

"What was it, Donna?"

"Well, when I got here to set up for the night, there was a strange man already here. I assumed he was here to play bingo and told him he was early."

"Are you sure about that, Donna?"

"I am. I know that I get here around 5:15 to set up. The bingo players don't usually start arriving for a good half hour. I told him the pizza would be delivered shortly, if he was hungry."

"What did he say?"

"That's the strange part. He never said a word. He just stared at me and ran out the side door. I never gave it another thought until just now. I wonder what business he had here that night, if not to play the game."

168

"Can you describe the man, Donna? Any information would be helpful."

"Let me think. He was here so briefly." Donna excused herself to scoop some popcorn and serve pizza to the people in the short line that had formed. "Sorry about that, but the refreshments are my responsibility."

"Of course. We understand. Please, continue."

"Okay. Not to be judgmental, but he was pretty grungy looking. Really dark, greasy hair and quite a bit of stubble on his face. Definitely not anyone I'd seen here before. But, now that I'm thinking about it, there was one thing about him that stood out."

"Really? What?"

"He had a tattoo of a cross on his neck. It struck me as quite odd because, believe me, he didn't look like a church going man."

Ethel and Nellie felt the hairs on their arms rise. Why would *he* be here at the bingo hall? And why would *he* be in the refreshment area before anyone was there? Their thoughts were one.

"Is there anything else you can think of?" questioned Ethel. "Even the tiniest detail might prove to be important."

Donna seemed more pensive and focused than the two women had ever seen her. "I'm sorry. Nothing else I can remember."

"You probably don't realize this, Donna, but you've just given us a clue. And it may just help us solve the case."

"Really?" replied Donna.

"I can't say for sure, but the man with the tattoo on his neck may, in some way, be tied into what happened to Priscilla."

Donna suddenly showed more emotion then either woman had ever seen. "Are you saying that I may have been alone with a murderer?"

Ethel was not surprised that, in Donna's eyes, everything was about her. "I'm not saying that, Donna. I'm just saying that you've provided us with a very good lead. But there are a lot of loose ends that need to be tied up before we can be sure of anything. At this point, everything is speculative."

"Will you keep me informed?" Donna seemed far more interested and concerned than she had been prior to her remembering the detail that may have put her in the same room as the possible killer.

"Absolutely, Donna. And thank you for your help. Oh, before I forget, can I have a diet coke and a bag of popcorn?"

"Sure," replied Donna.

As they walked away, Ethel could not contain her emotion. "Oh my God, Nellie. I can hardly believe what I just heard. Finally, we have another possible lead. I'd like to think Priscilla would be proud."

"I think she would be, Ethel. I'm surprising myself at how all this detective stuff is really getting into my blood." She gave a quick smile, despite the circumstances. "I've even been waking up in the middle of the night thinking about the case and all that's happened."

"I knew it, Nellie. I knew you had it in you. You're becoming quite the sleuth."

"I've had a great teacher, Ethel. But as much as we want to follow up on our leads, we promised that tonight was a night to put our worries aside and have a little fun. I guess knowing what we just learned won't make that an easy task."

Chapter Thirty-Four
Let's Google

"Golly, Nellie. I can't believe we're finally getting some real leads to investigate."

"I know. First the list and now the information about the strange man being at St. Angela's the night Priscilla was killed." Nellie paused a moment. "Where should we begin?"

"Well, we found the list first and it seems like it just might be the clue we've been waiting for. So, let's start with trying to decipher that."

"Seems like a good idea. But all we've got so far are a bunch of names with writing and numbers after each one. It makes no sense at all. It looks like some type of scribbly shorthand. Almost like hieroglyphics. We need to figure out who these people are and why they were on a list that may have cost Priscilla her life."

"Let's put on our best detective hats and brainstorm. We can do it," said Ethel.

Nellie's voice was filled with a sense of determination. "Of course, we can. Let's start with the obvious first step."

"And what might that be Madame Detective?"

"Why Google, of course! I mean there's hardly anything or anyone that you can't find out about with a proper search."

"Well, I am impressed, Nellie. It seems so obvious, but you were the one who thought of it. Not me.

Good going." Ethel smiled. "Don't laugh, Nellie. But, if I had a badge for good detective work, I'd pin it on you right now. Leading us to where the clues may be deciphered is a big step. I like how you're thinking."

"Why thank you, Ethel. That means a lot coming from you." She smiled broadly at her friend. "Let's head back to my house. My computer is set up and ready to go."

In a short while, the two women were eagerly perched before Nellie's computer.

"Which couple shall we start with?"

"I don't think it matters. I mean we don't know anything about any of them."

"True. So, let's start at the beginning."

Ethel removed the list carefully from her purse. "Dr. and Mrs. Harry Rockland."

Nellie entered the names in the Google search box. A flurry of activity followed and before their eyes several entries bearing the names Dr. and Mrs. Harry Rockland appeared.

"Hmm," exclaimed Ethel. "That was easier than I thought. Just look at the entries." Ethel and Nellie carefully scrutinized the information before them.

"I see several Harry Rocklands," declared Nellie. "But, look. Only two are doctors in the Kenmore area. That narrows it down a bit."

"You're right. Let's click on this one," Ethel added as she pointed to the first listing. "It seems as good a place to start as any." Nellie pressed the link and a picture of a very distinguished gentleman, probably close to seventy, appeared. Below the photo read, "Dr. Harry Rockland retires as a Board-Certified member of the American Academy of Ophthalmology. Dr. Rockland specialized in both glaucoma and cataract surgery." The article went on to discuss his education, accomplishments and volunteer work. The report stated that he and his wife,

Deidre, now reside in Boca Raton, Florida.

"Something tells me that this isn't the Harry Rockland that we're looking for. Click on the next one, Nellie."

Without hesitation, Nellie moved her mouse over the next article. "Oh my," she exclaimed, as the words spilled from her mouth. "Apparently, Dr. Harry Rockland has a son who followed in his footsteps. Another ophthalmologist. Only this time, he's living right here in our own backyard. Says he's a resident of East Amherst. Now that's a coincidence."

"Maybe," replied Ethel. "And maybe not." Ethel paused, deep in thought. "I think it might be prudent to pay a visit to Dr. Rockland."

"But it says that he is a retina specialist. Neither of us has any retina problem that we know of."

"My gracious, Nellie, where is your sense of adventure? We don't need to have a retina problem to find out about the Rocklands."

"Really?"

"Yes, really. Seeing Mrs. Rockland can accomplish the same result."

"I guess now is about the time when I say that you've stumped me. What are you thinking?"

"I'm thinking that since their address is right in front of our eyes, we stop over in a day or two."

"Stop over? That should go well," she said with sarcasm in her voice. "What in the world would we say we were doing there?"

"Don't be so naive, Nellie. I mean aren't you one of the best bakers in our city."

"What? What does my love of baking have to do with anything?"

"Think outside the box."

"I'm clueless. Run your thoughts by me."

"It's simple. You bake a bunch of your famous

molasses cookies and your one of a kind, lemon drop cookies. We both know how totally irresistible they are."

"And?"

"And we go to a few houses with them packaged beautifully, as only you can do, and tell the occupants that we're selling cookies for charity."

"For charity?"

"Why not? It's a good cause. Any money we make from the sale of your cookies can be donated to Haven House."

Nellie looked pensive, as she pondered what Ethel had suggested. "Hmm," replied Nellie. "I think you're onto something. And Haven House is an excellent choice, Ethel. So many mothers and children are living there safely who've suffered abuse at the hands of someone they loved and trusted."

"So, you'll do it? You'll start baking?"

"If that might somehow give us a lead into catching Priscilla's killer and help those at Haven House, I'm ready to hit the grocery store. I think I can finish baking what we need by tomorrow."

"Dr. And Mrs. Harry Rockland, here's hoping you'll be able to shed some light on why your names were on a list that someone may have been willing to kill for." Ethel turned to Nellie. "If we learn anything that could help us with the case, we can call your baked goods *Catch a Killer Cookies*."

Chapter Thirty-Five
A Visit to Mrs. Rockland

The well-manicured lawn and tall poplars that lined the side of the all-brick house gave it a mature, majestic feel. Ivy, twisting its way up the side of the stately home, only added to its refined look.

"I believe this neighborhood is called Deerhurst Park. It is beautiful, don't you agree?"

"Totally," replied Nellie, as she gazed about wide-eyed. "One house is more lovely than the next and each is so different. These homes must come with quite a hefty price tag."

The sound of children playing distracted them for the moment. Four little boys, about five or six, were tossing a football down the center of the cul-de-sac, in front of the Rockland's house.

"Looks like the children are having a good time."

"Yes. Maybe one of them is the Rockland's little boy."

"Maybe. So, now that we've stopped at two houses and already sold several bags of cookies, what do you say we ring the Rockland's doorbell." Ethel paused for a fleeting moment. "Remember, Nellie, it is important to act casual and natural."

"Got it, Ethel!" she responded as they walked slowly up the long driveway. The assorted flowers and shrubs that lined the walkway were magnificent. Bursts of color, intertwined with low growing ground cover, formed a colorful pathway to the front door. Nellie placed her baked goods in a position to be clearly seen, breathed in deeply and pressed the brass doorbell. "Here we go, Ethel," she uttered under her breath. "Let's hope for a clue."

The heavy wooden door opened and before them stood a woman who appeared to be in her early thirties. Attractively dressed in beige linen slacks with a delicate floral print silk blouse, she looked like she was ready to meet her friends for lunch. Her blond hair was swept back into a ponytail, while her makeup was understated. There was no denying she was a very beautiful young woman. Her smile seemed genuine and Ethel liked her immediately.

"May I help you?" Her words were soft and sincere.

"I'm sorry. Let me introduce ourselves. I'm Ethel Dinwiddie and this is my dear friend, Nellie Pearce. We are visiting different neighborhoods selling Nellie's homemade baked goods to raise money for Haven House. Are you familiar with what Haven House is?"

"Actually I am. I was involved in their fund raiser last October. I agree that it is an excellent cause."

"Well, that's wonderful to hear. We have homemade molasses cookies and homemade lemon drop cookies. Both are delicious." Ethel paused a moment. "Would you be interested in buying any today?"

"Without a doubt. Sounds good to me."

Ethel glanced towards the street where the boys continued to play. "Is one of those boys yours?" Without waiting for a reply, she added, "I know children love Nellie's cookies."

"I can imagine they would." She smiled briefly and then a melancholy look encompassed her face. "I wish one were mine. But my husband and I haven't been blessed with children yet. Maybe someday."

"I'll bet when you least expect it. God works in mysterious ways," added Nellie.

Mrs. Rockland smiled broadly. "Why you sound just like my priest. That's exactly what he said to us."

"Really?"

"Yes. I rather doubt if you know Father O'Leary from St. Angela's church, but he is an amazing man. He seems to understand how we feel and is doing everything in his power to help us. That's such a coincidence that you used the same phrase he did."

"Actually, we do know Father O'Leary. We attend St. Angela's, too. Maybe I heard it at one of his sermons."

"Really? What a small world." Mrs. Rockland invited them in, but the two women were anxious to discuss what they'd learned.

"It is so kind of you to invite us in, but we really must be going. We still have a lot of houses to visit."

Mrs. Rockland paid them for two bags of molasses and two bags of lemon drop cookies. "I'm so glad you stopped by. When my husband gets home from work, he's going to think I've been busy baking." She winked her eye at Nellie. "Maybe I'll let him think that I did bake these, before I tell him about the two lovely ladies that I met selling cookies for Haven House. I know he'll be pleased that we donated to a wonderful cause."

"Thank you," Ethel and Nellie said in unison. "Enjoy the cookies. Maybe we'll see you some Sunday at church."

Mrs. Rockland smiled. "You never know. I'll be looking for you both at mass."

"And we'll be keeping our eyes out for you," Ethel declared in a hushed tone, as they walked slowly down the driveway. "Mission accomplished."

Chapter Thirty-Six
God Works in Mysterious Ways

"So, my dear comrade. I'd say we've had a most successful encounter with Mrs. Rockland. We've gotten a few clues that may prove useful." Nellie was beaming.

"Agreed, Nellie. But now we need to reassess. Don't you agree?"

"You're our lead detective, Ethel! Whatever you think."

"Did you see the look on her face when we asked if one of those children playing in the cul-de-sac was hers?"

"It would have been hard to miss, Ethel. She looked as if she was holding back her tears."

"I know." Ethel looked pensive as she stared into the distance. "I'm wondering if it really was just a coincidence that she attends St. Angela's and that she actually quoted Father O'Leary's words verbatim. Couple that with what we suspect may be going on at Roxy's, what we overheard at the clinic, Annie's telling us about Skylar and....." Her voice trailed off without finishing her thoughts.

"And what, Ethel?"

"And Priscilla's murder," she replied with a shaky voice. "I'm just wondering if there is a common thread. Something that ties everything together."

"But what?" Nellie shrugged her shoulders.

Ethel took a deep breath and continued. "I don't know, Nellie. I'm baffled. But I think we need to pay another visit to Father O'Leary and then try to track down the next couple on the list."

"Sounds like a plan. And, while we're at it, I think we should definitely add this new information to the log we're keeping. We need a written record of everything we're finding. Like you said, no detail should be overlooked. If we end up going to the police eventually, with our *evidence*, it will be good to have everything written down with the precise date. I'll be glad to be our scribe."

"You are detail oriented and I think that would be very helpful. But for now, scribe Nellie, I think that we should head over to the church. I'll bet this is a good time to find Father O'Leary there. We can ask him about the Rockland family and see what he says."

The smell of rain was in the air. Ethel and Nellie grabbed their umbrellas before exiting Ethel's Civic. As they approached the walkway to the rectory, a light rain started to fall. As always, Father O'Leary seemed genuinely pleased to see them.

"Good afternoon, ladies. To what do I owe the pleasure of this unexpected, but welcome visit."

"Actually, Nellie and I just wanted to ask you something about an encounter we just had."

"An encounter? What do you mean?"

Nellie and Ethel had discussed *the list* and how it had come into their possession on their drive to the church. They decided to keep how they had acquired it under their hats. No need to divulge possible evidence, they thought. But we can say we saw Mrs. Rockland. He'd have no reason to know that we saw her on purpose.

"You know how much we enjoy doing charitable work, Father."

Father O'Leary beamed. "Of course, I do. You are two of our most treasured parishioners, as far as always being there to help others."

"Why it's the least we can do. We feel so blessed that we have our health and since we are both retired, it seems like the righteous thing to do." Nellie's words came easily.

"And it doesn't hurt that Nellie is a prized baker. Who can resist buying her delicious baked goods, particularly when the proceeds go to charity?"

"You know I've always supported giving to charity. And both of you have always set such a wonderful example for others. You certainly don't need my approval."

Ethel smiled. "We know that, Father. But we encountered a woman this afternoon who seemed quite delighted with Nellie's molasses and lemon drop cookies. She bought a few bags of each and was quite certain her husband would be very happy she did."

"That's nice to hear, but what does that have to do with me?"

"Well," added Ethel, "Mrs. Rockland is one of your parishioners. When Nellie told her that *God works in mysterious ways*, she said that was precisely what her priest had said." Ethel focused on the oversized cross on the wall before her and continued. "She said that you seemed to understand how badly she wanted a baby and would do everything in your power to help her. She clearly wants to be a mother."

"Yes. Dr. and Mrs. Rockland are a lovely couple. I had the honor of marrying them about six years ago. They would make excellent parents, in my opinion."

The look on Father's face changed to one the two women rarely, if ever, had seen. "It seems so unfair. The Rocklands are educated, loving, financially secure and have so much to offer a child. Yet, they are having trouble conceiving. Instead, these poor, uneducated women who don't know the first thing about raising a child are the ones that conceive without any problem."

"Sadly, that's life, as you have always pointed out to us, Father. Things aren't always fair."

"I realize that I am merely an instrument of the Lord. It is God's will as to what or how things happen. I will do whatever I can to help families like the Rocklands. I sincerely hope that one day, before too long, they will be blessed with a child that I know will be raised in His name."

"Mrs. Rockland certainly seemed like a lovely woman who would make an excellent mother."

"I couldn't agree more. Throughout scripture," said Father, "God is pretty clear about the responsibility He places in the hands of parents." None is clearer than that in Deuteronomy 6:6-7."

"I don't think I'm familiar with that scripture, Father. Can you explain to us what it says?" questioned Nellie.

"Of course. Deuteronomy 6 is concerned with each person's obedience to God. But it is also concerned with families. It repeatedly speaks of our children along with obedience. God cares very much about how we raise our children. It is important that we make His word a part of everything we do. Things as routine as eating a family meal, making sure our children get good schooling, playing a game of sports or attending worship should involve God's words. And nothing is more important than the role of the parents."

"Very interesting, Father. I don't think I've ever heard it explained in that way."

"One of my absolute favorite theologians is Robert Lewis Dabney. It was actually his quote that I came to greatly admire. It sets an excellent example on the importance of parenting. He states, 'The education of children for God is the most important business on earth.'"

"Those are pretty powerful words," Ethel exclaimed.

"Yes. And it is so clear to me how important it is to have a secure, loving family unit. It is through the teachings of family that His commandments shall flourish and be kept alive."

"That makes sense, Father. But, why did you tell the Rocklands that God works in mysterious ways? What did you mean by that?"

Father stared pensively into the distance. "I can't really say. I guess some things just can't be explained. But what I do know is that we need to trust in the wisdom of our Almighty God."

With those words, Father O'Leary turned towards the two women. "I sincerely believe Dr. and Mrs. Rockland will be able to become a family in whatever way God ordains. Only He knows what the future holds."

Chapter Thirty-Seven
Out of Jail

"Hmm," muttered Nellie.

"Hmm, what?" replied Ethel.

"I do believe we may be on to something, Ethel. But the proof is in the pudding, so they say."

"Haven't heard that old expression since my Leonard passed away. It seems to me that Father O'Leary knows far more than he's saying."

"I'm wondering the same thing myself. So, what do you say we pay a little unexpected visit to the next couple on the list? See if we can put our heads together and figure something out. Maybe there'll be some connection."

"I'm up for it, if you are. But," Ethel took a deep breath and continued. "Maybe we should wait until tomorrow morning. It's already close to dinner time."

"Okeydokey. Tomorrow morning it is. Actually, that will give me time to bake some more cookies."

The next day, as Ethel pulled into Nellie's driveway, the sight of the dark colored pickup truck in front of her house caused a frightened, uneasy feeling.

"Oh my God, Nellie. That's *his* black truck. I'd recognize it anywhere. I thought he was in jail."

"Me too. Well, he was in jail. But," her voice quivered, "do you think he got out?"

"Maybe it's just a truck that looks like his."

"Parked smack dab in front of your house, Nellie." Ethel grimaced. "Possible, but not probable."

"So, what should we do?"

"Let me think a minute."

"Think fast, Ethel. I'm really scared."

"I know. Me too." Ethel leaned over to make sure her car doors were securely locked. "I think we should call the police. No sense taking any chances with someone like him."

Ethel had the Kenmore police department on speed dial. A woman's voice answered. "Kenmore-Town of Tonawanda Police Department. What is the nature of your call?"

"This is Ethel Dinwiddie. I need to speak to Officer Malcolm as quickly as possible. This is an emergency."

Ethel and Nellie kept their eyes peeled on the black truck which did not leave its spot.

"Officer Malcolm here."

Ethel did not give him time to say another word. "Officer Malcolm. This is Ethel Dinwiddie. Nellie and I need your help."

"Okay, Ethel. Try to stay calm and tell me the problem."

Without hesitation, Ethel described their dilemma and their location.

"I'm on my way."

No sooner had she turned off her phone than they heard a loud knock at the driver's side window. Both women gasped, as their heads turned towards the noise. "Oh my God," shrieked Nellie. "It's him."

Thankful that she had locked her doors and that Officer Malcolm was on his way, Ethel sat speechless. It seemed to her that her body was frozen.

"Well, well, I must say that you two don't look too delighted to see me. What a pity! And to think that you ladies were my first stop after getting out of that hell hole of a jail." T-Bone gave an evil smirk that gave them both the chills. "I'm back," he smugly stated. He stood silently staring at the two women who were clearly frightened by his imposing figure. He glared at them before speaking again. "Pays to have friends in high places, wouldn't you agree?" The look on his face was sinister. "I was able to post bail far more quickly than I imagine you old biddies thought was possible." He stared at them while making a fist, as he spoke his next sentence. "I started a job and I intend to finish it. So, you two better rethink things or you might just find yourselves in a most unpleasant situation." His glare was filled with hatred.

Ethel mustered up all her courage, perhaps because the sound of police sirens was approaching. "Is that a threat?"

James Jesus Manzaro lowered his gaze. "Take it any way you choose, bitch. You tangled with the wrong man." His words were spoken with venom.

Ethel and Nellie did not doubt for a single moment that if he had the opportunity, he could do them serious bodily harm or worse. Never were they so happy to see Officer Malcolm approaching.

"Are you alright, ladies?" His tone was sincere and compassionate.

"We are now that you're here, Officer. This man ...." Ethel stumbled on her words and sat without speaking as she collected her thoughts. "This man threatened us, Officer."

"Hey, since when is it against the law to visit two old friends." He took a toothpick out of his pocket and began to pick at his teeth.

Ethel and Nellie found him totally disgusting. What a poor excuse for a human, thought Nellie.

Officer Malcolm addressed his words to the man who stood beside the vehicle. "I think it's pretty clear that you came here to try to intimidate these two women. All I can say is that I have this incident on file now and should anything happen to either of them, you will be my number one suspect. Do you understand what I'm telling you?" Officer Malcolm stared intently into Jimmy's brown eyes. "You have no business with them, from what I understand. And you should stay away from them all together. Am I making myself perfectly clear?"

James Jesus Manzaro was clearly not intimidated by Officer Malcolm's words. He continued to pick at his teeth, as he sarcastically responded to what Officer Malcolm had said. "I do understand, Officer." His words dripped with animosity. "But, as I see it, there ain't nothing illegal about visiting someone you know." He smiled that same evil grin at the two women. "Tell the officer the truth, ladies. Tell him how much you enjoy our little chats. Tell him how we have so much in common. I don't think he realizes how much you two need me."

Ethel and Nellie could barely contain their anger and disdain towards the man that stood so arrogantly beside the car.

"What is wrong with you? You need help. You are clearly disturbed and we would be happy to never have to see you again."

James Jesus Manzaro acted as if he'd never heard the words that Ethel had so clearly stated. He smiled broadly. "Why, what would Priscilla think of your acting so disrespectfully towards me? I, for one, think she'd be mighty disappointed in you both. She......"

Nellie cut him off mid-sentence. "How dare you speak about Priscilla." Hearing her name come from his lips sickened her. "Officer, please, make him leave."

"Listen ladies. Mr. Manzaro is clearly having trouble comprehending the seriousness of his actions and words. Perhaps it would be wise for you to consider taking out an order of protection against him." He turned

186

towards Jimmy and with great authority in his voice asked, "Am I making myself perfectly clear, Mr. Manzaro? It's time to leave."

Jimmy flippantly replied. "Whatever the crap your dimwitted order of protection is can't keep me away from them. And, just for the record, I ain't done nothing unlawful to these two busy bodies."

Officer Malcolm's voice was stern as he grabbed Jimmy's arm. "You can leave peacefully or I can call for back up. Your choice."

"Yeah, yeah, yeah. I get it. You police officers love to show off your authority. Love to boss people around. Okay. I'll leave. But no order of whatever the hell you told them about is going to scare me." He smiled cunningly, as Ethel and Nellie counted their lucky stars that Officer Malcolm had arrived so speedily. "I'll be seeing you, ladies. The pleasure's been all mine. Do have a nice, safe night."

James Jesus Manzaro smiled that same unsettling grin that had greeted them earlier, turned and walked back to his pickup truck.

Chapter Thirty-Eight
Sandboxes and Lemonade

As they approached the stately, pillared white colonial home, Ethel and Nellie were overwhelmed by the understated beauty of the entire neighborhood. One house was more regal then the next. There was an undeniable sense of refinement that graced the posh homes.

"Old money, Ethel. These are the kind of homes that are passed down from one generation to the next."

Ethel smiled. "I don't know about that, Nellie, but I do know I could never afford the likes of what I'm seeing here."

"I don't think most people could. Maybe Mr. and Mrs. Stuart Joslin won the lottery."

"I doubt that. I imagine at least one of them has a very lucrative job."

"They'd need to be very wealthy to live in an area like this," she exclaimed as she gazed at the surrounding homes. "Well, Ethel, I think we've arrived at 7997 Hummingbird Lane. I wonder if they'll be home. And I hope they don't suspect our using the guise of selling baked goods for charity as a means of finding out anything we can about them."

"All I can think of, Nellie, is that our plan worked so well on Mrs. Rockland that we have to hope it will go just as smoothly today. I mean it was successful largely because of you and your wonderful baking skills. Our little ruse worked like a charm."

"Lord knows that I've baked these lemon-drop and molasses cookies so many times that I think I could make them without my recipe card."

Ethel pulled into the circular driveway. The gardens, filled with a mixture of colors that looked as if they could be on the cover of a magazine, boasted poppies, hydrangeas, petunias and day lilies. Even the sweet aroma, as they walked up towards the front door, left them feeling euphoric. The stately pines that lined the side of the home formed a canopy. A glimpse into the yard next door showed densely twisted ivy creeping up the brown stones of the old Tudor home. "This is the kind of home," Ethel said to Nellie, "that I've read about in books."

"Baked goods and story ready to go," said Nellie as they approached the front door. The heavy brass knocker positioned on the ornate wooden door was all that separated them from the family who occupied this exquisite property.

"Are you sure you're ready?" Ethel asked Nellie.

"As ready as I'll ever be."

"Okay then. I'll knock."

A woman wearing a pale blue apron answered the door. A warm smile crossed her face. "Good afternoon, ladies. How may I help you?"

"We would like to see the lady of the house, if we may. We are selling baked goods for a charity we are working with."

"Oh. That would be Mrs. Joslin. She's in the backyard with the children. Come. I'll show you back. I'm Nadia."

"Nice to meet you, Nadia." This was most definitely the type of home where you would expect to see an abundance of help, thought Nellie.

As the woman led them through the house, Nellie and Ethel couldn't help but be in awe of the lovely decor and stunning Steinway Grand piano that graced the corner of the room. This living-room looked as if it could occupy a page in *Architectural Digest.* The delicate floral print chintz fabric that graced the sofa and chairs complimented the gorgeous oriental rug. Draperies flowed with a gentleness that gave the room a sophisticated feel. The kitchen beyond it boasted the biggest stainless-steel refrigerator they'd ever seen. Could I ever turn out some baked goods with that, thought Nellie, as she passed the elaborate Viking gas oven.

Ethel's mind imagined this home must have lots of children because why else would anyone need so many oversized appliances. As Nadia opened the French doors that led to the backyard, Ethel thought she was most certainly right. Three small children were playing in the sand box, beside the swimming pool, as Mrs. Joslin attentively watched them. She smiled at the two women as they approached her.

Mrs. Joslin was probably in her late twenties or early thirties with beautiful thick red hair that shimmered under the afternoon sun. Her green eyes sparkled, as she watched the children at play.

"I'm sorry to bother you, Mrs. Joslin, but I know how important charity work is to you. These two women are selling baked goods to raise money for charity."

"No bother, Nadia. I'm glad you brought them back. Thank you."

"You're welcome. May I get everyone some lemonade?"

Before anyone could reply, the biggest of the three children was out of the sandbox eagerly looking at the molasses cookies. "Can I have one?"

"Nellie smiled. "I'm glad they look so good to you, but you'll have to ask your mommy if you can have one."

Mrs. Joslin popped the child on her lap and nuzzled up warmly to her. "This is Lilly. She's five years old and has quite a sweet tooth."

"She's adorable and I like that she knows what she likes."

"That she does."

"So, is it alright with you if I give her one? I never like to assume it's okay without checking with the parent first. You know with allergies, it's better to be safe."

"I agree and I appreciate your being so cautious. I think it would be fine, but I'm not her mother. I'm her aunt. These three beautiful little ones are my sister's children. But I love them as if they were my own. They spend two and sometimes three days of the week with us. They are such a joy."

"They are adorable. How old are they?"

"As I said, Lilly is the oldest and she's five, Isabella is three and little Jack is two. My happiest days are the days my sister works and I watch the children. They are such a blessing."

Jack tugged on his aunt's pale green dress. "Cookie?"

"Mrs. Joslin's face lit up with joy. "Yes, Jack. You may have a cookie. And Lilly and Isabella may have one, too. Nadia, would you please bring us some lemonade to go with the cookies. That sounds good."

As Nadia disappeared into the kitchen, Mrs. Joslin asked them what charity they were raising money for. When they explained that it was for Haven House, she said that was a charity she felt everyone should give to. She told them that she and her husband had worked on several charitable projects there, as well, to raise money to help the women and children seeking to make a new, safe life for themselves. "Nothing is more important than the safety of children." And with those words, she told

Ethel and Nellie that she'd like to buy all the cookies they had. She then proceeded to write a check that far exceeded what they were asking.

Nadia appeared with a tray of freshly squeezed lemonade and Mrs. Joslin, who had told Ethel and Nellie to call her Meredith, invited everyone to sit at the large picnic table to enjoy the mid-afternoon treats. One thing was for certain. There were plenty of lemon drop and molasses cookies for everyone to enjoy. The children were all happy trying the different flavors and before long were back playing in the sandbox.

"This has been such an unexpected surprise and I'm so thankful you stopped by. I know my husband would have loved to have met you both. He is an advocate for the women at Haven House."

Ethel gasped with surprise. "I can't believe we didn't make the connection. Of course, you must be married to Judge Joslin. I've read about his helping women seeking safety there."

"Yes, that's my husband. Stuart is a wonderful man. He has a heart that is filled with so much love. I am so blessed to be married to such a compassionate, kind person."

"It seems like you both are lucky. He certainly has a lovely wife."

Ethel thought she saw Meredith's cheeks turn a soft shade of pink. "We have a wonderful marriage and we love each other more than anything. The only thing that could make things any better would be to be blessed with a baby to love." Meredith gazed down towards the children. "A gift from God. That's what children are. We just have to believe that one day we'll be blessed, too."

"I hope you are," said Nellie. "It's clear to see you love children."

"Thank you, Nellie. That means a lot."

Having had a most productive and enjoyable visit, there was one thing that they both immediately agreed upon. There was no doubt, in either of their minds, that Meredith Joslin would one day make an excellent parent. And knowing that the common thread that existed between her and Mrs. Rockland was their strong desire to become a family, it seemed quite obvious that this was something that needed further looking into.

Chapter Thirty-Nine
Skylar Shares Her Secret

Ethel and Nellie had barely pulled out of the Joslin's driveway when Ethel's phone rang.

It was Annie and she sounded upset and frantic. "Can you come over? Please come quickly. It's Skylar."

"Skylar?" Ethel questioned. "What's the problem?"

"Just come over, please. I'll explain everything when you get here."

Ethel did a quick U-turn and replied immediately. "We'll be there shortly."

Ethel pulled up to the curb in front of Annie's house in record time. As the two women exited the car, a clearly frazzled Annie bolted from the front door to meet them.

"I'm so glad you're here. I didn't know what to do." Annie's voice was trembling.

Nellie put her arm around the young girl and attempted to calm her. "I'm sure whatever it is, Annie, is something we can all figure out together. Ethel and I are here to help."

Annie gave a loud sigh of relief. But she was clearly flustered. "Skylar is beside herself." She paused. "I'm worried she might try to hurt herself or worse. Everything seems so overwhelming."

"Let's go inside," Ethel said as she held open the front door. "We'll talk this over."

"But, but...." Before Annie could finish her thought a very young, strikingly beautiful young girl appeared from the kitchen. It was obvious she had been crying. "This is Skylar," Annie declared as she motioned to the girl to take a seat. "These are my two dear friends, Ethel Dinwiddie and Nellie Pearce. They are the detectives I told you about and I promise you that your secrets are safe with them."

Skylar walked slowly into the living-room, her head down as she rubbed her tear-stained face. Annie helped her to a comfortable chair where she tried to regain her composure. But, as hard as she tried, her sobs overcame her. "What am I going to do? Now I'll never finish high school. I'll never be able to help my sisters or follow my dreams. All my......" She was crying so hard she could not speak.

"May I tell Ethel and Nellie what you shared with me when you first got here."

Skylar nodded. Her grief was overwhelming her, as her sobs intensified.

"I can see this is very difficult for you, Skylar, and you are obviously in a very emotional state. I just want you to know how grateful we are that you're brave enough to share whatever this is about with us."

Skylar's cries grew louder. "My life is ruined." She placed her hands over her face and trembled. "Tell them, Annie."

Annie took a deep breath. "Brace yourselves. This isn't easy to hear."

Ethel and Nellie sat quietly, as they awaited whatever Annie was about to tell them.

"About three months ago Skylar got home from school and, as she was fumbling in her purse for her house key, she remembers feeling a firm hand over her mouth and nose. She said that she smelled something that she described to me as a kind of sweet scent. She told me her

195

assailant did not say a word. She tried to scream, but the next thing she knew she felt dizzy and disoriented. Skylar told me that she felt as if she couldn't breathe. She doesn't remember much after that except that she woke up inside her house, lying naked on her bed, hours later. No one was there when she eventually came to, but there was blood on her sheets. She knew right then that she had been raped. And since then, she's missed two periods."

Without hesitation, Ethel stood and went over to give Skylar a hug. "I'm so sorry, Skylar. You know this wasn't your fault."

Skylar could not be comforted. She was beside herself. Eyes red and swollen, she could barely speak. "I, I, I ......I missed my period again. I'm pregnant and that's just what those pigs wanted. They want my baby."

"And what do you want, Skylar?"

Skylar attempted to compose herself, but it wasn't easy. She bit on her lower lip. "That's just it. I'm so confused. I don't know what to do."

"I don't think it's anything you need to decide today. But, have you thought about reporting this to the police?"

"No police." Skylar's voice was firm. She looked at Annie. "You promised me they'd understand. You said they'd be able to help. I don't want the police involved."

Ethel could see that Skylar seemed close to having a breakdown. She spoke calmly and quietly. "Of course, we will respect your wishes, Skylar. I'm so glad you shared what happened with us and I promise we will do everything we can to help you. In the meantime, try to rest and take care of yourself. We can talk again in a few days and, in the meantime, Nellie and I will poke around and see what we can find out."

"Thank you." Skylar placed her hands over her stomach. "It's funny. I hate whoever did this to me and I want him punished." Her eyes teared up again as she continued. "But strange as this must sound, I feel an obligation to the baby inside me. He or she is innocent and had nothing to do with the terrible thing that happened to me." She gave a long, pensive sigh. "I've got a lot of thinking to do."

Chapter Forty
A Possible Scandal

The phone call to Ethel came from out of the blue. All Bill said was, "Can you meet me at Shirley's Diner in about an hour?"

The call had most definitely piqued her interest. "Of course. We'll be there." She immediately phoned Nellie.

Bill sat in the rear booth farthest from the front door drinking a cup of coffee. He stood and smiled, as the two ladies walked in. "So glad you could come on such short notice. I think I may have come across something that may be of interest to you."

"Sounds intriguing, Bill." Ethel paused a moment. "We can use all the help we can get. We truly appreciate your assistance."

"Glad to do whatever I can." A pensive look overcame his face. "I'm kind of surprised myself with what I discovered. I've been doing a bit of poking around since I met with you last. One thing led to another."

"And?" Ethel's curiosity was getting the better of her.

"And I started digging around and doing more research on T-Bone. Interesting what I came across." He paused a brief moment. "Turns out the priest at your church, I believe his name is Father O'Leary, and T-Bone were involved in a very sketchy matter in Dunkirk, New York about seven or eight years ago. Dunkirk is barely over an hour from here. It's amazing what you can find out on the internet."

Ethel's face lost its color. "I know Dunkirk is pretty close. Nellie and I once visited a psychic community near there called Lily Dale. But what I don't understand is how in the world Father O'Leary could have ever been involved with anyone like T-Bone."

"How long has Father O'Leary been the priest at St. Angela's church?"

Ethel and Nellie thought. "That's a good question, Bill," replied Ethel. "Let me think." Ethel was silent for a few moments. "My Leonard died four years ago and Father O'Leary presided over his funeral. I'll never forget how compassionate and caring he was. But, now that I think about it, Leonard's two stents were put in about three years before that. It was actually Father Abbott who visited him in the hospital and provided us with spiritual guidance and encouragement. But Father O'Leary replaced Father Abbott shortly after Leonard's stents were put in."

"Interesting," said Bill. "About seven years ago, there was a huge scandal near Dunkirk at St. Theresa's Parish. And do you know who the presiding priest was?"

"Father O'Leary?" Nellie cautiously asked.

"Precisely. And from what all the newspaper articles I could muster up said, the church tried to keep the incidents as hush-hush as possible."

"Incidents? What are you talking about, Bill?"

"In a nutshell, ladies, your priest was suspected of somehow being connected to a baby selling ring." Bill swallowed hard. "But, because of his position and because the authorities couldn't directly connect him to the ring, he was quietly and discreetly transferred to a new parish."

"That new parish being our church, St. Angela's." Ethel's voice was grim.

"Exactly."

"But you said he was connected to T-Bone. How do you know that?"

"Well, I don't know for certain. I'm surmising from everything I read that they knew each other. James Jesus Manzaro was arrested on numerous counts. As I told you at our last meeting, he has quite an extensive rap sheet. He spent time in prison, but not as long as I thought he might have for his involvement in the ring. And as you two well know, he's out of jail and living here now. Why did he leave Dunkirk?" Bill took a long, slow sip of his coffee. "Another thing that I find rather perplexing and curious is the repeated references to a Doctor Kevin Miller. He is mentioned numerous times, as having a connection to the baby-selling operation. But apparently, no charges were ever filed against him. He appears to be squeaky clean. But I have my own theory about that."

"Very interesting, Bill. Thank you for everything you've done. You've given us a lot to think about and to look into."

"I should mention that I did a lot of digging around before contacting you. There were lots of implications in the news about seven years ago suggesting possible baby selling and illegal adoptions in the Dunkirk vicinity. One grandmother came forward on behalf of Dr. Miller." Bill pulled a news article out of his pocket. This story quoted the grandmother as saying that, "Dr. Miller was a miracle worker and that meeting him was the best thing that ever happened to her family." She went on to say that her daughter and her daughter's husband were unable to have children. But, because of Dr. Miller, she was now a grandmother and her daughter and son-in-law were forever grateful for his help in making them a family. She said that Anna Marie was the greatest blessing they could have ever hoped for."

"Do you happen to know where Dr. Miller is today?"

"Actually, I looked him up. He still resides in Dunkirk."

"Hmm. Very interesting. I'm pretty sure that Nellie and I will want to take a drive to Dunkirk this week to check out this Dr. Miller and to meet St. Theresa's newest priest. And while we're at it, maybe a stop in Lily Dale might just be in our future!"

Chapter Forty-One
A Visit to Father Darnell

It was a perfect early spring day. The welcome hints of greenery from the buds on the trees, along the side of the New York State Thruway, provided a picturesque drive. Because it was just a little over an hour to get to their destination, they were hopeful that they might have a little time left to visit Lily Dale following their visit to the priest and the doctor. Of course, because this trip was so spur of the moment, they had no guarantee that either person would be able to see them.

"Gee-whiz, Nellie. Can you believe what Bill told us? I must tell you that I'm feeling rather overwhelmed with everything he shared. It seems unbelievable, to say the least."

"I know. I can't get what he said out of my head either. But I think you're right about our checking it out. There are so many unknowns."

"Agreed. I was thinking we should start at the church. Don't really know why, but maybe the priest will be easier to see on such short notice." Ethel paused a moment and thought. "I hope we're not disappointed with what we find. I mean this could just be a wild goose chase, Nellie."

"True. But it was you who taught me that we need to go wherever the clues take us. And, plain as the nose is on my face, the clues are taking us to St. Theresa's and to Dr. Kevin Miller." Nellie's voice suddenly had a tone of melancholy to it. "I want to do right by Priscilla. No matter what we have to do or where we have to go, it will be worth it if we can figure out this mystery." Nellie looked up towards the heavens and in a whisper said, "We're here for you Priscilla. Ethel and I will never give up on you."

"I see it, Nellie! We're almost there." The church was quite a bit smaller than the one they attended and had a medieval look to it. A stained-glass window was clearly seen, as they slowly drove up the long, winding driveway. Two young men were busily raking leaves and twigs which had been covered by the winter snow. Daffodils and tulips were starting to sprout up through the rich, dark soil.

"So," declared Ethel. "This is where Father O'Leary worked, before he came to lead our congregation. I just can't wrap my head around what Bill told us yesterday. It seems inconceivable that Father O'Leary could have ever been involved in something so troubling and illegal."

"I know. It's just so *unchristian* that I can't believe it either."

From where the man appeared, they did not know. But, one of the men who had been tending to the lawn greeted them at their car. "Good day, ladies. May I help you?"

"Oh, my. You startled us." Nellie grabbed her purse from the car seat and continued to speak, as she stepped out of the civic. "My friend and I would like to speak to the priest, if we might." She cleared her throat. "It's personal."

The groundskeeper gestured towards the right. "Father Darnell is in the rectory. Do you have an appointment?"

"I'm afraid we don't. I know we should have called first, but we were just so anxious to speak with him that we decided to just stop by."

"Must be your lucky day. Father Darnell is here and he's in one heck of a good mood. Why we've been hearing him sing all morning. As you can see, the rectory windows are open and his voice definitely carries. I hope you like opera." He smiled warmly at the two women who appreciated his kindness. "Shall I tell him you're here?"

"Yes. We'd appreciate that."

Ethel and Nellie walked beside the grounds keeper towards the house that was just past the church. A simple building, vines of ivy crept along its walls giving it a quaint, old English look.

"It is beautiful here." Nellie's words did not go unheard.

As the door slowly opened, a robust gentleman, about forty-five, with a brush cut and dark brown eyes that seemed to sparkle, extended his hand. "Good day, ladies. I am Father Darnell, the priest here at St. Theresa's Parish. What can I do for you on this beautiful day?" His smile was genuine.

"Well, Father," replied Ethel. "Our visit concerns quite a personal, sensitive matter. May we speak privately?"

"I must say that sounds pretty cryptic. But, yes. Of course, we can." He opened the door to the rectory and gestured for the two women to enter. "I think you'll be comfortable in the study. We can talk freely there."

Father Darnell led the way to a small room at the rear of the house. Adjacent to a well-worn brown couch, adorned with plaid pillows, were shelves lined with books that filled the entire wall. "Please, ladies, be seated. May I get you some coffee or a cup of tea?"

"Thank you, Father, but I think we'd like to get right to the reason we're here."

"As you wish."

"Where to begin?" Ethel pondered her thoughts for a moment and then summarized, as best as she could, the reason she and Nellie were there. Father Darnell listened attentively.

"That's some story. It's hard to take in everything you've said. But I can tell you that there was quite a scandal here in Dunkirk before I began my job here at St. Theresa's. Rumors were abundant, as you can well imagine. But rumors are just that. I don't really know the extent of what was true and what was here-say. Hard to know."

"Well, Father, the main thing Nellie and I are hoping is that you can shed some light on what role Father O'Leary and Dr. Miller played in what allegedly occurred. Any insight you might be able to offer us would be greatly appreciated."

Father Darnell shrugged his shoulders. "I have to admit I don't know much. Everything happened really quickly. One day I was the Priest at St. Aloysius church in Derby, New York, and within days I was transferred here." Father looked around with a jovial expression on his plump face. "Can't say I'm not delighted with the move. Dunkirk is a quaint little city. I like being so close to Lake Erie. And the State Park here is a wonderful place to walk and clear my mind." Father Darnell gave a little chuckle. "I might share with you that, on more than one occasion, I have gone there for inspiration on writing my sermons."

"Sounds lovely, Father. But, please think hard. Anything you can tell us, even the smallest detail, may prove helpful."

"The only one I spoke with at length was Mrs. Boutet. She has been a parishioner here for years and is very active in the church. A charming woman, I might add."

"And?"

"Shortly after Father O'Leary left and I began my work here, she came to meet me. She made it quite clear that she was very upset that Father O'Leary had been transferred. She shared with me that her daughter, Mary, and her husband had been trying to have a baby for years. She told me that Father O'Leary had been instrumental in helping her daughter adopt a beautiful little girl. But she didn't elaborate on what role he played. Everyone in the family was thrilled and the child was the greatest blessing they could have ever hoped for. She said that Father would be sadly missed. She also mentioned a doctor that had been involved in the adoption. But his name escapes me."

"Was it a Dr. Miller?"

"That name sounds familiar, but I can't say for certain."

"I understand. But, do you know if Mrs. Boutet's daughter was the only one that Father and the doctor helped to adopt?"

"Actually, I believe there were others. But I don't honestly know for sure." Father paused a moment. "Perhaps you could speak to Mrs. Boutet. She is one of my most ardent parishioners and I'm quite sure she'd be happy to shed some light in any way she could. Perhaps she would know more than I do." Father rose from his chair. "Let me give her a call."

Chapter Forty-Two
Tea for Three

Mrs. Boutet's house was only a few miles from the church. Father Darnell had been somewhat helpful and was most assuredly a pleasant, God loving man. But Ethel and Nellie were hoping Mrs. Boutet would be able to provide more specific details as to what had happened in their sleepy little city that had caused two priests to be uprooted and relocated with barely any explanation.

The modest two-story blue-shingled home looked like every other one on the street. Aside from the varied colors, each house was the same as the next. A warm, jovial woman greeted them, as they stepped onto the tiny front porch. She extended her hand. "Good morning, ladies. I'm Arlene Boutet. Father Darnell told me to expect you." She gestured for them to enter. "Please excuse the mess. Sometimes I barely get a chance to clean up before my granddaughter visits again. So, I go with the flow, as the young people say. Actually, having Anna Marie here when my daughter works, is my greatest joy. To heck with the mess."

"I like your attitude," said Nellie. "This might sound silly to you. I don't have any grandchildren. But my cat, Matilda, means the world to me. And, if she leaves her yarn balls and catnip around the house, I just look the other way. Life is too short to get riled up over things that don't really matter."

"Couldn't agree more," declared Arlene. "Please, sit down. I'll make us some tea."

Arlene Boutet disappeared into the kitchen. Ethel and Nellie waited patiently for a few minutes before she appeared with a pot of tea and some store-bought shortbread cookies. "I apologize for the cookies. No time to bake on such short notice. Forgive me."

"Don't be silly. They look delicious."

Arlene poured each of the ladies a hot cup of lemon spiced tea and offered them a cookie. "So, ladies, how may I be of help?"

Ethel reiterated everything she had shared with Father Darnell. She added that she was hoping that Mrs. Boutet would be able to provide some more specific details about Father O'Leary's sudden departure from the church and information about Dr. Miller.

"Well," replied Arlene Boutet, "I'll certainly do my best to answer anything I can."

"Could you tell us how your daughter, Mary, became involved with Dr. Miller."

"Oh, that's an easy one to answer." Arlene smiled. "Mary and Bob had been married nearly eight years. They both wanted nothing more, from the day they said *I do*, then to become parents." A look of melancholy encompassed her face. "But, the longer they tried, the more it seemed that it was not in God's plan. Mary and Bob consulted several doctors that specialized in trying to help you to conceive. I think they're called infertility specialists. Oh, my! They had their share of seeing them. So many tests and procedures. They tried to remain hopeful. But, try as they might, nothing seemed to work. I never saw my daughter so upset and dejected. It broke my heart."

"I can imagine that must have been very painful for you to see your daughter so unhappy."

Arlene stared into the distance and said nothing for several long minutes. "Then, one Sunday at Mass, Father O'Leary asked to speak with me privately. I had shared with him, several months earlier, how Mary's inability to conceive was causing much unhappiness among the whole family. I remember his words, as if it were that very day. He said, 'God works in mysterious ways.' Then, he wrote down the name of a doctor and told us to have Mary set up an appointment with him. He said that he had heard, through other congregants that he was not at liberty to mention, that Dr. Miller sometimes was able to place unwanted babies in good Christian homes. The following week, Mary had an appointment with Dr. Miller."

Arlene began to fidget with her hands. It is what she said next that Ethel and Nellie found so disturbing.

"My husband and I are not fancy people. As you can see, we live very modestly. So, when Mary told us that babies were available, but with doctor fees, lawyer fees and fees for the biological mother's medical care, the total cost would be $25,000, I was taken aback, to say the least. We don't have that kind of money."

Ethel and Nellie exchanged glances and immediately knew what the other was thinking.

"My husband, Ray, is an electrician. He works hard and makes a good living. And we've religiously put money away for our retirement for years. But, that's a lot of money. We had close to $18,000 saved, but didn't know how we'd ever accumulate the rest. Mary became more and more depressed. To be honest, I was very worried about her."

Arlene cast her eyes downward. "Ray and I had quite a difference of opinion about what I suggested next." She took a long, drawn out breath. "I wanted to go to my parents and ask them to help. But Ray felt that was wrong and a huge imposition. We don't usually argue much, but this was causing a real rift between us. Finally, he agreed. We approached my mom and dad and explained everything to them. We really didn't even need to ask. Without hesitation, my mom asked how much we needed. When I told her, she looked at my dad, he nodded, and mom said it would be their pleasure and that was that."

"You are very lucky. And Mary and her husband are definitely fortunate to have such caring parents and grandparents."

"As my mom said, it's only money. And if you can't use it for something that will bring great happiness, then what good is it to have?"

"Your mother sounds like a very smart, loving woman. And she must be thrilled to be a great grandmother."

"She and my dad are over the moon. Anna Marie brings them so much joy. That little bundle really brought the whole family even closer together than we already were. And now that she's in school, we are all thrilled to see her thriving so well. She's a very special little girl. But, then, I guess I'm just a bit prejudiced!"

"As you should be. I'm happy for all of you." Ethel took a sip of her tea. "I'm just wondering if your daughter or you met the biological mother or her family? And, if you don't mind my asking, how was Father O'Leary involved? Also, you mentioned a lawyer was consulted. Are you able to tell us his or her name?"

"I know it was only a few months after Mary saw Dr. Miller that he contacted her to say there was a baby being born who needed a mom and a dad. And once she was able to tell Dr. Miller that we could provide the money, she was sent to meet with a lawyer."

"Was the attorney here in Dunkirk?"

"Yes. His name is Paul Kliner. He has an office not far from here. He actually met us at the hospital the afternoon of the adoption. And it was he who handed the baby over to Mary."

"That's very helpful information, Arlene. Did Mary meet the biological mother?"

"No, not the mother. But she did meet the grandmother. Needless to say, it was a very emotional day for everyone."

"I can only imagine."

Mr. Kliner assured us that everything was legal. He told us that some of the money had been used to help the girl with her expenses while she was carrying the baby. Then, the doctor and he needed to be compensated. I don't know if there was anyone else who got paid. But what he told us seemed fair."

"Did anyone ever discuss with you where this baby came from?"

"No. But, maybe that was our fault. We didn't ask. We were only too happy that Mary and Bob were going to become a family."

"You've been a big help, Arlene. We now know for sure that it is Dr. Miller who locates the babies. And we know that it is Mr. Kliner who does the legal work for the adoption. We just aren't sure yet how it all fits together and exactly what part Father O'Leary plays in all of this. Thank you so much."

"I wish I could have been more helpful, but I've told you everything I know. All I can say about Father O'Leary is that he knew we were a good Christian family and he knew how badly Mary and Bob wanted to become parents." Arlene suddenly got an odd look on her face that caused Ethel to ask her if anything was wrong.

"It's probably nothing, but now that I think about it, I do remember something Mary said the day she went to meet with Dr. Miller."

"What was it, Arlene?"

"She said the room had several very young girls

waiting to be seen. Mary mentioned it to me because she said it seemed so unfair that they were probably in high school and pregnant without a husband. And here she was; happily married and ready to start a family and couldn't get pregnant." Arlene shrugged her shoulders. "I agree with my daughter. It just doesn't seem fair." Arlene exhaled. "I don't think I was too helpful. I wish I could have given you more information."

"To the contrary, Arlene. You've given us a lot to really explore and think about. What you just shared may prove more useful than you could imagine."

Chapter Forty-Three
Arrogant Dr. Miller

"Well, detective Nellie. What do you think?"

"I think I'm more confused than ever."

"Come on, Nellie. Focus. We got some great clues. Now, we need to follow the leads and connect the dots, so to speak."

"Okay, Ethel. I admit that it was great to be able to get the name of the lawyer and to confirm that Dr. Miller is somehow connected to the babies that are being given up for adoption. But I still can't wrap my head around what role, if any, Father O'Leary plays in all of this."

"We can be quite certain that the couples that are adopting the babies are all from good Christian homes with a strong sense of family. Father O' Leary has made it pretty clear that he finds that a major prerequisite."

"So?"

"So, what we still don't know is how these families are chosen and how the girls are found and selected to relinquish their newborns. That is still an unknown. But Father O'Leary certainly has access to knowing private things about the congregants who may choose to share with him their struggle to become a family. I'm sure it is very painful to want to conceive and not be able to. I'm pretty sure it would be completely normal for a woman, in that situation, to seek guidance from her priest."

"True."

"And what he does with that knowledge is what we need to figure out. But I think it might be prudent, as long as we're here in Dunkirk, to stop over at Dr. Miller's office."

"And do what, Ethel? Don't you think it's going to look a little ridiculous when two old geezers walk into a doctor's office that specializes in pregnancies and adoptions. I mean we'll stick out like two sore thumbs."

"You've got a point there, Nellie. But, maybe that's a good thing."

"And how can that be? What's good about it?"

"Let me think a minute." Ethel sat pensively staring into the distance. "I've got it! We'll say we're from the Ladies Christian league doing an article on how babies change lives for the better. If he goes along with it, at least we can sit down and scope things out with him. See what he says. What his thoughts are."

"Sounds a bit contrived to me, Ethel. But, hey, you're our lead detective. I guess it's worth a try."

The two women stopped at the drugstore and picked up a sturdy binder for their entries. "We look pretty official, don't we Nellie?"

"I suppose so. Hope springs eternal," declared Nellie.

"Well, no time like the present," added Ethel, as she opened the door to the doctor's office.

As they quickly surveyed the room, they noticed several young, very pregnant girls. They smiled broadly at them, as they approached the receptionist who had barely looked up when they entered.

"No, I'm not pregnant," Ethel joked. "Thank goodness. I don't know what I'd do with a baby at my age."

The woman behind the glass partition smiled. "And how may I help you?"

"We're wondering if Dr. Miller might have a few minutes to spare. We're writing an article for the Christian Women's League that I think could help many women. We want them to know they have choices."

The receptionist seemed to like that explanation and briefly excused herself. When she returned, Ethel and Nellie were delighted with her reply. "Dr. Miller has a few more patients to see this afternoon and then he would be happy to sit down for an interview, if you don't mind waiting."

"Thank you so much," said Ethel. "We're happy to wait until it's convenient for him."

Before too long a middle-aged man with a genuine smile appeared. His gray hair gave him a distinguished look. "Good day, ladies. I'm Dr. Miller." He extended his hand and then gestured for them to come back to his office.

Ethel surprised herself at how easily her lies flowed. She had always considered herself to be an honest, upstanding woman, but this meeting called for drastic measures. "We are so glad to meet you, doctor. The article we're doing for the ladies Christian League is going to be written to raise awareness for women as to their choices. We believe this is such a critical issue."

Dr. Miller smiled broadly. "I couldn't agree more ladies. That is actually a topic that is near and dear to my heart."

"Really? That's wonderful to hear." Nellie positioned the notebook before her and thought to herself how official she looked. "May I take notes, doctor, while my partner asks you some pertinent questions?"

"Of course. Whatever you need to do."

"Well then. Where to begin?" Ethel composed herself before asking the first question. "Is there any common thread that links together the women who come into be seen by you?"

Dr. Miller replied without hesitation. "I'd have to say that no two women or their needs are alike. As you can well imagine, some have been trying to become pregnant for years and are delighted to find themselves in the family way. Others are newly married and usually find themselves to be quite excited with the news. And then, sadly, there are a large number of unwed, under aged women who, for a variety of reasons, find themselves pregnant and do not want to have the baby."

"Are you saying they want to abort their pregnancy?"

"Yes. Sadly, in some cases, that is the only option that makes sense to these young girls. They don't realize they have options."

"Options? Like what?"

"Well, I, for one, am opposed to ending a life. Especially that of an unborn fetus. It is morally wrong, in my opinion. So, I try my best to explain to these young women that they are not trapped. That they do have other viable options. I feel for them. I really do."

Oh, I bet you do. You're nothing but a greedy, self-serving man who's making oodles of money from these young girls. You are using your position to exploit their misfortune. Ethel kept her thoughts to herself, as Nellie meticulously jotted down notes as Dr. Miller spoke.

"I'm sure you do," Ethel lied. "Tell me, is there anything you advise these young women to do that might improve their situation? Are you able to offer them any shred of hope?"

This is where Dr. Miller really began to boast. "These girls would be lost without me. Sometimes, I am their only hope. I can do what no one else can. The women who walk through my door are lucky indeed. They have a big problem and I have a solution. It's as simple as that."

"Really? Well, that sounds wonderful." What an arrogant, ego-maniac, thought Ethel. "So, in a way you are their salvation."

"Oh, not in a way, my dear. I clearly am their salvation."

Nellie felt as if she wanted to put her finger down her throat. What a narcissist, she thought.

"My practice is the biggest in the area and just continues to grow and grow."

Ethel couldn't resist her next remark which she said in a sickeningly sweet tone. "How lucky are we that you were able to squeeze us in."

His reply should not have surprised the two women. "When Claire, my receptionist, told me that you were writing an article for the Christian Women's League, I was only too happy to meet with you. I know how many people read that publication and, to be quite honest, it may bring more women to my office. I guess my sitting down with you and giving you my time and expertise, could be considered a win-win." He paused a moment. "You get the article you want and I, hopefully, get more patients."

What a repulsive ego-maniac, thought Ethel. But, knowing she had a job to accomplish, she just smiled. "You mentioned earlier that you are able to help these young women by providing other options to them. What options are those and do any of the women still choose to end their pregnancy?"

"Good question. Glad you asked. Unfortunately, there are always some women who insist on ending their pregnancy. Their mind is made up from the beginning and there is virtually nothing I can say or do to change their minds." Under his breath, Ethel swears she heard him mutter, "stupid, ignorant lowlifes."

"What was that?" questioned Ethel.

"Nothing."

"But fortunately, the vast majority are open to finding out about other choices. No need to kill your baby, I always tell these young girls."

"What happens to the babies, once they are born?" Ethel wanted to hear him say the words. Without missing a beat, he complied. "Do you have any idea how many well-educated, good Christian couples are unable to conceive?"

Ethel shook her head. "No, I don't doctor."

"Well, I do. And the number is staggering. So, I do what I consider, in my eyes, to be the Godly, righteous thing. I encourage these poor, wayward girls to carry their babies to term and to surrender them to homes where they will be well provided for both materialistically and spiritually."

"And they readily agree?" questioned Nellie, looking up momentarily from her notepad.

Dr. Miller did not reply immediately. He pondered the question for a while. "Not always. To be perfectly honest, some of these girls require more coddling than others. I need to sweeten the pot, so to speak."

"Sweeten the pot? I don't understand."

"Look. These girls are not like you and me. They often come from very poor families and haven't even finished high school. They wouldn't know the first thing about raising a child, let alone bringing up a child properly."

Ethel was fuming inside, but did not want the interview to end on a sour note. "I see what you're saying, doctor. But, what did you mean about sweetening the pot?"

"Just that I understand what a difficult decision this is for a young girl and how her life will definitely be affected for the months she is carrying the baby. So, I may offer her some compensation for her troubles. Doesn't that seem like the Christian thing to do?"

It was all Ethel could do not to confront him for what she already knew. But she realized that would be against her best interests. Instead, she swallowed hard. "You've been very helpful, Dr. Miller. I think this article will definitely raise awareness about the choices women have today."

"Glad to help. Please be sure to include my name and phone number, in case a woman wishes to contact me."

"You can be sure we will, doctor," Ethel responded with sarcasm in her voice.

"Oh, do you need my photo for the article? Might add a nice touch," Dr. Miller added as he tightened his necktie and buttoned his white coat.

"I think we're good, doctor. But we'll be in touch if we think we need one."

Chapter Forty-Four
Psychics and Butterflies

"Can you believe how pompous he was?" Ethel's voice was filled with annoyance.

"Pompous and entitled. And did you hear how condescendingly he spoke of people less fortunate than he? Their only sin was being born into a poor family that struggles financially."

"I know. He made it pretty clear that he believed a better choice for a parent is someone Christian, educated and well to do." Ethel shook her head. "But those words may just be the clue we needed. Think about it, Nellie. Those words rather mimic those of Father O'Leary, wouldn't you agree?"

"I guess so. Are you implying what I think you're implying?" Nellie shrugged her shoulders. "Do you think they are in cahoots?"

"I think there is a good possibility. But there are a lot of loose ends we need to piece together before we can draw any definite conclusions."

"Agreed. But I think we've accomplished a lot today. What do you say we allow ourselves a little bit of fun? Lily Dale is so close. Should we stop there?"

"Absolutely. I think it's just the diversion we need."

Ethel set *Reginald GPS* and they were off. Barely fifteen minutes later they turned onto Dale Drive in the Village of Cassadaga. The Lily Dale entrance gate was less than a mile down the winding, wooded road. A feeling of serenity immediately overcame them, as they entered the psychic community.

"This is so exciting," exclaimed Nellie. "I just love it here. Imagine, this spiritual meeting place has been here since the late 1800's."

"I know. It's amazing. And even though we've only been here one other time, there's something about the tranquility of this setting." Ethel checked her watch. "We're in luck, Nellie. The next activity is the service at Inspiration Stump. And maybe, if we're lucky, one of the mediums will speak to us."

"Oh, that would be something, wouldn't it, Ethel? Let's see. If we look at the guide the man at the front gate gave us, it says to follow the quiet trail to the retreat that's found at the end of Leolyn Woods. Come on. Let's follow the crowd."

The two women were in awe at the peacefulness they experienced as they entered the woods. In the distance, rows of benches, much like at a church, were filling up quickly.

"Over here, Ethel," Nellie whispered. Two end seats in the third row were available and the two women quickly sat down. Nellie inhaled deeply. "I can feel the spiritual energy."

"I can too. I really hope we receive a message."

Almost immediately a hush fell over the crowd, as Reverend Barbara Dubois introduced herself and addressed the group. She positioned herself behind the podium and spoke clearly.

"Welcome to all. Whatever brings you here today, we hope that you will find your experience to be positive and one of spiritual awakening. These services have been held since 1898. If a medium should ask if he or she may come to you, please let them hear your voice. And please be considerate of those around you by refraining from talking. Cell phones should be silenced out of respect for the mediums and for those receiving a message. Each psychic will give three or four short readings and then the next medium will begin. I am pleased to share with you that we have six mediums, two visiting mediums and one student medium here with us today. And now, without further delay, let me call upon our first psychic, Reverend Edward Shelbury."

Ethel and Nellie remembered him from the last time they had been there. A bald man of slight build with piercing eyes, he immediately focused on the woman in the row behind them who was wearing a red scarf.

"May I come to the lady in the bright red scarf?" he asked.

"Yes," she replied, with a tone that clearly indicated she was happy to have been chosen.

Reverend Shelbury gazed into the distance for a brief moment or two. "I was immediately drawn to you," he said. "I keep getting an image of a bicycle lying tangled on the ground. Does that mean anything to you?"

The lady in the red scarf began to sob. "Yes," she replied. "My son, Daniel, was on his bike when a car came from out of no-where and hit him." She placed her hands over her face and cried. "He is lucky to be alive, but he was badly injured."

"The man who hit him had been drinking. I assume you are aware of that?"

"Yes. The police arrested the man for driving under the influence." She inhaled deeply. "He will face time in prison."

"As he should. But I just want you to know that I see your son making a full recovery. It will be a long, slow road, but he will regain the use of his legs."

"How did you know that his legs were the problem?"

"The vision came to me quite clearly. That's all I can tell you. You must be strong for him. He needs you now more than ever. He will get better."

The woman wearing the red scarf sighed loudly with relief, as Reverend Shelbury continued on to the next person. Several psychics followed, but neither Ethel nor Nellie were chosen. And then registered medium, Eleanor Lucas, approached the podium and solemnly gazed into the audience. "May I come to the lady in the teal- colored top?"

Nellie nudged Ethel. "That's you."

Ethel took a breath and replied without hesitation. "Yes, please do."

"I can see that your heart is filled with worry and sadness. Something very heavy is troubling you."

"Yes, that is true," responded Ethel.

Medium Eleanor Lucas closed her eyes and looked up towards the heavens. "Is that your sister beside you?"

"No. It's my dear friend."

"But I'm getting a message that you are sisters. Does that mean anything to you?"

Ethel felt goose bumps form on her arms. "There were three of us. We were so close that sometimes we felt as if we were sisters."

"And one has died. Is that correct?"

Ethel could hardly believe her ears. "Yes. Our dear friend, Priscilla, who was like a sister to both of us, was taken from us."

"I am so sorry. She wants you to know that she is safe and at peace."

Ethel and Nellie's eyes filled with tears. "But, may I ask you something?"

"Yes."

"Can you tell us how she died?"

The medium went into a trance. Ethel and Nellie

223

sat in awe. "Her death was not natural. But I think you are aware of that. She's trying to give you clues that will lead you to her killer. She says you must not give up. She is so grateful to you both and wants you to know how much she loves you."

At that moment a white butterfly flew towards Ethel and landed on her chest. It did not go unnoticed. "Before I go on to my next reading, may I say that having that white butterfly land on you did not happen by chance. It has a very deep spiritual meaning. To many, a white butterfly is a message from heaven. It could be a response to your prayers. I think you need to look into all possibilities." The medium was silent for a moment. "And I will leave you with those thoughts."

Ethel and Nellie were dumbfounded. They could hardly believe what the psychic had said. As they drove towards Kenmore, they reviewed everything that had happened that day. It had been filled with so many potentially important clues. They knew they had many more roads to travel. Yet, their visit to Lily Dale had left them both feeling renewed and content with the knowledge that Priscilla was at peace.

Chapter Forty-Five
Matching Bingo Sweatshirts

"I must say that visiting Dr. Miller was quite enlightening. That man was a real piece of work."

"That's the understatement of the year, Nellie. But we got a lot of information out of him. And now, like Medium Lucas suggested, we need to explore other possibilities."

"Easier said than done. Let's start by going over what we found out today. Maybe that will spur us on to investigating something new."

"Okay. I'll summarize. For starters, we discovered that both Dr. Miller and Mr. Kliner have offices in Dunkirk, New York. And, up until about seven years ago, Father O'Leary was the priest at St. Theresa's church in Dunkirk."

"That gives new meaning to the Holy Trinity, wouldn't you agree?"

"Very funny, Nellie!"

"I don't mean to sound sacrilegious, but you've got to admit that the three of them are pretty high and mighty."

"Without a doubt. Not to change the topic, but I can't seem to get Skylar out of my mind. She was so forlorn. But she has a maturity about her that is astonishing for a girl her age."

"Agreed. And if, in fact, someone targeted her to become pregnant and give up her baby, maybe that in itself holds a clue."

"What do you mean?"

"I'm not really sure. But I think it would be prudent for us to keep a close eye on what Skylar decides to do. If she does decide to carry through with giving birth, we'll need to find out what happens to her baby."

"Thanks to Annie that shouldn't be too difficult."

"Maybe it would behoove us to call Annie and set up an impromptu meeting with Skylar. We can feel her out about which way she is leaning."

"Now you're thinking."

Without delay, Ethel took out her cellphone and called Annie. A broad smile filled her face, as she returned her cellphone to her purse.

"What's so amusing?" Nellie asked.

"Just that Annie said she'd take care of inviting Skylar, if we'd wear our matching bingo sweatshirts!"

"Hey, I think that's a great idea. Those sweatshirts are becoming like our logo."

"And I have no doubt that Priscilla would have had a good chuckle knowing that. That's reason enough to dress as twins."

"Then it's settled. But, for now, I'm exhausted. What do you say we call it a day? And since we're not getting together tomorrow till late afternoon, as much as cleaning my house is nowhere near as stimulating as our detective work, I know what I'll be doing."

"Not a bad idea, Nellie. My house could definitely use a good dusting and vacuuming. I've kind of put my housekeeping on the back burner since we've been so busy trying to solve the murder."

Nellie and Ethel awoke feeling refreshed. They puttered around their own houses doing laundry and cleaning. With the smell of Pine-Sol in the air, Ethel grabbed her keys, locked her front door, got in her Civic and headed over to pick up Nellie. In a very short time, they pulled up in front of Annie's house.

Annie's living room provided a comfortable place for them to talk.

Skylar's stomach had a definite baby bump and Ethel surmised she was probably seven or eight months along.

"Nellie and I just couldn't get you out of our thoughts, Skylar. You are truly a remarkable young lady and have been through so much."

Skylar seemed more relaxed and far less upset than the last time they had seen her. She was quite composed as she spoke. "First of all, thank you for caring about me. It means a lot. And secondly, I have given my options more thought than you can imagine. Deciding what to do is a huge decision and not one that I am taking lightly." She bit down on her lip and brought her hands to her stomach. "I know this baby was not conceived in a loving way. That is a certainty. But it is not the fault of this unborn child. It is alive within me and I believe it is my responsibility to nurture it and bring it safely into the world. Why I was chosen I do not know." She paused and looked down. "Maybe I will never know. But this innocent child should not die because of me. I have decided to do what I believe in my heart is the only righteous thing to do. The only Christian thing to do. And, through my pain, it is my hope that a loving couple will be blessed and find joy in raising my baby. That is the choice I have made, with God's help, for I believe that was His plan."

Ethel and Nellie's eyes filled with tears. Skylar's maturity and comprehension of the problem were well beyond her years.

"You are an amazing young woman, Skylar, and I want you to know that we are here to help you in any way we can. You are not alone," Ethel said with great compassion in her voice.

"All my life, I have felt that nothing has gone my way. My father was never there for any of us and now he is in prison. My mother is an alcoholic who barely functions, let alone takes care of her own children. And my two sisters are struggling with everyday life. It is so hard to watch. I've tried my best to be there for them and to guide them, but it hasn't been easy. I worry that Daphne, my youngest sister, is falling in with the wrong crowd." Skylar bowed her head and spoke in a hushed tone. "When I was raped, I am ashamed to say that I considered taking my own life." Skylar inhaled deeply and sat without speaking for several long minutes. "But," as Father O'Leary told me, "God works in mysterious ways. He shared a quote by Paul, from Romans 12:21, that really made me think. Would you like to hear it?"

"Yes," the two women replied in unison. '

"Do not be overcome by evil, but overcome evil with good. I didn't really understand the impact of his words at first. But, the more I thought about them, the more I realized that maybe good could come from evil, just as Father had explained to me."

"What else did Father say?" Ethel innocently asked.

"Just that a baby is a blessing from God. It is a divine gift that must never be taken for granted, no matter what the circumstances. By having this baby and giving it up for adoption, I would be doing the ultimate act of unselfishness and would shine in God's glory."

"But all your prenatal care will require a fair amount of money. Has Father discussed that with you?"

"Actually, he has. This may sound crazy to you, because I know it sounded unbelievable to me. But apparently there are couples in his church who have been trying for several years to have a baby. Father told me that these couples would gladly cover all of the expenses for the baby and even provide some additional money for me for my troubles." Skylar flipped her thick red hair over her shoulder. "When Father explained to me the enormous impact this baby would have on an infertile couple's lives and the act of godliness that I would forever be remembered for, it suddenly seemed like the only right thing to do. And now that my morning sickness has finally passed, it doesn't seem like the burden it once did."

"You are an amazing young lady, Skylar. Thank you for having the courage to share all of this with us. I'd be lying if I said I wasn't flabbergasted by what you just told us," said Nellie.

"I know. I was pretty surprised myself when Father asked to speak with me. I have Annie to thank for confiding in him on my behalf. His talking to me and explaining things has truly given me a new outlook. To end this little one's life would be a sin. I am finally at peace with my decision and no longer feel guilty." Skylar cradled her stomach and looked down lovingly. "What Father said to me really left a footprint on my heart."

Chapter Forty-Six
A Bit of Poking Around

"Well, Nellie. That was quite an earful! Can you believe what we just heard?"

"Blow me away, Ethel. Who would have ever thought that we would be able to gather so much information in such a short time? Skylar, without knowing it, has corroborated what we were thinking. There can be no doubt now that Father is somehow involved in whatever shenanigans are going on."

"I think there are more layers to this mystery than we realize. We need to proceed with a plan in mind."

"I do love being your assistant, Ethel. And, today I feel like a real detective. I have this feeling in me that we're very close to cracking the case." Nellie looked up to the heavens. "Priscilla, it's been a long, slow process, but we're not giving up. Come hell or high water, we're going to catch your killer. And that's a promise."

"That a girl, Nellie! I like your enthusiasm."

"Now let's think. What's next?" She pondered her thoughts for several moments. "I think we need to pay Father O'Leary another visit. You know that old adage that honesty is the best policy."

"I do. But, do you really think we should share with him what we found out today?"

"I think it's imperative to get everything out in the open. Remember Medium Lucas told us to explore new ways. Laying it all out on the table, so to speak, would definitely qualify as something we haven't tried before. And there's no time like the present."

Ethel and Nellie put a little squirt of lilac scented perfume, something Ethel always carried in her purse, on their wrists as they approached Father's door.

"Even if we don't get any information, at least we'll smell pretty," Ethel mused.

The knock on the door was immediately answered. Father looked happy to see them.

"Good afternoon, ladies." His smile was genuine, as he glanced down at his watch. "Or, should I say good evening."

"May we sit, Father?"

"Of course. Please do."

"You two look as if you have the weight of the world on your shoulders. Whatever is the matter?"

Ethel cleared her throat. "Father, Nellie and I took a little trip yesterday."

"Why that sounds lovely. This time of the year is so beautiful with the ...."

Ethel cut him off mid-sentence. "Father, you need to hear what we have to say. It's important."

"I'm listening."

"Nellie and I went to Dunkirk. We did a bit of poking around."

The uneasy look on Father's face did not go unnoticed. "And what did you find out with all your poking about?"

"Actually, we found out that you used to be the priest at St. Theresa's Church and that you left in quite a hurry."

Father replied without hesitation. "I left because the diocese felt I could be of more use at our church here in Kenmore. Simple as that. As a matter of fact, they hired a new priest, Father Darnell, to take over for me in Dunkirk."

"Yes. We know. We actually met with Father Darnell. He was very informative. He referred us to a lovely lady whose daughter had adopted a baby. We had quite a nice little chat with her at her home."

"I'm surprised. I never thought the two of you would take things this far. I guess I underestimated you." Father crossed one leg over the other and Ethel felt they had definitely touched on a nerve.

"I must say that Father Darnell and the grandmother were very helpful. But I'd have to say that our greatest information came from a Doctor Miller, wouldn't you agree, Nellie?"

Ethel and Nellie saw the color drain from Father O' Leary's face. "What? You met with Dr. Miller? Why?"

Ethel was rather enjoying the banter between them. "Nellie and I suspect that somehow our dearly departed Priscilla found out something she should not have known. And, we think that's why she was killed. Should anything happen to Nellie or me, I should tell you that we have been to the police and shared with them everything we know." Ethel amazed herself at how easily the lies flowed. She took a gamble that he would believe her and he seemed to accept the bait.

"No need to have done that, ladies. I have done nothing wrong."

"Be that as it may, Father. All we want is justice for Priscilla. And we will do whatever it takes to see that her killer or killers are made to pay for their crime."

"I think that's what we all want, Ethel. And I must say that you two have truly amazed me with your dedication and persistence. It takes a lot to surprise me, but kudos to you both."

"We are on a mission, Father. And we won't rest till Priscilla's tragic demise is accounted for and the people who killed her are brought to justice."

"I understand. But, how can I help? What can I tell you that you don't already know?"

"Well, for starters, we know that Priscilla came to confession the night she was murdered. We need to know if you have any idea what she did before she entered the confessional booth. That could be crucial information."

Father appeared a bit more relaxed. "Now that's something I can help you with."

Ethel and Nellie's ears perked up. "Please, go on."

"Actually, Priscilla stopped by the rectory before we headed over to the church. She had a lot on her mind. Poor soul. I'd never seen her so distraught. We shared a cup of tea together. She was a bundle of nerves that day." Father wrung his hands together. "It hurt me to see her in such a state. As I mentioned to you before, she was worried Fred may have started gambling again. And she was very worried about Annie. So much on the poor woman's mind. She brought up Roxy's, but wouldn't elaborate when I asked her to. She eventually broke down and told me she was afraid someone was trying to kill her. That night at bingo, when you asked me to call the police, I had already intended to do so based on what she'd shared with me at confession."

"But, when she was with you in the rectory and in the confessional booth, she was alive."

"True. Very much so."

"So, what could have happened to Priscilla in that brief period of time, before bingo, that could have killed her?" Nellie spoke her thoughts aloud.

Suddenly, Donna's words were crystal clear. Ethel's voice was filled with enthusiasm. "Wait a minute. I just thought of something. And I think it might be really important. Donna told us that the man with the tattoo cross on his neck was standing near the snack bar well before the start of bingo."

"You're right, Ethel. I remember her sharing that with us."

"And, he's the same man that pushed me down. He's also the same man that threatened to kill Fred and hurt Nancy. Surely, his being at the church on the very night Priscilla was killed has to be more than a mere coincidence."

"You two seem to have several leads to explore," Father declared.

"That's true. But I have another pressing question that is perplexing me. If T-Bone was at the church bingo hall the night of the murder, did you see him or have any contact with him, Father?"

Chapter Forty-Seven
A Baby Girl is Born

The phone call came quite unexpectedly. "Ethel, I just wanted you to know that Skylar's baby came early." Annie's voice was filled with enthusiasm. "She's a little peanut. But the doctor on call, who delivered her, assures her she should be fine. She only weighs 4 pounds 2 ounces."

"That is a tiny one. And how is Skylar doing?"

"She had a long, hard labor, but is glad it's finally over. She's resting comfortably here at the hospital. I was a bit surprised, pleasantly surprised, when she asked for you and Nellie to come see her."

"We'd love to. Are you sure she's up to it?"

"I think so. The doctor didn't give her any restrictions that I'm aware of, other than to rest."

"Okay. Let me just give Nellie a call and we'll try to stop by later this afternoon. And, Annie, please tell Skylar we're proud of her. That was a lot for a young girl to endure. Thank goodness she has you, Annie."

"I was only too happy to help. I was a bit worried when I got the call that the baby was coming early. But things worked out well. Skylar was a real trooper." Ethel could hear the sadness in Annie's voice with what she said next. "It was so sad to me that Skylar's mother chose to embrace the bottle, rather than to support her daughter." Annie was silent for a moment. "I guess we can't judge someone else unless we've walked in their shoes."

"Now you sound like Father O'Leary," added Ethel.

Annie laughed aloud. "Maybe I do. So, shall I tell Skylar that you'll be stopping by?"

"Yes. We'll come as soon as we can."

Ethel was glad that her preoccupation with being well organized had paid off. It was about a month ago that she and Nellie had attended the church craft sale and had seen a beautiful hand knit sweater and bonnet. And that it was in yellow was perfect, as they had no idea what the sex of the baby would be. They decided then and there to purchase it for Skylar. Nellie had taken it home to wrap. Perfect, thought Ethel. I'll call Nellie right now and tell her to get the gift and herself ready.

The maternity floor at Kenmore Mercy Hospital did not have the sterile smell that Ethel remembered so vividly. As they walked by the nursery, they stopped to admire all the beautiful newborns in their little incubators. They imagined Skylar's baby would be in a special area for preemies. As they entered room 307, they were delighted with how happy and excited Skylar seemed when she saw them.

"Thank you so much for coming. It means a lot to me."

Ethel and Nellie went over to her bedside and each gave the young girl a hug. "You look remarkably well put together for someone who just had a baby," exclaimed Ethel.

"Thank you. It was a lot of pushing and a lot of pain, but now that she's out, it's a huge relief."

"Can we see her?"

"She's in the NICU. The nurse told me that they put her there to closely monitor her. She's in an incubator to help control her temperature. Everyone here has been so kind to me and I know the baby is being well looked

236

after. If you'd like, I can ask the nurse if we can look in on her."

"I, for one, would love to see her," said Nellie. "Oh, but before I forget, Ethel and I got her a little something to welcome her into the world." She handed the decorative bag to Skylar.

When she opened the gift, her eyes filled with tears of joy. "How can I begin to thank you both. I am so lucky that you two are in my life." Skylar held up the delicate sweater and bonnet. "She'll look beautiful in these. The yellow is so cheery and it will keep her nice and warm. Thank you so much."

"Our pleasure. It's not every day, at our age, that we get to shop for a newborn. It was quite a treat."

"I think that's what they call a win-win in high school lingo," said Annie.

At that moment, the nurse entered the room and gave them permission to look in on the baby. They needed to scrub their hands and arms before entering the isolated area. Incubators lined the room in neat rows.

Skylar whispered, "She's right over there," pointing to the incubator at the end of the second row.

Ethel and Nellie were speechless for a moment. Her little arm had an IV and she was so tiny that they wondered how she would ever be strong enough to leave. She was wearing a little cap to help keep her warm. Skylar bent over and gently removed it for just a moment and smiled broadly.

"Oh, my word! Why I've never seen so much hair on such a little baby. And such a beautiful shade of red, just like her mother's."

Skylar beamed. "She is such a pretty little thing, if I do say so myself." Suddenly, her demeanor changed before their eyes. Her voice became melancholy, as she bent over the incubator and gently caressed her tiny, frail little face. "How I wish times were different and I could

237

keep her. I love her already. But," she continued with tears in her eyes, "I'm not ready to be a mother and I want her to have the best life she can. I want her to have a mother and father who will cherish her and be able to give her all the things I can't, at this point in my life." Skylar bent over and kissed her baby's forehead. "A loving family is my gift to her."

"And a wonderful gift that is," said Nellie.

"I never knew how strong a bond I would have with her in such a short time. It's pretty remarkable." Skylar tried to force a smile, as she continued to stroke her baby. "I love you. I always will."

Skylar wasn't the only one who was teary eyed. Ethel put her arm around the young girl. "We should probably get you back to your room so you can rest."

Skylar reluctantly turned to leave and then turned back. She threw a kiss towards the baby. "Love you always," she whispered, as she left the room.

Skylar was barely settled in her bed, when there was a knock at the door. "Come in," she declared.

The door opened and who stood before them but Dr. Miller. Ethel and Nellie were truly startled to see him and the expression on their faces must have spoken more loudly than words.

Dr. Miller immediately walked over to Skylar's bedside and said something in a hushed tone. He then nodded and smiled at Annie. Lastly, he turned towards Ethel and Nellie. "Ladies, it's nice to see you again. I never did receive a copy of the article you were writing for the Christian Women's League." Ethel found it difficult to decipher whether his tone was sincere or sarcastic.

Ethel didn't miss a beat in replying. Once again, the ease with which her lies flowed amazed her. "We are still working on it, doctor. We want the article to be perfect and it involves a good amount of research, as I'm sure you can understand. It should be ready soon." Ethel smiled warmly.

"Fair enough." He looked towards Skylar and back at them. "I didn't know you knew one another."

Skylar innocently replied. "Oh, Ethel and Nellie have been like mothers to me." She leaned over and picked up the bag with the gifts they had brought. "Look. Isn't this the most beautiful sweater and hat set you've ever seen?"

Dr. Miller smiled. "They are very pretty."

"I'm so lucky that Annie introduced them to me. They've been keeping tabs on me throughout my entire pregnancy."

There was no denying the skeptical look that overcame the doctor's face. "So, Annie introduced you?"

"Yes. Aren't I lucky to have two such lovely ladies care so much about me and my baby?"

Dr. Miller looked over towards Annie and the look he gave her left no doubt that he was clearly not pleased with what he'd just been told. A forced smile encompassed his face. "Well, Annie, I guess we have some talking to do." An uneasy silence overcame the room. "I don't mean to be rude ladies, but I really need to speak to Skylar privately."

Nellie chuckled. "Hey, we can take a hint. Anyway, we were just leaving. You should have a look at the baby, Dr. Miller. She is a beauty."

"About that, I have no doubt." He stood and opened the door, as he gestured for Ethel and Nellie to leave.

"We'll be in touch, Skylar. Take care of yourself. The baby is beautiful."

"Thank you again for coming to see me and for the clothes."

"Our pleasure."

"Ladies, I'll be anxious to read that article. I

239

assume it will be finished before too long. Seems to me you've had more than enough time to complete it." His voice was cold and accusatory. "That is if there ever was an article. I'm beginning to wonder."

Chapter Forty-Eight
Just Ask the Nurse

"That was weird."

"Weird and confusing."

"I know. I thought Dr. Miller's office was in Dunkirk. What is he doing here? And, I don't get what the relationship is between him and Annie. It almost seemed to me like he knew her."

"Me too. And why didn't he ask her to leave too? He seemed as if he was in quite a hurry to get rid of us."

"Next time we see Annie why don't we just ask her."

"Probably a good idea. And the most logical one." Ethel's next thought caused her to laugh aloud. "I don't know how convincing we were with our Christian League article. I think he's on to us."

"Oh well. We did the best we could. And we did accomplish learning a lot, so I guess it was worth the deception. He's a sly one that Dr. Miller. And, call it feminine intuition, but I think there's far more to him than meets the eye. I'm still perplexed why he wound up in Skylar's room."

Suddenly Ethel got a look on her face that Nellie knew all too well. "What? What plan do you have now?"

"Have a little faith, Nellie," she answered as she walked towards the nurse's station.

A young nurse addressed them. "How may I help you ladies?"

Ethel cleared her throat. "Our dear friend's daughter is pregnant and looking for a doctor. She is several months along and just moved here from Arizona. We were so impressed with Dr. Miller. I believe that's his name. He is in the room now with our niece, Skylar. I would appreciate it if you could just give us his contact information, so I could pass it along to my friend for her daughter."

The young nurse smiled. "Of course. I'd be happy to write that down for you. Just give me a minute. It should be in the file."

As the nurse stepped away, Nellie turned towards her friend and said, in a hushed tone, "Bravo! That was good thinking, detective Ethel."

Within moments, they were leaving with the information in hand. As soon as they were in the car, Ethel locked the doors and immediately read what the nurse had written down. The paper read: Dr. Miller 527 High Street 716 812- 4773.

"Oh, my word, Nellie. That's the place we went to with Annie. But I don't recall seeing his name on the door."

"Neither do I. That's strange."

"Let me try to call there. It's still early," Ethel said as she got out her cell phone and dialed the vaguely familiar number.

"Oh, Ethel. You think of everything."

"Please, Nellie. This idea isn't exactly rocket science."

"Good afternoon. Women's clinic."

"Yes, good afternoon. I'm hoping you can help me. My dear friend's daughter just moved here and needs an OB/GYN. My niece speaks so highly of Dr. Miller. I was wondering if he still works at the clinic?"

"Oh, yes. Dr. Miller is one of our most sought-after doctors. But he is only at our Buffalo office once a week. His primary practice is about an hour away in Dunkirk."

"I see."

"But, if you'd like to make an appointment with him, he is here every Friday."

"Thank you so much. I'll let my friend know and give her the number."

"Certainly. Glad to help."

"Hmm," said Nellie. "That is a little curious. Why does he come here once a week? Surely he has more than enough patients in Dunkirk."

"That, my dear, is what we are going to try to figure out. And, once we've done that, maybe we'll be a step closer to solving the case."

"I never thought I'd say this, Ethel, but I'm finding all this detective work to be quite exhilarating. I'm really anxious to talk to Annie. Maybe she'll be able to shed some light on all the suspicious things we noticed at the hospital."

"That is at the top of our list for tomorrow. Perhaps, Nellie, you could even whip up a batch of your delicious *Catch a Killer Cookies*! Maybe they'll lead us to more clues."

"Consider it done."

Chapter Forty-Nine
Amanda Rose

"We're so happy you were able to spare some time to speak with us today, Annie." Ethel unbuttoned her hunter green cardigan and continued. "To be honest, we were a bit taken aback yesterday with Dr. Miller. So, we did a little digging around and discovered he works one day a week at the Women's Clinic. The same clinic that we went to with you several months ago. It seems rather unusual to us that he works here in Buffalo considering his primary office in Dunkirk seemed quite thriving the day we were there."

A puzzled look overcame Annie's face. "What? You went to Dr. Miller's office in Dunkirk?"

"We did." Ethel collected her thoughts. "We found out about him from a lovely grandmother that Father Darnell put us in contact with. I believe her name was Mrs. Boutet. Anyway, her daughter adopted a baby with the help of Dr. Miller. We wanted to speak with him."

"And?"

"And what? We discovered that he, in our humble opinion, is an arrogant, self-righteous man who has little compassion for those less fortunate."

Annie looked down and bit on her lower lip. She began to fidget with one of the charms on her bracelet. She did not speak.

"What's the matter, dear?"

Annie continued to sit without uttering a word.

"To be honest, we were a little surprised that he all but kicked us out of Skylar's room yesterday, but never asked you to leave. His demeanor just seemed rather unsettling to us. We sensed that you were somehow familiar with the doctor. Or, more aptly put, that he was familiar with you. Do you know him?"

Annie began to wring her hands together and Ethel knew, without a doubt, that they had touched on something.

"I don't mean to make you feel uncomfortable or to pry. But Nellie and I are really perplexed. And I guess we just want to know if you have ever interacted with Dr. Miller before."

Annie breathed in deeply, covered her face with her hands and began to sob uncontrollably. Her cries grew louder.

"What is it, Annie? It can't possibly be so bad that you can't share it with us. We are your friends. I hope you know that by now. And you know you can trust us."

Annie's cries continued. Ethel and Nellie exchanged sympathetic glances and waited patiently for her to say something.

After a long while, Annie spoke between muffled sobs. They had never seen this beautiful, self-confident young lady in this state. "I am so ashamed. I've never told this to anyone. And I need you both to promise me that you will never divulge what I am about to tell you."

"Promise," they uttered in unison.

"This is just so difficult to share."

"We understand, dear. Take your time."

"I don't know if you are aware that I grew up in Dunkirk."

"No. We never knew that."

"Well, I did. I lived there all my life until I moved here for my teaching job. When I was in high school, I was a cheer leader. Pretty popular and thought I knew everything."

"I think that's typical of teenagers these days."

Annie shrugged her shoulders. "I guess so. Anyway, I had a big crush on one of the football players. His name was Drew. Naturally, when he took an interest in me, I was flattered. I also was stupid, but I didn't see it back then." She began to cry again. "I should have known he was only after one thing. My mother warned me, but I basically told her to leave me alone and that it was my life. I was in love." Her sobs grew louder. "One night after a big game, we had a few drinks and one thing led to another." Annie hung her head down and gazed at the floor. "I'm sure you can figure out the rest." She moved uneasily from side to side in the chair. "When I missed my period, I thought it was just late. But, when I missed a few more, I realized the impact of that one night with Drew. It cost me my dignity and created another life." She looked up at the two women. "There. Now you know the truth. I'm not the prim and proper school teacher you two probably assumed I was. And, not surprisingly, Drew wanted nothing to do with me or our baby. I was such a fool."

Ethel and Nellie got tears in their eyes seeing Annie so distraught. "You were young and naive. And you did what lots of girls do. But, seeing as you don't have a child, I'm wondering what happened to the baby. Did you carry it to term?"

"It was the hardest decision of my life. I could never have gotten through it without the love and support of my parents and Dr. Miller."

"Dr. Miller?"

"Yes. Dr. Miller was amazing. He was the obstetrician I saw in Dunkirk and he was wonderful to

246

me. I knew I didn't want to abort. Being a devout Catholic, I knew that would be a terrible sin. But, thanks to Dr. Miller, I was given another option."

"Now it's all beginning to make sense to me," said Ethel.

"Dr. Miller said that because I was pretty and had done so well academically and because Drew was a handsome football player, our baby would be in great demand. He promised me that there were many wonderful, loving couples that wanted a baby more than anything in the world, but couldn't conceive for one reason or another. My baby would be given every opportunity life had to offer. It seemed like the answer to my prayers." Annie cleared her throat. "What I really wasn't expecting was that Dr. Miller even gave me money, once I agreed. He said it was for my medical expenses and miscellaneous things I might need. At first, I didn't want to accept it. But he insisted."

"How gallant of him," Ethel sarcastically replied. I can only imagine what was in it for him, she thought to herself.

"So, that's how you know Dr. Miller. We suspected it wasn't the first time you'd met."

"No. We go back a long time."

"And may we ask if you gave birth to a boy or a girl."

"A beautiful little girl. She was so sweet and tiny. Only five pounds at birth, but healthy as could be. I only wish times had been different." A melancholy look came over Annie's face. "Although I knew she was going to a good family, it was the hardest decision of my life. I named her Amanda Rose. I'm sure the adoptive family chose a new name for her. But, in my heart, she'll always be my little Amanda."

"Did Dr. Miller ever share anything with you about the family who adopted her?"

"Not too much. I wish I knew more. Only that the father was an attorney and the mother was a preschool teacher. He said they had a very loving marriage and that the baby would be showered with love and lack for nothing. That's all I could hope for."

"Sounds like it was very difficult, but the right decision for you at the time."

Finally, Annie smiled. "You sound just like Father O'Leary."

"Really? What do you mean?"

"When I became pregnant and was considering my choices, I was very distraught and upset, as you can well imagine. At the time, Father O'Leary was the priest at St. Theresa's parish where my family attended mass. I spoke with him on numerous occasions. It was through his guidance and compassion that I was led to Dr. Miller."

"So, it was Father O'Leary that put you in touch with Dr. Miller?"

"That's right. I don't know what I would have done without the two of them. They were my godsends. I owe them both so much."

Chapter Fifty
A Glass of Chianti

"Well, Nellie. That was a most productive visit, wouldn't you agree?"

"Definitely. I almost fell off my chair when Annie tied Dr. Miller and Father O'Leary together. I could hardly keep from gasping."

"I know. This case is like an onion, Nellie. It seems to have lots of layers. But through our tedious detective work, we are slowly peeling back each one. Slow and steady, Nellie. That's how we roll."

"You're a funny one, Ethel. But I think we're making some real progress. I have a feeling that soon we are going to tie all of this together and figure out why Priscilla was killed."

"And by whom" added Ethel.

"That, my dear friend, is the $64,000 question." Nellie cleared her throat and took a swig of her bottled water.

"Let me put on my thinking cap." Ethel gazed into the distance. Deep in thought, she was silent for several minutes. "I think it's important to find out how and why Priscilla ended up with the list in her office drawer. I know it's a feather in our caps that we got to interview some of the people on that list. But, let's face it, Nellie. We still don't know how that list wound up in Priscilla's possession or why she went to Roxy's the

Thursday night before she died. These questions still need to be answered."

"But, the only one who might know about Roxy's is Annie. And we just left her."

Ethel looked at her watch. "It's barely 5:00. What do you say we call Annie and say we'd like to take her out to dinner? We can tell her we thought of a few other things we'd like to ask her and wanted to thank her for being so open with us."

"Good idea. Where can we go?"

"First, let's call and see if she's agreeable to the idea. Then, I think somewhere near her house would be preferable. Maybe Chef's. That's not too far from her and always delicious."

"Oh, I love their eggplant parmesan. It's the best in the city, in my opinion."

Within the hour, the three were seated at a cozy corner table at Chef's.

"I was so happy when you called me to have dinner. I really had nothing planned and Chef's is my favorite for Italian food. I love their spaghetti and meatballs."

"We're glad you could join us. How about if we order some wine. Do you like Chianti?"

Annie smiled. "Chianti is my favorite. Especially with Italian food."

"Then it's settled. I'll order a carafe of Chianti for the three of us."

Wine in hand, Ethel broached the first question, as delicately as she could. "I'll be perfectly honest with you, Annie. Nellie and I were pretty surprised with what you shared with us earlier. We had no idea that Father O'Leary and Dr. Miller were friends."

Annie replied in a very nonchalant, matter of fact tone. "I don't think it's a secret. They've been friends for a long time. As I told you earlier, they both really helped me in my time of need. I was so lost."

"I'm happy to hear that, Annie. I know your faith is strong and I can imagine having Father O'Leary's guidance and support made a very difficult time more bearable."

"Exactly. It was still really tough. But knowing Amanda Rose would be part of a family that could really take care of her and love her forever made it the choice I felt most comfortable with."

"I think it was the right thing for you at the time." Ethel contemplated her next thought. "I know that you and Father O'Leary were at Priscilla's house for bible study the Thursday before she was killed."

Annie's face took on a very serious demeanor. "That's true. There were several of us there that evening. We felt so blessed that Father was explaining his sermon to us. He's such a busy man and it was so generous of him to volunteer his time." A confused look overcame Annie. "What does our being at bible study have to do with Priscilla's death? I don't understand."

"Maybe nothing. Nellie and I are just trying to sequence Priscilla's steps those last few days of her life."

"We know there was a list that Priscilla had that a very, how shall I say this, unsavory man tried to get. He was willing to kill for that list. Do you know anything about that?"

Annie's eyes doubled in size and her facial expression took on a look of total fear. She looked as if she were about to cry.

"What is it? What's the matter?"

Annie found it difficult to speak. She fumbled for her words, but they would not come.

"Annie," Ethel said in a soothing voice. "We are not here to judge you. Please, if there is anything you can tell us that may shed some light on the importance of the list, I beg of you to share what you know."

Annie began to tremble. Her voice quivered, as she spoke. "I never meant for anything bad to happen." She put her hands over her face and started to sob. "When I was in Father's office a few months ago, I saw the list on his desk and it really piqued my curiosity. I strongly suspected what it was for. So, when Father was called away for a bit to speak to a parishioner, I made a few quick copies and shoved them into my purse." Annie bit down on her lip. "His copy machine was right there and it seemed so easy. I know it was foolish and dishonest, but I felt compelled to see what was on the list."

"And?"

"And, as I suspected, it was a bunch of names. But beside each one, were notations that I was unable to decipher. It just looked like scribbles to me. I had no idea what it all meant. I'd rather not share with you how this all relates to me, but suffice it to say that I am involved and want to do what's right."

Ethel and Nellie were baffled. How any of this related to Annie they did not know.

Annie continued to cry. "I am ashamed to tell you this, but I mailed the list anonymously to Priscilla. I attached a note saying they were important church papers and to please put them in a safe place and not give them to anyone. I wanted someone else to have the list in their possession, someone I could trust. With Priscilla being in bible study with me, I believed she was an honest, righteous woman."

"We'd certainly agree with you about that, dear."

"I never told her it was from me or anything about the names on it." Annie shrugged her shoulders. "I intended to tell her at some point, but then she..." Annie's sobs grew louder. "I never imagined her keeping the list would cause her any harm."

"We know that. How could you have known."

"As I said, there are certain things I'm just not comfortable sharing with anyone. Things that happened in my past. But, as I've learned, the present is often intertwined with the past.

Chapter Fifty-One
The Baptism

Sunday Mass was something both women had attended for as long as they could remember. They always felt spiritually renewed when services were over. When Leonard and Edwin had been alive, the foursome had often gone out for breakfast after church. Now, Ethel and Nellie went together every Sunday. They could not recall Fred's presence at Sunday morning services since Priscilla's untimely passing.

Father's sermons inevitably gave them something to really think about each week. The Thursday night bible study group, Priscilla had informed them long ago, was merely a chance to get together with other like-minded people in the church to explore the various interpretations of some of Father's sermons. Ethel and Nellie wished that they had been involved in the Thursday night group. Perhaps they would have a better idea as to exactly what had happened on that fateful night.

Their thoughts were interrupted as Father O'Leary walked to the altar. He looked out at his congregants and said, "In the name of the Father, and of the Son, and the Holy Spirit."

With those words, Ethel and Nellie crossed themselves, as the word *Amen* was heard throughout the church.

Father continued. "As we prepare to celebrate the mystery of Christ's love, let us acknowledge our failures and ask God for pardon and strength."

Ethel leaned over and whispered to Nellie. "And maybe we should say an extra prayer to ask the Lord for help in bringing Priscilla's killer to justice."

"Agreed. We need all the help we can get."

Services continued as they had for most Sundays before them. But, when Father announced that a baptism was to be performed, Ethel and Nellie were thrilled. They loved nothing more than to see a beautiful newborn, surrounded by his or her loving parents, becoming a member of the church. So tiny and fragile, baptism was something both women felt blessed to be a part of witnessing.

Father O'Leary's words were clear and concise. "What do you ask of the church for this child?"

"Baptism," the couple replied in unison.

"Oh, my word, Nellie! Do you see what I see? Look at the woman holding the baby."

Nellie turned her head to get a clearer look at the couple whose child was being baptized. She let out a quiet gasp. "Why that's Mrs. Joslin. I'd recognize her beautiful, thick red hair anywhere. And that must be Judge Joslin beside her."

"I guess God does truly work in mysterious ways," whispered Ethel. "They look so happy."

Father went on to explain to the family and to his congregants the importance of baptism as a sacrament of initiation, cleansing, strengthening and welcoming. He explained how it offers us a new life in which we become the children of God, followers in the footsteps of Jesus.

Shortly thereafter, the sign of the cross was traced on the forehead of the tiny infant. The baby's head was sprinkled with water three times as Father said the words, "I baptize you in the name of the Father, the Son and the Holy Spirit." He then anointed the tiny baby with sacred oil representing the belief that the Holy Spirit lives within the heart of this newly baptized child.

Although neither Nellie nor Ethel was proficient in speaking any foreign language, they had come to recognize the Latin words, *Ite, Missa Est,* as the concluding prayer heard every Sunday at Mass.

The two women could hardly wait to offer their congratulations to the Joslin family. They scurried, as quickly as their legs would allow, to the front of the church where the couple proudly held their beautiful baby girl. Both Mrs. Joslin and the Judge were beaming from ear to ear. When Mrs. Joslin spotted them, her smile grew even wider. She turned towards her husband. "These are the two ladies that baked those delicious cookies to help those at Haven House."

"Credit goes to Nellie" said Ethel. "We wanted to tell you both how absolutely thrilled we are for you. What a blessing."

"Yes. She is the greatest joy of our lives. She is more wonderful than we ever could have imagined. Would you like to hold her?" Mrs. Joslin repositioned the tiny bundle in her arms.

"I'd love to," said Ethel without a moment of hesitation.

The baby cooed, as Mrs. Joslin bent over and kissed her little forehead before carefully handing her to Ethel. "Meet Grace Elizabeth."

Ethel held the baby carefully in her arms. But neither she nor Nellie could believe their eyes. Over her little christening dress, she wore the sweater they had given to Skylar.

Nellie finally spoke. "She's a beauty. And her hair! It's the same red as yours."

Mrs. Joslin was glowing. "I know. Talk about miracles. Little Grace gives a whole new meaning to that term for us, doesn't she dear," she added as she smiled lovingly at her husband.

"I guess Father O'Leary was right. God does work in mysterious ways."

Chapter Fifty-Two
Made to Order

"Well, blow me away. Who would have ever thought that a morning at church would provide such a huge clue?"

"I can't fathom any other interpretation, Nellie. That was most definitely Skylar's baby. It looked like her clone. And she was even wearing the little yellow sweater we gave her."

"True. But she also looked like a duplicate of Mrs. Joslin with that thick red hair."

"There's one way to find out how this all transpired. Let's call Annie and arrange a meeting with her and Skylar."

Within a few hours, the four women sat together at Annie's house. Ethel and Nellie were a bit unsure how to broach the topic.

"It's so nice to see you again, Skylar."

"I feel the same way. You both treated me with such kindness and it was so thoughtful of you to bring the baby a gift."

"Our pleasure."

A melancholy look came over Skylar's face. "I know I shouldn't feel sad because my baby went to a really good home. Father O'Leary promised me that. I only wish things could have been different. I feel as if a part of me is missing. I loved her, even though I barely knew her." Skylar held back her tears. "I packed the beautiful sweater and hat that you gave her in a little bag, along with a letter to her explaining why I had to give her up."

"Did you meet the family who adopted her?" Nellie asked.

"No, but I included a separate note to them in the bag asking them to please carry out my wishes when she's older."

"That was a wonderful idea, Skylar. I'm sure one day your little girl will appreciate and understand what a difficult decision this was for you."

Skylar gazed into the distance. "I hope so. It was the hardest thing I've ever had to do. But I know they truly appreciated becoming a family and they were very generous to me."

"Really?"

"Yes. I don't know how they knew I wanted to go to college one day. But they gave me a check for $50,000 which provides me with so many opportunities. That is more money than I could have ever imagined. I am very grateful."

"But, if you didn't meet them, how did you get the check?" Ethel's voice was calm and non-accusatory.

"Father O'Leary gave it to me. Once my baby was safely in the adoptive parent's arms, he and Dr. Miller stopped by to see me. I thought that was very thoughtful of them."

Ethel smiled. "Yes, it certainly was." But her thoughts were totally different. This baby was definitely *made to order,* so to speak. They knew that Judge Joslin and his wife wanted a baby more than anything in the world and they also knew they were financially very well to do. What a perfect combination to exploit them for their own gain, she thought. Also, Ethel couldn't help but think how the baby's having red hair was the icing on the cake. Why I imagine they'd have paid whatever was asked for a baby that looked like Mrs. Joslin.

"One other thing was pretty remarkable," Skylar innocently added.

"What's that?" asked Nellie.

"Dr. Miller said that he knows how difficult it is when a young girl, particularly from a home that is in my area of the city, finds herself in the family way. He said if I tell any girl who finds herself pregnant about him, and she uses him as her obstetrician, not only will he help her to find the best possible home for her baby, but he will pay me $5,000 for sending her to him. I could hardly believe it. He is such a generous man."

Ethel felt like screaming and exposing Dr. Miller as the criminal he was. But she knew that would be a mistake, at this time. "I guess it was a blessing that you found one another."

"I was very lucky," Skylar replied. "Thank goodness for Dr. Miller." She then looked over at Annie who had been sitting quietly beside Maxwell, taking everything in. "And I owe so much to my teacher. She has always been there for me. Why, without her, I truly don't know what I would have done."

Annie's cheeks grew pink. "I don't deserve any credit, Skylar. It was you who carried the baby."

"Yes. But it was you who supported me from the moment I confided in you. Speaking to Father O'Leary the way you did, arranging for Dr. Miller to visit me at the hospital to figure everything out. You have been like a mother to me."

Ethel was taken aback with what she just heard. She turned towards Annie. "You introduced Dr. Miller to Skylar? You spoke to Father O'Leary about her? Why?"

Annie was clearly flustered. "I did what I had to do. I did the best I could do in a situation that wasn't easy."

"But why would you call in Dr. Miller? There are lots of good doctors in our city."

And then it struck her. "Oh my God, Annie. You got money for doing this, didn't you?" Ethel stared in disbelief at the young woman who sat across from her. "Dr. Miller paid you." Ethel's eyes quickly scanned the interior of the home. "To be honest, Nellie and I wondered how you could ever afford this expensive townhouse and all its beautiful furnishings. Not to mention your cashmere sweaters and Tiffany charm bracelet. Just not possible on a teacher's salary. But now, I think I'm finally putting it all together."

Annie bowed her head and did not speak.

Chapter Fifty-Three
Nervous Nellie

"If you live to be our age, I guess nothing should surprise you."

"Yes, but Annie being involved in this baby selling. I mean she's such a wholesome, sweet young woman. Who would have ever thought she could be involved in anything so sinister?"

"Exactly. Which is probably why Dr. Miller and Father O'Leary recruited her. No one would ever suspect her of being involved in anything illegal."

"We need to visit Father O'Leary. I'd say he has some explaining to do."

"I do agree with you, Ethel. But I think it would be prudent if we shared what we've found out, along with our whereabouts, with Officer Malcolm first. Just so he's up to speed with what's going on." She paused a moment before continuing. "I really don't think anyone would call me a nervous Nellie for wanting police backup. There are quite a few unsavory characters involved with a lot to lose if they're exposed."

"You're right, Nellie." Ethel took out her cell phone and dialed the Kenmore Police Department. She explained quickly and concisely to Officer Malcolm the reason for the call. She tried not to leave out any crucial details.

"Sounds to me like this is something for the police to handle."

"I agree, but Nellie and I have come this far. We really want to see what Father will say when confronted with the evidence we have."

"It's against my better judgment. But, you two ladies have proven to be remarkably capable, in spite of some pretty dangerous obstacles. Call me when you get to the church and I'll send backup. We'll park in the church parking lot and wait. If you need us, at any time, just send a text that says, HELP, and we'll come right in." Officer Malcolm paused. "If I don't get anything from you in a reasonable amount of time, we'll be busting in."

"Thank you, Officer Malcolm. I'll write the text out now, so all I'll need to do is press send. Ethel's voice took on a frivolous air. "I do believe that my partner, Nellie, may need to bake you another cake. You are being most accommodating."

"Let's not think about that right now. You both need to focus on staying safe."

"I agree with Officer Malcolm. I think I'm living up to my name. I feel like a nervous Nellie. What do you think is going to happen when we confront Father?"

"Only one way to find out," declared Ethel, as she pulled in beside the rectory. She dialed Officer Malcolm, as promised.

The two women exited the car, as Ethel slipped her cell phone discretely into her cardigan sweater's pocket. Before doing so, she pressed record on her voice recorder app. Nellie knocked firmly on Father's door.

"My gracious! You two do get around. Please come right in. I just heard you were at Annie's having a nice little heart to heart. Not a good decision, ladies." Father cleared his throat. "You know you two have always been such stellar parishioners. I could always count on you to do the right thing. But, sadly, you've gotten involved in something that is way over your heads.

What a shame that no one will ever know the good work you've done in the Lord's name."

At that moment Red stepped out from the next room, wearing the shirt with the missing gold button.

"Oh, my word, Ethel," Nellie gasped, as she pointed at Red's shirt. "That's the same gold button I saved as evidence."

Red's evil smile encompassed his smug face, as he arrogantly pointed to the spot where the button should have been. "Lost it under an oak tree months ago," he snickered. "But that's of little consequence now. I have far more important things on my mind then some old button. I must say that I, for one, was extremely delighted with the intense red color of Skylar's baby's hair. Are you two lovely ladies at all perplexed about who the father might be?" His voice dripped with sarcasm.

"You are disgusting, Red. Poor Skylar. How could you have done that to her? She's just a young, innocent girl. It's unconscionable. You ruined her life."

"I beg to differ with you. We saved her life." Red's haughtiness sickened Nellie and Ethel.

"What? That is the most ridiculous thing I've ever heard."

"Her father's in prison. Her mother does nothing but drink all day. Where would she have wound up? I'll tell you where. In the gutter. That's what happens to girls like her."

Ethel could not contain her anger. "Girls like her? Why you disgusting low life. How dare you talk about Skylar that way."

"And who's gonna stop me? You? Clearly your dearly departed Priscilla couldn't."

"How dare you speak of Priscilla, you scoundrel, you."

"I should tell you that Priscilla and I shared a cup of tea in this very room the night she croaked. Such a pity."

Ethel turned to Father O'Leary. "Is that true, Father? I remember your telling me that Priscilla stopped by the rectory before confession and that she had a cup of tea. Was Red here?"

Father O'Leary glared at the two women. "You two should have left well enough alone. Putting your noses where they don't belong was a huge mistake." He walked toward the door that separated them from the outside and bolted it shut.

"But, Father," Nellie pleaded. "Surely you understand that…."

"Quiet," he ordered. "I've heard just about as much as I care to from the pair of you. Since you ladies seem so hell bent on knowing what really happened to your dearly departed Priscilla, sit down."

"You heard the man. Sit down now and no funny business," Red added, as he pulled a revolver from his pocket.

Chapter Fifty-Four
Blackmailed

Ethel realized her options were limited with Red holding a gun over them. Her heart began to pound and her body felt like she might pass out at any moment. Pull yourself together, Ethel, she thought. She knew that she wanted to get as much information as she possibly could, before texting for help. Her adrenaline was flowing.

"Father O'Leary, I'm really surprised that you would ever be involved in anything illegal." She looked up at Red with hatred in her eyes. "Now, this degenerate not upholding the law doesn't surprise me in the least," she said as she glared at Red. "Nellie and I felt it in our bones that he was up to no good, from the moment we first saw him at the Sheridan Family Restaurant. Such a sleaze."

Red seemed to find her words amusing, which really enraged Ethel. "What's that old saying? Oh, yes. Sticks and stones may break my bones, but words will never hurt me." He smiled that sinister grin that the two women had seen many times before. "It just breaks my heart that you two old biddies won't be around to see the case solved. I mean you've worked so hard. You actually got much farther than we ever imagined you would."

Ethel gathered up every bit of courage she had. "At least clear things up for us. We're baffled as to what role Annie could have ever played in this dreadful operation."

"Ah, Annie. Yes. She was quite an asset, wasn't she Father?" Red chugged a big gulp of the beer that sat on the table beside him. "Who would have ever suspected our sweet school teacher of being our prize recruiter. We did good using her. That's for sure, huh Father?"

"That Annie was religious and that she worked in the prime location for directing, shall we say, misguided girls to the clinic proved to be invaluable." Father paused and inhaled deeply. "And I do believe she grew quite accustomed to those rather large *finder fees* we paid her over the years. She lives quite well on a teacher's salary. Beautiful home, stylish clothes. And to think at first she didn't want to cooperate."

"What?" questioned Nellie. "What changed her mind? Annie seems like such a good, honest person."

"As we now know, Annie shared with you the fact that she isn't nearly as pure and pristine as she'd like everyone to believe. She certainly strayed and used poor judgment when she was a teenager. But, thanks to Dr. Miller and me her problem disappeared. It seemed almost too good to be true when she finished college and was offered a job at Roosevelt High School. It doesn't take a genius to know what kind of girls go there."

Ethel felt as if she were talking to Dr. Miller. Father sounded much like him with his preconceived notions and bigoted attitude. "Just because a girl is poor and less advantaged doesn't give you the right to exploit her."

"Exploit her? Why Ethel, don't you see? We are giving these girls a chance for a good life. Without us, most of them would probably never leave that shit hole neighborhood they call home."

Ethel bowed her head. "I can't believe how you're speaking, Father, and how judgmental you're being. This is a side of you I never expected to see."

267

"I believe I am doing what God would want. You have no right to judge me."

"But I clearly know right from wrong. And what you are doing is wrong. Plain and simple."

"Think what you like, Ethel. But, sometimes compromises need to be made for good to prevail over evil. When we first approached Annie, she wanted nothing to do with our plan and refused to help us. She was dead-set against it." Father hesitated a moment before continuing. "But, as you now well know, we have ways of persuading people to see things our way. Only Dr. Miller and I knew where her baby had been placed. And although we hated to have to threaten her the way we did, it gave us the leverage we needed."

"Now I'm beginning to understand," said Ethel. "Annie told us, some time ago, that she'd confided in Priscilla the truth as to why she was so afraid to go to the police that night after Roxy's. But she never told us."

"Enough already," chimed in Red. "Hey, all we told Annie was that it would be a shame if that beautiful baby girl she'd given up for adoption years ago had a bad accident, if you get my drift?"

"You despicable man. Poor Annie never agreed to do what she did for the money. She agreed to your demands to protect her child. And I'm sure she knew, if she went to the police, the outcome would have been the same. Annie was blackmailed."

Red shrugged his shoulders. "I suppose you could call it that. Don't really give a crap why she agreed, just that she did. And she's been quite helpful over the years, wouldn't you agree Father?"

Father was deep in thought. "Annie is the least of our problems, Red. We need to figure out what we're going to do with these two. They know far too much."

Ethel and Nellie had never been so frightened in their lives. Nellie's hands felt sweaty and she was beginning to hyperventilate. Where she got the courage to ask her next question, she didn't know. "If you're going to kill us, at least let us know why Priscilla was killed and how she was involved in all of this?"

"I'm not one to mince words," said Father. "I guess that's the least we can do before you join your dearly departed busy body friend. Sad to say, she was much like you, sticking her nose where it didn't belong."

"Some people never learn," added Red. "It's just too bad I didn't knock Nellie off the night I killed Priscilla. Killing two birds with one stone, isn't that how the saying goes? That would have been so satisfying. But that lightning storm ruined my plan."

Nellie gasped. "Why you murderer. You useless, disgusting excuse for a man. I wish you'd......"

"Shut up, bitch. Shut up. I'm sick of you two old bags getting in our way." He paused and looked towards the kitchen. "Father, fill them in, if you like. I'll put the kettle on for tea." The look on his face was chilling. "Your dear friend, Priscilla, so enjoyed her final cup of my special tea. I'm sure you two old geezers will too." And with those words, he headed into the kitchen.

Chapter Fifty-Five
Purple Flowers and Tea

It was pretty clear, from Father's demeanor, that this was not an easy task for him. He hemmed and hawed and, were it not for Red yelling at him to wrap it up, Ethel felt they may have been able to reason with him. But, with Red there, they were clearly in grave danger.

Ethel mustered up all her courage and took in a very deep breath. "Listen, Father. I rather doubt Nellie and I will ever get out of here alive. But I know that I, for one, would have a tremendous load lifted from me, if I knew what happened to Priscilla. I beg of you, Father. Please let us leave this earth knowing what we have tried so desperately hard to figure out."

Father seemed to struggle with his words. "You should know that I was not at all happy when Priscilla met her demise. But she was a huge liability, just like the two of you." Father bowed his head. "It needed to be done and so it was. And, believe it or not, what happened to Priscilla is very troubling to me. I didn't want things to end like they did. I really didn't." Father inhaled and mumbled something under his breath. "I guess I can lay it all out for you, ladies. I doubt you'll be able to tell anyone from where you'll be within the next few hours."

Nellie thought she was going to pass out. She struggled to breathe. Her skin felt clammy and she suddenly felt very light headed. She feared the end was near.

Ethel had never been this frightened in her entire life. But her need to find out, once and for all, what happened to Priscilla filled her with a sense of strength she didn't know she had. "Go on, Father. We're listening."

"Very well then." Father knew Red would be in shortly. And he knew, all too well, that Red would not hesitate to do something terrible. "As you both know, Priscilla was a devout Catholic. She was someone I admired. Her character was pure and she loved to help others. Much like the two of you."

"We know all that, Father. Why was she killed?"

"That Thursday night at bible study, I got a phone call that troubled me. T-Bone, whom I understand you ladies had a run in with, had brought in a young lady to Roxy's who was, how shall I put this, not cooperating. I knew she was one of Annie's students and hoped she could reason with her. The young girl said she'd changed her mind. She was adamant that the baby was hers and that she intended to keep her. But her baby, much like Skylar's, had been conceived with a specific adoptive family in mind. That baby had already been spoken for and a very sizeable sum of money had already crossed hands. It just wasn't right."

"But it was her baby. Wasn't it her choice, as to whether to keep the child or not?"

Father snickered, which really annoyed Ethel. "You sound just like Priscilla. The girl is only fourteen years old, Ethel. What does she know about raising a baby? Not to mention that the adoptive couple had already laid out thousands of dollars for her medical needs. She had been given the finest care. And that couple specifically paid for an infant with blond hair and blue eyes." Father's irritation grew. "Stupid girl. She doesn't know the first thing about raising a baby. Especially a baby who will be raised in a loving family with good

271

Christian values."

"And, so, you were going to have Annie go to Roxy's that night to try to reason with the girl and change her mind."

"Now you're catching on. I thought, if anyone could inspire the young girl to make the right decision, it would be her teacher. These young, uneducated, poor girls can often be swayed by a person they respect. We thought that Annie could encourage her to do the right thing. And, if you recall, Priscilla insisted on going with her."

"So, basically, you wanted Annie to bribe an innocent girl to give up her baby?"

"Ethel, dear. I wouldn't call it a bribe. It would have been so easy, if that ignorant girl had just shown some common sense. But there was no reasoning with her. And that posed a huge problem for us."

"A lot of money at stake, I imagine," said Ethel with disgust in her voice.

"Don't I know. Thousands and thousands of dollars." Father's expression grew even more angry. "Things might have been okay if goody two shoes, Priscilla, had kept her thoughts to herself and stayed out of things that didn't concern her. Her heart went out to the young girl and she tried her best to convince Annie to do what was right."

"That must not have set well with T-Bone," Ethel added.

"That's an understatement. T-Bone wanted to kill Priscilla that very night, but we decided to give it a little more time."

"How gracious of you," Nellie said with total sarcasm in her voice.

"T-Bone told us that Annie had tried, half-heartedly, to reason with her student. We knew right then that we had a big problem. And it needed to be resolved.

272

But we were confident there was no way Annie would go to the police. She knew, all too well, the outcome that action would have on the child she'd given up for adoption. As we said, we'd made it pretty clear that, if she crossed us, that little girl might wish she'd never been born." Father smiled. "I guess you could say we had Annie in our back pocket. But, Priscilla. Well, I don't have to tell you two how righteous she was. And that posed a threat. A big threat. Priscilla's big mistake was telling everyone that, if they didn't leave that poor girl alone to make her own decision about her baby, she was going to go to the police and tell them everything she knew. And we certainly couldn't have that, now could we?"

"You killed Priscilla!" Horror filled Nellie's voice.

"No. I didn't kill her," Father replied without any emotion.

"Well, if you didn't, who did?" Ethel was so frightened that Red would return before all her questions had been answered that she blurted out the one other thing that had been troubling her before Father had a chance to reply. "What about the list? Priscilla never told us a thing about its details. How did she get the list and what was so important about it that T-Bone was ready to kill Fred for it?"

"Priscilla was her own worst enemy. Her compassion is what did her in. And, if she hadn't stuck her nose in where it didn't belong, she'd still be playing bingo with the two of you."

"I don't understand."

"Actually, the thing that amazes me is that I had no idea how Priscilla came to have the list or that she even had it, for that matter. I kept it in the rectory. Then, as fate would have it, in she came one Sunday, a month or two ago, to attend confession."

"Confession? I don't understand. I thought the last time she attended confession was the night she died."

"That is correct. But this was at an earlier confession." Father gazed into the distance. "She told me that she was very puzzled by a list she had anonymously received. She was troubled by what the list meant and why it was sent to her, of all people. And, that it was sent with no name, address or explanation of why she was receiving it, weighed heavily on her. Apparently, there was a sticky tab on the envelope that read: Important Church Papers. Please put this in a safe place and do not give to anyone. Will explain everything as soon as I can." Father paused. "I guess, because it was church related, that's why she shared it with me."

"That sounds pretty cryptic. So, what was on the list?" Nellie persisted.

"If you must know, it was a very private, highly confidential list of couples willing to pay a lot of money for a baby. And the more specific their wishes, the higher the price. Names, phone numbers, money agreed to be paid. Even bank account and stock holdings were on that list. Actually, much of it was written in code. Extremely valuable information was all there on that one piece of paper."

"No wonder that list was so important to you."

"You're not kidding. And I thought about it a lot after her confession. The only one person who could have gotten that list to Priscilla was Annie. And the more I thought about it, I remembered Annie being left alone in the rectory office, a while ago, with the list in plain view. It took me a while, but it finally all fell into place. I think she stole the list and planned to somehow get it to the police. But nobody pulls a fast one on me and lives to tell about it."

"What? You don't intend to hurt Annie, do you? Have you no conscience?"

Ethel's words didn't seem to affect Father at all. "Once you two are no longer a threat, T-Bone will pay a little surprise visit to our sweet Annie. What a pity to think that she'll be joining the two of you. But the way I see it, she's a traitor."

"You are more of a demon then I ever could have imagined. How can you preach goodness and godliness, when you are a monster?"

"I wouldn't say that, Ethel. I have done much good in the world." Father glanced down at his watch. "Let me just finish clearing things up for you both before Red comes back. Once he joins us, we may not have the opportunity to finish our little chat."

Ethel and Nellie sat frozen in fear; but eager to hear what Father was about to say.

"When I realized the list was in Priscilla's possession, I had no choice but to recruit T-Bone to retrieve it. If anyone could make her give up that list, it was him. That was my list and the names on it would potentially bring us hundreds of thousands of dollars." Father wrung his hands together. "I know I had the original list, but if that copy had gotten into the wrong hands, our entire business could have been exposed. And we certainly couldn't risk that."

Ethel and Nellie sat aghast at what Father was saying. Suddenly, his face broke into an enormous grin. "I still admire myself for how clever I was that day you two grand inquisitors came into the rectory nosing around. I graciously agreed to share what Priscilla had told me in confidence at confession. I even made out that it had been a difficult decision to reach." Father laughed aloud. "I had you two actually believing that Fred had a gambling problem. That was so smart of me to concoct such an absurd story. And that I did it so spur of the moment seemed really brilliant on my part. I knew you'd take the bait and look at things through different eyes. Oh, the looks on your faces when I told you that ridiculous story and sent you off on a wild goose chase. I still find it amusing that you believed me. My intention was to divert attention from the truth. But you two just wouldn't let it go. And, now, here we all are."

"Ladies," exclaimed Red, as he entered the room. "The tea is ready. Before I give it to you, did either of you happen to notice those beautiful purple flowers in the vase on Father's end table?"

Ethel and Nellie sat numb and speechless, as their gaze turned towards the flowers.

The threatening expression on Red's face did not go unnoticed. "Lovely, aren't they? They're called Monkshood and they contain a deadly poison. As you can see, each blossom is shaped like the hood worn by a medieval monk. The plant is sometimes called Aconitum and it is highly toxic. Should it enter your body, through a refreshing cup of tea for example, it mimics a heart attack. A deadly heart attack, I should add. Can you imagine that?" He seemed to take delight in sharing the gruesome details.

"You murderer," Ethel cried out. "How could you kill an innocent, God loving woman?"

"It really wasn't a difficult choice," he callously replied. "Only Father knew that Priscilla was stopping at the rectory before confession. Surely, she would never suspect *his* motives. So, I stayed in the background, completely out of sight. My job was that of the preparer of the tea. I had secured the flowers from an old friend who specializes in promoting death through unnatural causes that appear quite natural. Pretty clever, wouldn't you agree? All Father did was deliver the special beverage to her and watch her enjoy it. The deed had been done. And we knew it would take a few hours before it would take effect and that worked out perfectly for us. Oh, I almost forgot to tell you. Our good friend T-Bone was part of the plan. We used him as our look-out man that night."

Nellie thought she was going to be sick. Suddenly everything came together. "You killed Priscilla. You poisoned her," she shrieked.

The expression on his face was contorted and evil. "It was my pleasure. She got in our way. Do you have the remotest idea how much money our baby business brings in? She should have listened to us and minded her own damn business." Red seemed insanely wrapped up in his thoughts, as he ranted on and on about how it was Priscilla's own fault that she'd been killed.

So, Ethel decided there was no time like the present and, in one split second, pulled the telephone out from her cardigan pocket and quickly hit send.

Chapter Fifty-Six
Almost Goners

The instant Red noticed her phone in her hand, he became even more enraged. "You bitch. You stupid bitch. Give me that," he shouted, as he pointed his gun at her. "What the hell do you think you're doing?" He grabbed the phone from her and violently threw it across the room. It smashed against the wall before crashing to the floor.

But it was too late. Officer Malcolm and his back up team were at the door. "Open up." His voice was firm. "Either open up this minute or we'll be forced to break the door down. Your choice."

Red gritted his teeth and glared at Father. "How many times have I told you that we should have killed these two good-doers when we had the chance. They've always been trouble. But, you and your righteousness. Always thinking things would work out. Look around, Father. Does it look like things are going to go our way now? All our hard work down the toilet because of these two old busy-bodies."

Ethel and Nellie froze in fear, wondering what would happen next.

Father bent his head down and walked slowly over to unbolt the door. "I'm sorry, Red. I never thought it would end like this."

"Saying that you're sorry means nothing. It didn't have to be like this." Red's voice was filled with hatred.

Officer Malcolm and his backup entered. "Hands up, you two. But first, place your gun and any other weapons you may have on the floor."

Ethel was never so happy to see anyone. She burst out of her chair and threw her arms around Officer Malcolm. "You were right, Officer. Nellie and I had no idea how dangerous these men could be. We are so thankful you got here when you did."

"It was your quick-thinking, Ethel, that got us here so speedily. Calling me earlier with all the details was spot on. Great detective work. I don't mind telling you and Nellie that I'm pretty darn impressed with how this whole case went down."

"That means a lot coming from a seasoned officer like you."

Ethel looked over to see Father O'Leary and Red in handcuffs, being read their Miranda Rights. "Well, you two aren't quite as smug and condescending as a few moments earlier, are you?" she said when the Officer in charge had finished. Ethel glanced over at the purple flowers that looked so beautiful. But she knew quite well that looks could be deceiving. "Oh, and Officer Malcolm, you may want to take in the flowers and tea as evidence. I think that they will prove exactly how our dear friend was killed."

The two men glared at her, but neither uttered a word.

"I'll be honest. For a moment, I thought Nellie and I were goners. My whole life flashed before me. And then, you appeared. Talk about blessings."

"Talk about timing," Nellie chimed in. "I cringe to think what could have happened to us had you not arrived precisely when you did." Nellie's face took on a look of relief, as she saw the two culprits being led away.

"What a day!" exclaimed Ethel. "Would you like

us to come down to the station, Officer, and give you a statement as to everything that led up to Priscilla's death. Now we even know how she was killed and why."

Officer Malcolm smiled so broadly that the space between his two front teeth seemed even more accentuated.

"I think you two deserve a break. But, if tomorrow morning is convenient, that would be soon enough and very much appreciated. Say around ten o'clock." His smile grew wider. "And, if I haven't already said so, great work, detectives."

"Holy cow, Nellie. He called us detectives. I think I could get used to that. Except," she grimaced, "today was much too close for comfort."

"I'm still shaking. It's hard to believe everything that's happened. Poor Priscilla. But at least now we can let Fred know what happened to her and why. Maybe knowing will bring him some comfort."

"I hope so. No time like the present, don't you agree, Nellie?"

Within a few minutes, Celeste Civic was on the move. "122 Hartford Avenue, Reginald. We have some news to share that can't wait."

Chapter Fifty-Seven
The Catch-a-Killer Detective Agency is Born

Even though Fred had been terribly sad to hear the gruesome details surrounding his beloved Priscilla's death, he was glad he finally had some answers. He found it incredibly contradictory that the Church, the very thing Priscilla loved so much, was what had eventually led to her demise. Learning about Father O'Leary and his involvement in something so sleazy was hard for Fred to accept.

"As sad as what you just shared with me is, I have some good news," added Fred.

"What is it?"

"Even though I've told Nancy a hundred and one times not to move back because of me, she insisted it was for the best. She even got herself a teaching job with the Kenmore School System that she'll start in September. She will be the newest English teacher at Kenmore West High School. Hard to believe that was Priscilla's and my alma mater.

"Why that's wonderful news, Fred. We know that will make life much easier for you."

"That it will. Having Nancy here will be such a blessing in so many ways. I know Priscilla would be very happy. I know I am."

"It's always good to hear happy news, Fred. I can hardly wait till Deborah and Sarah return from Thailand. Not even five months now and they'll be home for a long visit."

"I remember Priscilla always said what lovely girls they were."

"I'd have to agree. Having them back will be something to look forward to. But, now, Nellie and I had better get going. We have a big day ahead of us tomorrow."

"Of course. But there's something I'd like to give each of you before you go. I think it would make Priscilla very happy." Fred walked into the bedroom and returned with something in each hand.

"Why it's Jasper and Seymour!" exclaimed Nellie. "I'd know those little fellows anywhere. They were Priscilla's good luck trolls."

Fred smiled. "Indeed. Two of her many good luck trolls. But I think Jasper, with his orange hair and Seymour, with his green hair, were her two favorites. I'd like you each to have one."

Ethel and Nellie were touched by his kind gesture and each gave Fred a hug.

"I'm so glad you like them. I remember Priscilla telling me how she used to put all her trolls in a row above her bingo cards for good luck. But it seemed like Jasper and Seymour had a special place in her heart, just like the two of you. Maybe it will even seem like a part of Priscilla is with you at bingo." Fred managed a tiny smile; something they had not witnessed in a very long time. "I know she kept her lucky rosary beads out, too. Those I gave to Nancy."

"I imagine those will always be very special to her".

"Yes, I'm sure they will." Fred was silent for a moment. "I guess I'd better let you two be on your way. I know what a stressful, trying day this has been for you. When you visit the police tomorrow, make sure those evil men pay dearly for what they did to my Priscilla. Life in prison is what they should get."

"We'll do our best, Fred."

That night Nellie could not sleep. She tossed and turned and just couldn't get out of her mind how close she and Ethel had come to being killed. So, as was often the case when she had time on her hands, she decided to go down to the kitchen and bake. Something for Officer Malcolm seemed like the appropriate choice. After all, she reasoned, he saved our lives. It's the least I can do. She remembered that she and Ethel, when they had visited Mrs. Rockland, had joked that they'd call her cookies *Catch a Killer Cookies*, if they helped to solve the crime. And, by golly, Nellie thought, help solve the crime they did! There was no denying that. "I guess I'll bake a batch of molasses cookies and some lemon drop cookies, too. Sounds like a plan," she said aloud to no-one.

By the time she finished baking, it was nearly time to get ready for the day. Somehow, she didn't feel tired at all. Rather, she felt invigorated and ready to take on the day; a day where she would be known as Detective Nellie Pearce. "I still can't believe we solved the case, Matilda. Detective Nellie Pearce. I like the sound of that. Don't you girl?" Matilda meowed, almost as if she understood.

"Well, well, Nellie. Don't those look delicious," Ethel exclaimed, as Nellie stepped into the Civic. "When did you ever find the time?"

"Couldn't sleep, Ethel. And you know nothing takes my mind off my troubles like baking."

"Don't I know. And I rather imagine Officer Malcolm won't protest. I really think he's going to look at us in a completely new light considering we, two amateur sleuths, solved a pretty high-profile case."

"Agreed. And to think he had his doubts!" Nellie's tone was flippant.

The young lady at the desk was the same one they had seen on their previous visits. Only this time she seemed, in Ethel's eyes, to greet them differently. Her voice had an upbeat quality to it. "Officer Malcolm told me to send you both right back when you arrived. He's expecting you." She paused and smiled. "Love your matching outfits! My mom likes to play bingo. I know she'd think your sweatshirts are adorable."

"Thank you. I think they helped us solve the crime," Ethel said with a bit of levity in her voice.

"Really? Well, that's amazing." The young girl smiled broadly. "Speaking of amazing, Officer Malcolm raved about your baked goods. Your carrot cake was delicious."

"Thank you, dear. I love to bake. It's been a hobby of mine since I was a young girl. My husband used to say that the way to a man's heart is through his stomach." Nellie winked. "Maybe there is some truth to that."

"When Officer Malcolm told me to send you right back, he said he hoped you'd baked something. Said your confections are the best he's ever had. Looks like he's going to be in a very good mood."

"Well, that's nice to hear. People do seem to love my molasses and lemon drop cookies. I'll be sure to have him save you a few of each."

Ethel and Nellie headed back to the familiar office. But the greeting they received was a far cry from how they had been treated the first time they'd come in.

"Welcome, ladies," said Officer Malcolm. "Please, sit down. May I introduce you to Sergeant Gugino; one of our finest."

Sergeant Gugino bent down and firmly shook each lady's hand. "I believe we owe you both a great debt of gratitude. Officer Malcolm filled me in on everything and I must say it's one heck of a story. It certainly isn't every day that the public gets involved in a crime as horrific as this one and then goes on to solve the case. Well done."

"We were only too glad to help. Now our dear friend Priscilla can finally rest in peace."

"And she owes it all to her two best friends. You persevered and never gave up. You followed the clues and put them together like seasoned pros. Very impressive, ladies."

"What happens now?"

"Father O'Leary and Red are being held in jail without bail, pending trial. They were both quite eager to give us a list of the names of all their accomplices. They thought it might reduce their sentences by cooperating. But murder is murder. They will not be harming anyone for a very long time. We will be investigating each and every person they implicated. I can personally assure you that anyone who was involved in this case will be prosecuted to the fullest extent of the law. Recording them the way you did was brilliant. And luckily, our tech guy was able retrieve everything from your phone's memory. What a confession you got!"

"That does our hearts good, Sergeant. Goodness shall prevail." Ethel paused a moment. "I think you may also want to speak to Annie, the teacher who was at Roxy's with Priscilla the night T-Bone brought in the young, pregnant girl. I can give you Annie's phone number and address."

"That would be helpful. Thanks."

"We phoned her last night to tell her what had happened. But, in all likelihood, she may have some vital information to add to the case. I think she'd definitely be a prime key witness. Annie was being blackmailed by Dr.

Miller and Father O'Leary. And Father told us he planned to have T-Bone kill her, too."

"What can I say? Your help has truly been invaluable." Suddenly his mood appeared to change. "Listen, ladies. I certainly want to give credit where credit is due. But, in honesty, we're glad things turned out the way they did. This case might have had a much different outcome. You two very easily could have been killed."

"We know that and we were mighty scared yesterday when Father O'Leary bolted the door and Red pulled out his gun." Ethel felt shivers run down her spine. "Not to mention how close we came to having a cup of Monkshood tea. I'd never even heard of it before. But I guess it's a pretty clever way to kill someone if you want people to think the person had a heart attack. Red was even more sinister than we imagined."

"I was just a bit curious as to why Father called the police the night Priscilla collapsed. I mean he knew what had really happened. He could have just let everyone assume it had been a heart attack. So, I asked him yesterday, once he was in custody," said Officer Malcolm.

"And?"

"His answer was actually pretty clever. He told me if foul play was ever suspected that we would never suspect him, since he was the one who called the police that night. Why, he had asked me, would he ever have called the police if he had played any part in her demise. Also, he told me that Priscilla had come to confession that night and had confided in him that she believed someone was trying to kill her. His calling in the police actually made perfect sense. We never suspected his involvement." He smiled warmly at Ethel and Nellie. "Catching him the way we did was because of your hard work and insightfulness and we are eternally grateful."

286

The two women could not have felt more fulfilled. "We appreciate your vote of confidence, Sergeant. We finally feel we did what we set out to do. We've achieved justice for Priscilla." Ethel felt as if a huge burden had been lifted from her. She smiled broadly. "You never know when another case may require our special expertise."

"But, for now," added Nellie, "we've brought some molasses and lemon drop cookies for you to enjoy. Time for a break."

"Happy to oblige," said Officer Malcolm. "You do make the most delicious baked goods."

Nellie beamed. "I love to bake. And I should tell you that my molasses and lemon drop cookies were instrumental in our solving the case."

Officer Malcolm looked perplexed. "How so?"

The two ladies went on to explain the sequence of events and how the cookies had gained them access to two homes where they were able to gather some pretty significant clues.

Officer Malcolm and Sergeant Gugino listened eagerly as the story unfolded.

"So, if I'm hearing you correctly," said Officer Malcolm, "these *Catch a Killer Cookies* were used not only to help charity, but also to garner evidence for the case."

Sergeant Gugino shook his head. "Now that's thinking outside the box. Our officers could learn something from the two of you and I'm not kidding. That was pretty unbelievable police work."

"Thank you," declared Nellie, as she placed the assortment of cookies on the rectangular desk. "And now, why don't we each take a *Catch a Killer Cookie* and toast our dearly departed Priscilla. May she rest in peace."

"To Priscilla's memory," said Officer Malcolm, as he picked up a molasses cookie. "And to her two friends to whom we shall be forever indebted."

Sergeant Gugino chimed in. "Maybe there's something to these cookies." His voice was frivolous. "I, for one, wouldn't mind if they were available at the station every week. Maybe our officers would be as inspired as you two were to solve a crime that seems unsolvable."

"Why Sergeant Gugino," Nellie exclaimed. "I do believe you're on to something!" She thought a moment. "You know I would be happy to bake something for the officers every week, if you think that would help them to work more efficiently."

Officer Malcolm took a bite of his molasses cookie, his face beaming. "I never thought I'd say this, but you two ladies have been a breath of fresh air. That we doubted your abilities, shame on us. We know you've solved a very difficult case. And that leaves us no choice but to view you both in a whole new light."

Ethel and Nellie could hardly believe their ears. "What are you saying, Officer?"

"Just that, in the future, we will not look at you in the same way we first did. You have clearly proven yourselves to be competent detectives who, unlike any officers here, do not hesitate to utilize, how shall I say this, unconventional methods to catch your killer. And I admire that. I really do. So, let's keep in touch."

As Nellie and Ethel turned to leave, they looked back one final time. Officer Malcolm and Sergeant Gugino were each enjoying another cookie. They waved a final goodbye, as Officer Malcolm rose. "Take care, ladies. And stop by any time."

"Case closed," declared Ethel, as she gave Nellie a high five.

"Yes! And it turned out to be a much better ending than I'd expected yesterday."

"That's for sure. We're alive to talk about it."

"And one thing is pretty clear. I think we make one heck of a team," added Nellie.

"I couldn't agree more." Ethel suddenly had a thought. "Hey, Nellie. What would you think about opening up our own detective agency?"

"I never thought I'd say this, Ethel, but I think that's a great idea. And I've got just the name. How about if we call our agency The Catch-a-Killer Detective Agency."

"I like it, Nellie! I like it a lot. And our signature trademark can be your special *Catch a Killer Cookies.* No other detective agency will ever have those."

Nellie smiled. "If only Edwin and Leonard could see us now. How proud they would be."

"I'm pretty proud of us, too, Detective Nellie. We did it. We solved the case for Priscilla and brought her justice, just as we promised."

"And I've got a feeling in my bones that we're going to get involved in another case sooner than later. Let's have a toast when we get home to The Catch a Killer Detective Agency!"

"Great idea. But, for now, Detectives Nellie Pearce and Ethel Dinwiddie over and out."

Nellie's Catch-a-Killer Lemon Drop Cookies

1 cup of granulated sugar
½ cup of butter that has been softened, but not melted (Nellie usually sets the butter on her counter to soften a good hour or so before using it)
1 large egg
¾ teaspoon of vanilla
1 and 1/4 Tablespoons of fresh lemon juice
1 and 1/8 teaspoons of the zest of a fresh lemon
1/8 teaspoon salt
¼ teaspoon baking powder
1/8 teaspoon baking soda
1 and ½ cups of flour
1/2 cup of powdered sugar

Preheat your oven to 350 degrees. Lightly grease your cookie sheet and put it to the side. Now it's time to make your cookie dough! Mix together your butter and sugar. (Nellie uses real butter for the best flavor!) Next add an egg, vanilla, lemon juice and lemon zest and mix with butter and sugar. Now stir in your flour, baking soda, salt and baking powder. Mix all together. Then form your cookie dough into small balls (Nellie uses a good-sized teaspoon) and gently toss each ball in a bowl of confectionary sugar until each is lightly covered.

Evenly space the balls on your cookie sheet and place the sheet in your preheated 350-degree oven. Bake for about 10 to 12 minutes until the bottom of each cookie is light brown. The insides will be chewy. If you are using a nonstick, darker cookie sheet, bake about 9 or 10 minutes. Remove from the oven and cool about 5 minutes before transferring to a serving plate.

Exercise caution when using this recipe to catch a killer!

Catch-a-Killer Molasses Cookies

1 cup of butter that has been softened

1 large egg

1/3 cup of dark molasses (not light molasses)

1 and 1/2 cups of sugar (set aside another ¼ cup of sugar to roll dough balls in)

1 cup of firmly packed brown sugar

2 and 3/4 cups of flour

1 and 1/2 teaspoons of baking soda

1 teaspoon of ground ginger

1 tablespoon of ground cinnamon

1 teaspoon of ground cloves

2 teaspoons of nutmeg

1/4 teaspoon salt

Line your cookie sheet with parchment paper. Preheat your oven to 350 degrees. In a big mixing bowl, mix together butter, white sugar, brown sugar, egg, and molasses. Nellie uses a hand mixer. When nicely combined, gradually add in the flour, baking soda, cinnamon, ginger, clove, nutmeg and salt. Mix all well.

Shape your dough into one-inch sized balls. Dip the balls into your granulated sugar that you have set aside. and place them about 3 inches apart on your cookie sheet.

Bake for 10 to 12 minutes. Let them sit a few more minutes before transferring them to a cooling rack.

Exercise caution when using this recipe to catch a killer!

Murder at the Bingo Hall
Book Club Questions

1. How do you feel the setting of the book contributed to the mystery?
2. Do you think Ethel and Nellie were justified fearing for their lives? Explain your thoughts.
3. Who did you think the killer was? When did you think you knew and what clues did you use to deduce your conclusions?
4. How did your thoughts change about who did it, as the story progressed?
5. How was Donna's character different from the other women at bible study? Do you know anyone with a personality like hers?
6. Did you think Ethel and Nellie were believable characters? Did you like the banter between them? What were a few scenes that you recall where you especially enjoyed the conversation between the two?
7. How did humor weave its way into the mystery? Site some examples.
8. What did you think about their using Nellie's *Catch a Killer Cookies* to gain access to targeted homes? Do you think the clues they received helped them? Explain how.
9. How were Father O'Leary and Doctor Miller alike? What was the driving force behind each of their actions?
10. Why do you think Priscilla was so intent on going to the police?
11. How did blackmailing Annie affect everything she did? Do you think she was wise to do things

she knew were wrong or did she have no choice? What motivated her?

12. Discuss what went on at Roxy's. Did you believe Travis was fundamentally a good person? What about Red and T-Bone?

13. What did you think about how the mystery was solved and how it ended? Would you have ended it differently?

14. How did the use of bible quotations affect the overall story? Which one do you recall and why do you think it was used where it was?

15. Friendship is a major theme in this story. Discuss the relationship between Ethel and Nellie. What other special friendships exist? What is the importance of each?

Acknowledgements

I have so many people to thank for helping me to believe in myself and who encouraged me to keep writing. Perseverance paid off! Like Ethel and Nellie, I often say that hope springs eternal. And it was the positive comments and wonderful suggestions of so many people that really brought *Murder at the Bingo Hall* to fruition.

Beta readers were so helpful and I truly appreciate everyone who took the time to offer constructive criticism. A big thank you to Roberta Galler, Nanare Slepian, Linda Saland, Sue Sherman, Leslie Salomon, Carin Greenfield, Allison Tester, Leslie Sam, Toni Marshall, Virginia MacIsaac, Adam Testa and Kelly Vaiman. My two daughters, Elyssa and Julie, along with my niece, Nathalie, offered some excellent insight. The bracelet from Elyssa that said, "she believed she could…so she did" was a gift that I shall always cherish. Julie's help with my many computer issues and her eagerness to always offer a listening ear, were much appreciated. My niece, Nathalie, was kind enough to offer many valuable suggestions, even though she was struggling with Covid. Her ability to read critically and catch several mistakes proved very helpful. Dana would be proud. My brother-in-law, Larry Pohl, was always interested in my progress and supportive. He was even inspired to try his hand at writing. But, above all, my wonderful husband, Stuart, has been there for me every step of the way. He is my greatest blessing. Thank you for believing in me and for always loving me. He not only helped me with computer problems that needed resolving from time to time, but he proofread my entire book, even though cozy mysteries are not his favorite genre!

And a big thank you must be given to Ethel Dinwiddie, Nellie Pearce and Priscilla Hatfield. In the midst of my rewriting, after several drafts, I was diagnosed with breast cancer. Rarely a day went by, that I did not look forward to sitting down at the computer and spending time with these feisty ladies. Without them I don't know how I would have ever survived the many days and nights when things often seemed so frightening and uncertain. Being able to write about their courage and determination helped me face my troubles and deal with them in a positive way. I drew strength from their character. I feel blessed to say that after surgery and radiation, I am cancer free.

Thank you to anyone who has read my book. I truly hope that you enjoyed it. I cannot begin to express how truly grateful I am. I am currently working on my next Catch a Killer Murder Mystery and hope you'll check it out when it's available. Meanwhile, why not take a quick look at some of the other books I have written. Check me out at www.lindapohl.com

*If you enjoyed reading this book, I would be most appreciative if you would leave a review on Amazon.com. Thank you.

Printed in Great Britain
by Amazon

47285791R00172